BOOK THREE OF THE MACHINISTS

MARTYR

CRAIG
ANDREWS

To receive *Heritage*, a free prequel novella
set in the world of The Machinists, sign up
for the Craig Andrews mailing list at:

http://eepurl.com/IEjIr

For additional bonus content, and to be the first to hear
about giveaways and
promotions, follow Craig Andrews on Facebook at:

https://www.facebook.com/craigandrewsauthor

For Ender and Callan, the two best sons I could ever ask for. I love you to infinity and beyond—and back!

PROLOGUE

THE CHILL EASTERLY WIND PUSHED at Emelina's back, threatening to shove her off the cliff. The howling breeze kicked up the loose top layer of snow, peppering her back and neck, accumulating in her wild, raven-colored hair. She paid it little mind, continuing to let her legs dangle over the bluff, instinctively leaning into the wind, silently fighting back. Deep down, she understood this was what the magi did. They were always on guard. Always fighting. But today, her attention was on the quiet village three hundred feet below.

The Ferdii Village was already bathed in shadow, the sun too low in the western horizon to clear the mountainous peaks of the Alps. In another fifteen minutes, the entire valley would be covered in darkness, and she would have lost. She chafed at the thought. The only thing worse than losing was losing to a *boy*—and Marcellus was worse than most boys. She could already see his patronizing expression, his narrow eyes disappearing under his squishy face as it contorted in victorious laughter.

"Hunters is a *boys'* game," he would say.

Lina wanted to prove him wrong. She wanted to shut

him up. But most of all, she wanted to win and rub his pig nose in it. Yes, she was a girl—and younger than he was by almost two years. But those things shouldn't matter. She could wield, just like he could—*better* than he could, in her opinion—and that should have been enough to make him take her seriously. It wasn't, though. He always won, and he never let her live it down.

On the good days, he would tell her, "I told you so." But more often than not, he would just smile and walk away. His smug condescension was worse than anything he could say, and it left Lina wanting to blast him in the butt with a fireball. Not to hurt him, of course, just knock him down and dirty his plump ass.

The wind gusted again, taking her out of her fantasy. It might have been her imagination, but the shadows seemed to have climbed higher up the mountainside. Like a ticking clock, they were counting down toward the end, and the clock was almost at zero.

Hunters was a game that could be played in large groups or with as few as only two people, requiring the hunter—in this case, Lina—to find a target, stalk and incapacitate them. The games were usually timed, with more time allotted when more people played. Today's game was between only Lina and Marcellus, and it would be over when the sun set and the entire valley was covered in shadow.

Lina stood and stepped away from the edge until she felt the cool rock of the mountain wall behind her. The path was narrow, only a few paces wide, and it cut into the mountain in a series of cutbacks until it reached the top, where the ruins of the ancient watchtower stood over their remote valley. She'd come up to the outcropping to gain some clarity after having looked everywhere she could think of.

Marcellus hadn't been in any of the places he'd hidden

during their last three games or in any of the other spots favored by the other magi children. She sighed, frustrated. Marcellus had probably doubled back and hidden in a place she'd already searched. That or hid in the watchtower or well-house, but those were forbidden to magi children.

Lina froze.

The watchtower and well-house were *exactly* the type of place Marcellus would hide. He wasn't a cheater, but he liked to shift the rules mid-game. "Improvising," he called it. Lina took another look at the valley. The pinks and purples of the sunset had turned a darker shade.

Even my favorite colors taunt me tonight.

The well-house was on the outskirts of the village, and she was too high to get there in time, but the watchtower was only forty feet above her at the top of the range. If Marcellus had hidden there, she still had a chance.

She bounded forward, running as fast as she dared on the slick rock, navigating the switchbacks until she came to the top. She slowed, valuing silence over speed, then dropped to a crouch and approached the crest of the mountaintop on her hands and knees.

The watchtower, one of Ferdii's Eyes, was only a few dozen yards to her left—and perilously close to the cliff's edge. Long before Lina had been born, a similar watchtower, the second Eye, had stood on the other side of the wide valley. Together, Ferdii's Eyes had been manned by watchful magi, ready to warn their Family below of incoming invaders, but the watchtower's twin had fallen to ruin centuries ago, and the one in front of her was closer to a relic than anything else.

Their need had disappeared in the ages following the Fracture. Their magi community, while secluded, wasn't entirely hidden—and enough time had passed that they were never hunted. Any outsiders who passed through, rare as they were, assumed that, like so many of the other small communities living in the Alps, the Ferdii Family were just the last remains of an ancient people clinging to a primitive way of life. That sentiment wasn't altogether inaccurate.

No longer needed, the towers had fallen into disrepair. The pale-gray stone, having weathered so many brutal winters, was porous and brittle; and the old timber door that led into the structure had disintegrated so long ago that Lina's elders didn't even remember it. The top half of the structure had collapsed so that the top of the tower was open to the sky. Fallen stones littered the ground behind the tower, and if she looked at them from the correct angle, they resembled a set of stairs leading to its uppermost floors.

Lina watched from the path for several long seconds. The inside of the tower was dark, but as the seconds ticked by, she thought she could see traces of movement inside.

It's only your imagination, she told herself. But she couldn't risk it. She sprang from the ridge and raced toward the fallen stones at the rear of the tower. Eyes focused on her destination, she let her hearing drift, willing it toward the entrance of the tower. But above the gusting wind and the soft crunch of her footfalls, she couldn't hear anything.

She cut across the front of the tower, her focus faltering for a moment as she snuck a peek in the entrance's direction. Still seeing nothing, she rounded the edge of the tower and ducked behind the fallen stones. Her breath was heavy with apprehension. When Marcellus didn't emerge from the entrance, Lina began her ascent, climbing the rubble and mindful not to look at how close the broken tower was to the cliff's edge.

The stone was rough and flaky against her hands, and the corners and edges were weakened by age. Halfway up, her footing gave way, and she tumbled toward the cliff's edge.

Lina grasped desperately for a handhold, but it was her foot that found purchase, catching in a crack between stones. Lina's upper body was thrown backward with momentum, her head and back slapping against the sharp rock.

Lina's vision went white, and she tried to blink away the pain. When her sight returned, she found herself with her back against the rubble, her head dangling over the cliff's edge. The world was upside down, and the valley floor at the top of Lina's vision showed the onset of spring—green grass and colorful wildflowers growing through the thinning layer of snow.

Vertigo seized her, and Lina slammed her eyes shut, swallowing the rising lump in her throat. When it subsided, Lina opened her eyes, craning her neck to look at her leg. Her foot was caught between two large stones and bent at an odd angle. Strangely, she felt no pain. Lina rolled forward, searching for something to grab onto, found it, and pulled herself up.

Once she was sitting up and out of immediate danger, Lina pulled her leg free, and after shooting a nervous glance toward the cliff's edge, she crawled a few feet farther away.

That was close.

She didn't want to admit it, but Lina finally understood why the town elders had forbidden young magi to venture up to the towers unsupervised. It was *dangerous*. Lina stood, slowly testing her leg under her weight. It was sore, but not unbearable. If she found Marcellus and won, the pain would all be worth it.

But before she began searching again, she heard something she shouldn't have. Voices. Not Marcellus or another boy's voice. Men's voices. Strange voices. And they were coming from inside the tower.

Despite her better judgment, Lina crawled closer to the

opening, stopping just short of the precipice. Voices carried above the wind. Someone *was* down there, and it wasn't Marcellus.

As slow as Elder Ulrich's gait, Lina slid forward, peering into the tower. Her eyes took several moments to adjust, and the first thing to come into view was the narrow staircase that hugged the curved interior walls of the structure. Made of the same stone as the tower, and shielded by the exterior walls, the stairwell was in remarkable condition. Bolted to the walls were iron sconces that had once held torches. The black metal was pitted with rust, orange with age. The stairs and sconces spiraled twenty feet down to the ground, where two dark figures huddled over a fallen third. The only light entering the tower came through the opening at the base, where the door had been, and the open roof.

Dressed like the night itself, the two figures wore clothing that reminded Lina of a carapace. Bulky and metallic, the two figures looked more like black ants standing on their hind legs than men. The one nearest the door wore a helmet with a glass visor that covered his face and muffled his voice, while the other had removed it to expose a square face that matched his broad shoulders. She'd never seen anyone like them.

The third figure, motionless at their feet, was more familiar, and Lina's blood froze at the sight of him. *Marcellus.*

The men below spoke a language Lina didn't understand, but she knew their tone. Short. Angry. Commanding. And she didn't trust it.

She pulled away from the precipice, confused. Terrified. *Who are those men? And what did they do to Marcellus?*

She knew she had to tell someone, to warn the Village, but how? The only way down was the same way she'd come up, and that meant passing in front of the tower again. And others might be out there. Telling someone also meant leaving Marcellus in their custody, and if his slumped position was any indication, they hadn't been kind. She might not like Marcellus, but she couldn't abandon him. The only thing she could do was wait until the strangers left—and hope they left Marcellus behind unharmed. It wasn't a good plan, but it was the best she had.

Something tickled the back of her mind as she peered over the precipice again. How long had those men been up here? And how had they scaled the mountainside without anyone knowing?

A third man entered the tower. Like the others, he resembled an insect, but he held something that neither of the others had. A *gun*. Lina had never seen a gun before, only heard the hushed stories that the magi boys liked to tell. Stories of life outside their village. Stories of Silent People. Truth be told, the gun wasn't overly intimidating in person, little more than a tube of metal, but the casual confidence in which the man held it terrified her.

Helmeted like the first man, the newcomer's features were also hidden behind a visor, but he was taller and broader than the others and held himself with an air of superiority. The other two men snapped to attention, the helmeted man shooting a glance at another gun leaning against the wall near the door.

The newcomer followed his gaze, and his body stiffened when he saw the weapon. He turned to the helmeted man and took a powerful step toward him, stopping only inches from the man's visor. The first man held his ground, but his shoulders dipped slightly, wilting under his leader's intensity. Like the conversation that preceded the newcomer, the words were harsh and angry—even more so now than before.

The newcomer pointed angrily at Marcellus, kicked the

boy's limp body, then motioned to the door. The square-faced man protested. The leader turned on him, barking orders in his face. Squareface held his ground, meeting the other man's gaze, and said something else. Defiant. A terrible tension filled the tower, and Lina resisted the urge to slip back behind the safety of the ancient stone.

The leader spoke again, his voice cold with anger. The words seemed somehow familiar, as if the man had repeated himself. He pulled something from his hip—another gun— and pushed it into the man's chest—not barrel first as if he were going to shoot him, but as if he were forcing the man to take it.

Squareface looked at the gun then back up to the newcomer before finally taking the weapon. The leader's anger lost a bit of its edge, and he said something more before stepping aside. Squareface looked at the gun in his hand and sighed, clearly at odds with his orders. Shaking his head, he stepped over Marcellus's limp body and pointed the gun at his chest.

No!

He hesitated.

Don't do it! Lina silently protested.

Squareface fired. Marcellus's body shook slightly under the impact, and just like that, it was over.

Lina cried out, then realizing what she'd done, ducked behind the precipice—but not before the shooter spun around and looked straight up at her.

Lina covered her mouth. *How could I have been so stupid?* A cold sweat chilled her. She wanted to scream. She wanted to cry. Vomit. Run. Hide. But she was too frightened. The man had shot him—he'd shot Marcellus!

And he saw you.

Lina rested her forehead against the cool stone, wishing

more than anything in the world that she could melt into it. She was exposed with nowhere to go. Trapped.

Frozen in terror, she waited for the inevitable. But instead of the three men rounding the outside of the tower, she heard their voices inside. Was there a chance they hadn't heard her? That the man hadn't seen her?

No, she thought. The man's eyes had been as black as his deed—and they'd locked onto hers. *He knows I'm here.*

Not knowing what else to do, Lina crept back up to the ledge. She kept her body low, exposing only the top of her head. If the men looked up, they would spot her for sure, but she had to risk it. She had to know. She couldn't wait any longer.

The men were already moving by the time Lina peered over the edge. The helmeted man had his rifle in hand, looking it over. The newcomer and Squareface slid Marcellus's body against the wall and covered him with a tattered blanket they'd found on the floor. Squareface never looked in her direction, and Lina got the distinct impression that he was purposely avoiding it.

A radio on the leader's hip squawked. He grabbed it and barked a short response. Within moments, he and the helmeted man were out the door. Squareface lingered. He grabbed his helmet from a pile of rubble and, before putting it on, shot a glance toward Lina.

She met his eyes defiantly, refusing to give him the satisfaction of seeing her fear.

Squareface nodded solemnly and brought a finger to his lips. *Be quiet.*

Lina blinked, and the man entered the night.

CHAPTER 1

ALLYN WATCHED IMPATIENTLY AS EMERY struggled to wield. The young Hyland magi crouched on his haunches, hands inches above the small firepit that held a pyre of dry timber. Allyn couldn't make out the young man's face in the twilight, but his narrow shoulders were tight, his breathing shallow. Allyn could only imagine the look of determination on his face—a look that was closer to frustration than concentration. Eyes narrow. Lips pursed. Forehead creased.

The rest of their squad had formed a wide circle around them, blending into the dense foliage of the forest. Layers of thick clothing with hoods and knit caps protected them from the lingering winter chill. A few shifted irritably, and Allyn could almost hear the whispers of derision on their lips.

There were a number of their group that could wield a fire; Maleah and Flynn in particular had grown quite deft at wielding in the week since they'd ventured from the Hyland Estate. But this was Emery's rotation, and he had to believe he was alone. He had to feel the weight and burden of the group, because failure meant the squad would go to bed cold and hungry for the third time in as many nights—since the responsibility had rotated to him.

Allyn shivered at the thought of another sleepless night—the thought of a fire and a warm meal was nearly enough to convince Allyn to step in and do it himself. They'd ran out of dried meat in the time it had taken Maleah to *ascend*—to break through her block—and the bread in the day it took Flynn to do the same. Allyn had chosen to pack light, knowing it meant they would run out of rations, but he hadn't anticipated it happening so quickly. The hunger had been meant to be an uncomfortable motivation, but it was rapidly turning into something more dangerous. If Emery didn't overcome his block within the next couple of days, Allyn would be forced to replace him in the rotation, and that meant risking losing him.

Movement out of the corner of Allyn's eye pulled his attention from the faltering magi. Vonn had stepped forward, and the frosty ground crunched softly under his weight. Though most of his bulk had softened with time, he was a larger man who was roughly twice Allyn's age, with gray peppering his temples and beard. Where Jaxon had used intimidation and indifference as methods of training, Vonn was kinder and more personable, treating the student-teacher relationship more as a mentorship. And like many of the young magi, Allyn had instantly gravitated toward him, trusting in the man's genuine authenticity.

The Hyland trainer caught Allyn's eye and cocked his head to the side in question. *Now?*

Allyn nodded, and Vonn approached Emery from behind. He knelt beside the younger magi, keeping his distance, but making sure he was firmly in the young man's field of vision.

"Let's take a break," Vonn said, his deep voice warm and compassionate.

"No." Emery's shoulders stiffened as he worked to refocus.

Allyn had thought the young magi was close to breaking, but now he wasn't so sure. Emery was plainly frustrated, likely even a bit embarrassed, but he wasn't weak. He would have continued until Allyn called for him to stop, just as he had the previous two nights. And even then, after Allyn had ordered him to take a break, Emery had kept trying—albeit alone and away from the group.

Allyn walked slowly through the circle of magi, gaining a better vantage.

"Wielding isn't something you can force," Vonn said. "Encourage? Of course. Stimulate? Sure. But not force. Wielding is only possible when the mind and body are acting in unison, and right now, they're telling you something is wrong."

Emery looked up at Vonn sharply. "I know what's wrong. I'm tired, I'm cold, and I'm hungry. And I know I'm letting all of you down."

"No." Vonn's soft voice carried just far enough that everyone in the group could hear him. "We're letting *you* down. We're a Family, Emery. We're supposed to stick together, but sitting here with you, I can feel their negative energy. I can hear their unspoken words just as I'm sure you can. The expectation that you're going to fail."

"I will," Emery whispered.

"I know you can wield." Vonn inched closer and laid a gentle hand on Emery's shoulder. "I've seen it."

"That was different."

"Why?"

Emery looked as though he wanted to say something, but bit it back and remained silent.

"You're succumbing to expectation," Vonn said. "They believe, so you believe, and therefore, you fail. It's a self-fulfilling prophecy. But I know you're more stubborn than that. I know deep down you believe you can do it, because I can feel *that* too. You just have to prove yourself right."

Emery looked back at the pyre with an expression Allyn didn't recognize. Not determination, acquiescence, or resignation. *Acceptance, maybe?*

Shoulders relaxing, Emery breathed slowly, deeply. The forest went quiet, almost as if the trees, wind, and animals held their collective breath along with the magi. Anticipation hung thick in the air, but it wasn't the anticipation of failure. This was different. The very air tingled with excitement. With trust. With positive energy. And in the span it took Allyn to blink, a fireball ignited in Emery's palm.

Surprised, Emery fell back, and the fireball winked out of existence. On his backside, Emery held his hands up in front of him, studying them in disbelief.

Vonn's laughter boomed through the night, and he moved to stand over Emery. "Good. Now do it again. I'll grab the food." He stepped away, leaving Emery to try again.

Allyn met Vonn on the edge of the camp, where a fresh deer carcass hung from a thick branch. The fist-sized hole where Vonn had felled the animal with an ice blast was barely visible in the dim light.

"Well done," Allyn said.

"You too," Vonn said. "The idea that the group was at fault resonated with him. Gave him confidence to try again on his own terms. We'll have to be careful, though, not to cultivate a mindset that failure is always someone else's fault."

"Agreed," Allyn said. "We can cater to his need for positive reinforcement and encouragement to keep him involved, but we need to separate him from the group as quickly as possible. That's his next step."

"We're walking a fine line with him."

"So far, it's the only thing that's worked."

"Who's next?"

Allyn looked back toward the group. Emery had succeeded in lighting the fire, and flickering orange flames danced in the center of the squad, making the various onlookers appear as little more than silhouettes. The other magi were congratulating Emery, slapping him on the back and pushing him between them as if he were a pinball.

"I'm not ready to move on from Emery," Allyn said. "We need to be sure he wasn't a one-hit wonder."

"A what?"

"A one-hit wonder," Allyn repeated. Then, when it became apparent that Vonn's lack of understanding was a deeper issue than simply not understanding the reference, he said, "A fluke."

Even after living with the McCollum Family for several months, Allyn still often forgot how far removed the magi could be from outside influences. Like many of the Hyland Family members, Vonn was more aware of pop culture than the members of the McCollum Family, but their knowledge was still the equivalent of someone from another country. By the time a fad or turn of phrase had reached magi consciousness, it had already left the culture it was born into well behind.

"Give him another day," Allyn said. "If he succeeds again tomorrow, we'll move onto Kaira."

"Do you have a plan for her?" Vonn asked.

"I'm working on that."

"Can I make a suggestion then?"

"Of course."

"Before we move on to Kaira, think about Devon."

"Devon?" Allyn dismissed the idea with a shake of his head. Allyn had first met Devon months before, when he arrived at the Kaplan Cabin with his parents, Brandt and Juniette Hyland. They had been among a small group of refugees who had fled Darian's wrath and been drawn to Jaxon's message that the McCollum Family had discovered a new way to unlock magi abilities in those previously thought unable to wield. After Jaxon and Parke, acting grand mage of the Hyland Family, had tasked Allyn with employing those new strategies with a mind for unlocking Machinist abilities, Devon had been one of Allyn's first attempts. And one of his first failures.

"What makes you think he's ready to try again?" Allyn asked.

"He's active," Vonn said. "He's worked himself into the group by being one of the first to congratulate someone when they ascend, and one of the first to offer encouragement when they fail."

"That's new."

"Exactly. And like Emery, I think we can use the power of the group to influence him."

Allyn contemplated the idea for a moment. Devon had not only failed to wield, he also hadn't shown any signs of improvement. The entire reason he'd been invited on the exercise was to boost his morale by providing encouragement through mutual success—something that seemed to be working. But Devon's failures aside, Allyn wasn't sure if *he* was ready to try again. Although, if Devon had indeed turned a mental corner, that was a small victory, and maybe Allyn could keep the momentum going.

The very fact that Allyn was even having this internal debate was a cause for celebration. Flynn and Maleah, two magi previously thought not to have the ability, could wield. As could Boyd and Aidyn, whose abilities had been discovered shortly after settling in at the Estate. For the first time since the turn of the century, the number of wielders was growing. And in the face of that kind of positive news, who was Allyn to say Devon wasn't ready?

"Put together a couple of exercises," Allyn said. "We'll bring him along slowly. If he shows signs of regression, we need to pivot."

"You don't sound very confident."

"It's not about confidence," Allyn said. "It's about being prepared."

"I can respect that. Just..." Vonn winced. "Just remember that we're a part of the group too. Like their collective energy, we radiate positive or negative feelings, as well. And by position alone, ours is more powerful. It's a fine line to walk—being challenging and accepting failure—but we can't let them know we expect it. That will break them, and we may never get them back."

"Understood." When Allyn had accepted the role of training the non-wielders, he'd imagined himself becoming a drill instructor, yelling and spitting in the faces of his squad. Breaking them down. What he hadn't realized was that these magi were already broken down. They didn't need a hard ass. They needed a collaborator. A positive influence. A friend. In practice, he was much closer to a therapist than he was to any one of the clichéd drill instructors he'd seen in Hollywood war movies.

"I'm guilty of it too," Vonn said. "We just need to keep each other in line."

Allyn doubted that. The other man didn't seem to have a negative bone in his body, but Allyn didn't press the issue. "I'll keep you honest."

"Good."

"Give Emery some time to celebrate, but have him find me when he's done. I need to let him know he's not off the hook."

"Back to business?"

Allyn nodded. "It never ends."

He left Vonn and made his way to where Liam and two other magi were huddled over a fallen tree. Splayed out across the wet bark and encased in clear plastic was a detailed map of the local terrain. The western hemlock, Douglas fir, western red cedar, and red alder trees that made up their surroundings and filled the brisk mountain air with a sweet scent of pine, were illustrated with various green swatches dictated by the density of the forest. The countless mountain runoffs that made their way west to the Pacific Ocean were blue.

Liam held his finger in one spot while his other hand operated a compass.

"How are we looking?" Allyn asked.

"We're too far south," Liam said, not looking up.

"Too far south? How is that possible? I thought we were heading south until we came to this creek." Allyn pointed at a blue line on the map.

"We were," Liam said. "But that creek isn't there anymore."

"I don't understand."

"This region has had a very dry winter," Liam said. "My best guess is that there hasn't been enough mountain runoff, and the creek dried up."

"What does that mean for us?"

"It means we'll have to circle back around and approach base camp from the west."

"How long?"

"It'll cost us at least half a day."

Allyn rubbed the week-old scruff on his chin. *Another couple days?* They would be completely out of rations by this time tomorrow, and the deer that Vonn had slain was difficult to move and would spoil before long. Not to mention they were running low on water. During any other given year, the range would be covered in a thick blanket of snow, and they would be able to collect and boil water to refill their reserves, but as Liam had said, the season had been abnormally dry. More than anything, their navigational oversight was a blow to their morale. Yet another setback.

You wanted them to face adversity, he reminded himself. *It was the foundation of the entire exercise.*

Allyn fingered a cylindrical metal device in his pocket. Liam had assembled the transmitter before they'd left, and all Allyn had to do was push the small red button at the top of the device to send an alert to Jaxon. It was to be used only in an emergency, if they needed immediate extraction. The current situation didn't qualify.

"Plot a course," Allyn said. "But measure twice. I don't want any more setbacks."

Liam's face soured a bit—he wouldn't like having his nose rubbed in his mistake—but he nodded and set back to work.

Allyn turned, unsure what his next order of business was, when the sound of hissing steam carried on the wind and the fire went out. Allyn instinctively dropped to a crouch, hiding behind a large fern, his eyes probing the darkness. The camp had gone still as the magi settled into practiced defensive positions.

"What happened?" Liam asked from behind.

Allyn turned and placed a finger on his lips. He wasn't sure if Liam saw the gesture, but Liam didn't say anything more.

A twig snapped, and dry leaves rustled as a shadow moved toward him.

Allyn leaped up, wielding. Red coils of electricity sprang up around his arms, pulsing and filling the air with a metallic hum and a bloody light. The shadow slid to a halt and took a hurried step backward. A nervous young man stood in front of him. Flynn.

"People," Flynn said in a hushed voice. "In the forest."

Allyn cut the line to the coils, and the forest went dark again. "Where?"

"Follow me."

Moving as fast as silence allowed, Flynn led him to the other edge of the camp. As they passed, Allyn noticed the fire had been hastily smothered with soil. It mostly covered the orange glow of burning embers, but did little to mask the smell of thick smoke that hung heavy in the canopy of leaves and pine needles.

On the outskirts of camp, Flynn slowed, falling into line with the magi that were already waiting. Ren and Vonn found him immediately.

"What've we got?" Allyn whispered.

The woman's sleek black hair covered half of her face, making it appear as if she were looking at him from behind a dark veil. "Movement."

"People?" Allyn asked, repeating what Flynn had told him.

"Don't know yet."

Allyn silently rebuked Flynn for having passed along incomplete information; he would have to talk to the young magi about that. "What's the play?"

"See if they get closer," Ren said simply.

"And if they do?"

Ren didn't answer. Instead, water pooled in her hands, immediately freezing into lances of ice.

"There!" Vonn whispered.

The white light of flashlights danced through the distant trees, so bright they might as well have been blaring bullhorns—and they were heading directly toward Allyn's squad.

They know we're here. They saw the fire—or me wielding.

"I count three," Ren said.

Allyn quickly cycled through their options. They could hide and hope whoever it was slipped by them in the night. But their camp was large, and the odds of that happening were slim. They could wait for them to approach and discover what the newcomers' intentions were, but Allyn hated letting the world come to him. He preferred taking control of the situation and forcing events to play out at his will, and that meant making their presence known.

"Give me fire," Allyn said to Ren and Vonn. "Make it look like a torch. And give me a bit of space, a couple paces to either side."

"We're going to confront them?" Vonn asked.

"We're taking control of the situation."

Allyn stepped forward, and Ren and Vonn fell into step behind him. The air *whooshed* as fire sprung over their arms.

The flashlights stopped.

"Who's there?" Allyn shouted.

The flashlights rushed forward, this time bobbing and swaying as the newcomers picked up speed.

"I said, who's there?" Allyn shouted again.

The flashlights didn't stop. If anything, they moved with even more vigor. Allyn glanced at Ren and Vonn then back to the movement in front of them, his hands tightening into fists as the newcomers drew ever closer.

Allyn wielded, and immediately the flashlights slowed, bobbing for a few more feet before stopping altogether. Closer now, three faint outlines appeared. The center figure was taller than the others and carried a flashlight in both hands.

"Allyn?" Nolan's voice carried across the space between them, nervous and hesitant.

"Give me light!" Allyn bellowed, and following his

command, anyone that could wield fire did, filling the forest with half a dozen more points of light.

Nolan stepped into the light, with Kendyl and Nyla at his side.

"What's wrong?" Allyn asked.

"Jaxon needs you back at the Estate," Nolan said. "Now."

CHAPTER 2

A LLYN HAD A THOUSAND QUESTIONS on the ride back to the Hyland Estate; unfortunately, nobody had any answers. Kendyl said that Jaxon had found her well before nightfall, saying that he needed Allyn and Liam to return to the Estate, and when pressed for answers, he'd said only that it couldn't wait until morning.

"Was he agitated?" Allyn had asked.

"It was Jaxon," Kendyl said with a sarcastic grin. "He's *always* agitated." After a moment, and an unamused expression from Leira, who sat in the front seat, she added, "But no, no more than usual."

Allyn pressed, often asking the same thing in a variety of different ways, hoping to elicit a new kernel of information, but Kendyl eventually shut him down.

"Jesus, Allyn. I'm not on trial here, and it doesn't matter how many ways you ask the same question. I can't answer what I don't know."

Frustrated and impatient, Allyn ceased his prosecution, though Kendyl had done little to ease the growing knot of tension in his stomach. If Jaxon needed to see them so urgently, something major was amiss.

Allyn's first thought was the FBI. Though he was still a wanted man, the heat he and Kendyl had previously been under had dwindled in the months following the climax with Special Agent Richard Maddox. Nolan and Liam's continued effort to sabotage the investigation using their shadow user in the FBI database had slowed Maddox's investigation, and eventually larger, more pressing issues had arisen. When law enforcement was forced to move on, Allyn and Kendyl had vanished again.

Nolan had once told him that the investigation would never end, that any agent worth the title would never give up. And Maddox had been a true predator, a lion in a suit and tie, and once he got his claws into something, he didn't let go. Had he taken the torch back up? Had he found a new piece of information that helped him reignite the investigation?

The latter was doubtful. Since arriving at the Hyland Estate, Allyn and Kendyl had ceased being Allyn and Kendyl Kaplan—they were now Allyn and Kendyl McCollum, complete with false identification and a digital history to back it up. Additionally, they were as far off the grid as possible. Even if Agent Maddox had found a new piece of evidence, it would be so outdated that it would be worthless.

Unless there's something I'm missing.

A little more than two hours after retrieving Allyn from the campsite, Nolan pulled the dark sedan around the circular driveway in front of the Hyland Estate. The clear night offered a full array of stars on display, and a full moon shined high overhead. The Estate itself, a two-story Victorian mansion, basked radiantly in the soft starlight, resting on the edge of a two-hundred-foot cliff. The surf battered relentlessly at the rocky ground below. At some point, hundreds of years in the future, the powerful ocean would carve out a swath of earth large enough to send the Estate toppling into the dark abyss of the water, disappearing from memory.

Spotlights lined the front of the Estate, shining ominously upward from the gardens like a flashlight under the chin of one's face. The black sedan they rode in joined a handful of other vehicles, all of which belonged to the Hyland Family, parked under a carport at the north end of the Estate. The grounds were still, many of the Estate's lights off, and save for the steady roar of crashing waves below, the scene was quiet.

The smell of salt, seaweed, and rotting sea life assaulted Allyn's senses as he stepped out of the vehicle. He'd long since grown used to the quirks of living by the sea, but having been away for a week, he had forgotten how assailing it could be.

He entered the Estate through a side entrance on the southern wing and quickly made for Jaxon's office. Located on the second floor and with a clear view of the Pacific, it had originally been home to a small Hyland library, but when Liam had settled in, he'd made it one of his first priorities to move the Hyland texts into the basement with the rest of the McCollum Library. And Jaxon, needing a private retreat, had quickly seized upon it.

The door was closed, and light poured through the crack at the bottom of the frame. Allyn knocked.

"Enter," Jaxon said from inside.

Allyn found Jaxon gazing out the salt-stained windows at the sea beyond. Jaxon was a large man, easily six inches taller than Allyn, with broad shoulders and a chiseled frame he liked to show off with sleeveless jerkins. At times, Allyn had thought Jaxon had more in common with a bull than a man. His dark, closely trimmed beard was just a little darker than the color of his skin, and it matched the length of the hair atop his head.

Allyn strode toward a dust-covered armchair in front of Jaxon's desk and took a seat as the other magi turned to face him. Allyn nearly started. Jaxon looked *exhausted*. Beyond his red, swollen eyes, his entire demeanor appeared defeated—his shoulders slouched, breathing labored, movement sluggish. Allyn hadn't seen him in such a state since they'd escaped the FBI's clutches.

"You made it back," Jaxon said. Even his *voice* sounded tired. "The beacon had you almost three miles south of where you should have been. You had me fearing the worst."

Surely *that* wasn't what was keeping Jaxon up at night.

"We had an issue with one of our landmarks," Allyn said. "And we didn't learn of the mistake until today."

Jaxon sat down and leaned back in his chair with a deep sigh, steepling his fingers in front of his mouth. Allyn readied himself for the rebuke. It wasn't so much Jaxon's expression that told Allyn it was coming, but his knowledge of the other magi—Jaxon wasn't one to let a teaching opportunity pass by. It was one of the many qualities that made him the perfect person to lead the McCollum Family. But Jaxon took a different tack than Allyn anticipated.

"What did you learn?" Jaxon asked.

"Not to use seasonal landmarks as checkpoints."

Jaxon chuckled softly, and it eased some of the tension in the room. "What was the landmark?"

"A creek on the west side of the range," Allyn said. "It was dry, and we must have missed it."

"Fair enough. What should you have used in retrospect?"

Allyn thought about it for a couple moments, and when nothing obvious came to mind, he shook his head. "I don't know."

"Your idea to use a natural landmark was a good one," Jaxon said. "Seasonal as it may be. The error wasn't in planning, but in execution. Even a dry creek bed should have been easy to spot and given you enough pause to re-evaluate your position."

Allyn nodded. Jaxon was right, and Allyn had long since learned to separate his personal feelings from constructive criticism.

"How did the rest of the exercise go?"

"It went well," Allyn said, leaning back and crossing his legs. "Flynn and Maleah ascended, and Emery is close. I'm confident he would have broken through completely if we hadn't been summoned back."

Allyn leveled his gaze on Jaxon, hinting further at the unspoken question. *Why am I here?*

If Jaxon caught on, he didn't show it. Instead, he rose from his chair and circled his desk to take a seat on the corner, closer to Allyn. His eyes flickered to the door then back to Allyn.

"Good," Jaxon said, his voice soft. "Any... any machinists?"

"No." Allyn shook his head. "Or, I should say, I don't believe so. Flynn, Maleah, and Emery all wielded fire. But that might have been a byproduct of the exercise's inherent prejudice. We crafted a need of warmth, of fire, and that doesn't lend itself to many of the machinists' known abilities."

Jaxon nodded again, poorly hiding his disappointment.

That's odd.

Jaxon had never expressed disappointment to such news before. The fact that the number of magi capable of wielding, regardless of whether they manifested traditional or machinist abilities, was increasing should have been cause for celebration.

"What's going on, Jaxon?" Allyn asked. "I have a hard time imagining you summoned me back here to question a training exercise that wasn't even halfway completed."

Jaxon crossed his arms, his eyebrows rising a degree. As acting grand mage of the McCollum Family and all but grand mage in waiting to the Green Family, Jaxon wasn't accustomed to being spoken to so directly. But being a member of Jaxon's personal council and de facto leader of the machinist movement lent Allyn certain advantages. So Allyn waited patiently, refusing to let the stretching silence unnerve him.

A knock at the door interrupted Jaxon before he could speak.

"Come in." Jaxon rose from the edge of the desk, standing straighter. He might be comfortable letting his guard down in front of Allyn, but that familiarity didn't extend far beyond him.

The door opened, and a heavyset man with a cleft chin and a round face entered. Parke Hyland was the acting grand mage of the Hyland Family, and in the few months Allyn had known him, Parke had proved himself to be a kind and generous man. Almost too much so. It seemed Parke was deliberately attempting to use his own compassion and munificence to counter the fear and rage Darian had used to govern.

Allyn couldn't complain or fault the man—so far his tactics were working. The Hyland Family was whole, and they'd provided the McCollum Family a place of refuge.

Parke nodded to Allyn and took a seat in the armchair beside his. Allyn studied the man. Not a hint of surprise had shown on his face. He'd known Allyn was coming, that the exercise was coming to a premature end. Whatever was going on, Jaxon and Parke were working together.

"It appears," Jaxon said, "that Arch Mage Westarra has finally decided to pay us a visit."

Allyn blinked. The leader of the magi Forum was the

most powerful man in the magi Order. That same man had ignored, rejected, and spurned every missive for audience the McCollum and Hyland Families had requested. Neither Jaxon nor Parke had heard anything from the arch mage since merging their two Families. It had almost seemed as if the magi leadership was attempting to splinter the two Families simply by refusing to acknowledge them.

"Why now?" Allyn asked.

Jaxon held out his arms and cocked his head to the side as if to say, "Your guess is as good as mine."

"He didn't say why?" Allyn asked.

"No."

"Nothing?"

"Nothing."

Shivers went down Allyn's spine, and the hair on the back of his neck stood on end. An unexpected visit from the most powerful man in the magi order didn't have a good ring to it.

"When will he arrive?" Allyn asked.

"Tomorrow."

"Tomorrow?" Allyn coughed, incredulous. "But... that's..."

"That's what we've been told to expect," Jaxon said, his voice taking on a stronger tone. "And that's what we'll prepare for."

Allyn closed his eyes and pinched his forehead. Silence crept into the room, seeping into the walls and bookshelves, so tangible Allyn could almost reach out and mold it. He wanted to say something. He knew he *should* say something, but he couldn't think of anything that the other two men weren't already aware of. They were in this together. Just as in the dark. Just as clueless.

That's why he called me back. Not to tell me that Westarra was coming, but because he doesn't know what to do. It terrifies him.

Allyn could see it now—Jaxon always carried himself with a cool confidence that bordered on swagger. He was commanding but didn't have to flaunt it. He spoke, always expecting people to listen to him. But now, his movements, facial expressions, even the cadence of his voice were the product of meticulous self-awareness. He wasn't just putting on a mask of leadership for Parke; Jaxon was putting on the mask for himself.

"I know what you're thinking," Jaxon said. "But we don't have any reason to believe his coming will bring ill news."

Parke met Jaxon's eye and shook his head slightly. It appeared the two didn't agree on this matter.

"Who received the notification?" Allyn asked.

"It came to me." Jaxon rounded his desk, opened a drawer, and pulled out an embossed piece of parchment. "Via this." He handed it to Allyn.

"This is very low tech," Allyn said, flipping the missive to look at the elegant script on the backside. "Even for the Order. How did it arrive?"

"It was nailed to the front door," Parke said.

"Excuse me? Nailed?"

"They want us to know that they're already here," Jaxon said. "That we're on their time and at their mercy."

"This is worse than I thought," Allyn said.

"Relax," Jaxon said.

"Relax? How can I relax? First it was Lukas, then it was Darian, and then the FBI. Now the most powerful magi in the Order has announced he's coming by nailing *this* to our front door, and you want me to relax?" Allyn barked a sarcastic laugh. "You're funny."

"Do you feel better?" Jaxon asked patronizingly. "The fact is, we don't know why he's here or what his agenda is. But we do know that if he wanted to attack, he wouldn't have left a note. We also know that he's watching us to see what we do. If we want to be taken seriously, as the legitimate Family that we are, we need to act the part. And that doesn't include stomping our feet and throwing a fit like a child who's had their favorite doll taken from them."

Allyn's face flushed, and he bit his bottom lip angrily.

"Now that doesn't mean I intend to go into this as a pawn," Jaxon added. "Once Westarra has entered the Estate, he's entered our realm and will be subject to our rules. If I need to flex, I have every intention of doing so. We are not a weak Family, and we will not be pushed around."

"What do you need me to do?" Allyn asked.

"Organize the machinists and be prepared to showcase your abilities. It's time to finally show the magi leadership who we are and who we're becoming."

CHAPTER 3

WORD OF ARCH MAGE WESTARRA'S impending visit spread through the Estate quicker than Allyn had expected. Jaxon hadn't mentioned who'd found the note, but based on the rate of velocity with which the word spread, Allyn assumed someone other than the grand mages had discovered it. The word circulating the Estate was a word of confirmation, not of possibility, and that, it seemed, traveled faster than light.

Jaxon and Parke had risen before the sun and roused their Families shortly thereafter, so by the time Allyn stepped from his room, the Estate buzzed with nervous excitement. Magi swarmed throughout the Estate, cleaning, organizing, and preparing. Some magi barked orders, while others engaged in mini power struggles over the proper way to polish the floor or if the baseboards really did need scrubbed. Even more worked in a quiet, determined fashion.

On more than one occasion while walking through the Estate, Allyn was yelled at for stepping on a newly mopped floor or grazing against a recently touched-up wall. He merely offered these people a simple smile of apology and continued on his way. Tensions were high, the stress deep, and some people, magi or not, dealt with it by taking it out on those around them. Allyn didn't need to exacerbate the situation.

To his surprise, the TVs, computers, magazines, newspapers, and other outside-world products scattered throughout the Estate had been taken down and hidden. It was one thing to be accepting of the outside world's influence; flaunting it was another.

Allyn didn't know how he felt about that. It felt like the Families were hiding who they truly were—who, in Allyn's opinion, they needed to be. But on the other hand, playing the game was important, and they needed to live up to expectations.

Allyn's squad of machinists waited for him near the north side of the Estate. They stood in a small circle near the edge of the cliff, watching as other magi cleaned windows, weeded flowerbeds, and scrubbed dirty siding. There were four of them in all: Kendyl, Liam, Nolan, and Canary. Each provided the Family with a unique ability. From communicating with computers, being a receptor of radio waves, or even manipulating emotions, their abilities were as unique as they were. And if Allyn and Liam were correct, these four represented the future of the magi race.

"Look who decided to wake up," Kendyl said as Allyn approached. Her sarcastic grin was a stark contrast to the rest of the group's overt nervousness. Her dark hair was pulled back in a tight ponytail, and she wore the pale-gray compression armor the Hyland clerics wore. Her black pants could have been mistaken for athletic gear, except that they were thicker, more durable, and fire resistant. As an *empath,* her abilities—the ability to channel, control, and *project* emotions—were closer to a cleric's than anything else, and she'd worked to integrate herself into that group. Dressing like one was a simple strategy for being accepted as one.

"I was up before dawn," Allyn said. It wasn't exactly true—he'd woken up to relieve himself and promptly gone back to bed—but it was close enough that he didn't feel guilty for lying to her. "What are you doing here anyway? Jaxon wanted the machinists together."

"I had nowhere else to be," Kendyl said. "I may not be a machinist, but if you're trying to make an impression, I can help you do that."

"Fair enough," Allyn said. Truth be told, he didn't care if she was with them or not. She was close enough to all of them that she wouldn't be a distraction, and besides, his sister might be able to offer additional insight and ideas that Allyn couldn't.

He turned to the rest of the group. Nolan and Liam stood shoulder to shoulder, but always aloof, Canary waited a couple paces away. Since her abilities had manifested, she'd kept her distance. Probably because her abilities made conversations difficult, getting in the way of her being able to listen and focus. As a result, she was socially awkward. Like an autistic child, she couldn't filter out the background noise from the rest. Life to her was like standing in a room with one hundred stereos, each blaring a different song.

Canary's yellow-and-black-streaked hair was tied in an intricate braid that hung over her shoulder. She looked at Allyn out of the corner of her eye, mumbling softly to herself. Allyn couldn't tell if she was talking to him, thinking out loud, or simply repeating the bits of conversation she heard on the radio waves constantly bombarding her.

Allyn nodded his head to the side, asking her to join the rest of the group. Casting her eyes to the ground, Canary shuffled forward.

"Thank you for meeting me," Allyn said. "You've no doubt heard the rumors. Jaxon and Parke received notice yesterday

that Arch Mage Westarra will be arriving at the Estate today."
Allyn paused to study the group and wasn't surprised when
none of them showed the slightest bit of shock. "We haven't
been informed yet as to the meaning of his coming, but it
no doubt has to do with the future of our Family. We have
some... unanswered questions."

"That's putting it mildly," Liam said sarcastically. Out
of all of them, Liam would understand the implications of
Westarra's arrival the best.

"You look like you've got a question, Nolan," Allyn said.

The former FBI agent wore a confused expression. Allyn
had attempted to explain as much of the magi culture and
leadership to Nolan as possible, but there were so many
details, so many layers of magi politics, that Nolan had
quickly become confused.

"I assume someone as important as the arch mage won't
travel alone."

"No," Liam said. "He'll have his Elemental Guard and
personal servants at his side."

"Then how many can we expect?" Nolan asked.

Liam shrugged. "I don't know."

"Why should it matter?" Allyn asked.

"The way I understand it," Nolan said, "the arch mage
is something like a president or prime minister of the magi
Order. They work with the Forum to rule and govern the
Families."

Liam shook his head. "Not exactly. The arch mage is the
leader of the Order, yes, but they aren't like a president—they
don't have unilateral control over the Families. Neither does
the Forum. They have influence, of course, and a lot of it,
but the Families are too spread out, too diverse to be under a
single rule. Think of the Forum less as a body of government

and more of a body of allies. Almost like..." Liam snapped his fingers as he struggled to make an apt comparison.

"Like the United Nations?" Allyn suggested.

"Yes," Liam said, pointing at Allyn. "That's not a bad comparison. Each Family governs itself and is responsible for itself, but drastic actions—like war, merging with another Family, or going public, anything that affects the entire Order—have to be approved by the Forum and ruled on by the arch mage."

"What happens if a Family doesn't seek approval first?" Kendyl asked.

"Then they're subject to the mercy of the Forum," Liam said.

"Which means?" Kendyl pressed.

"Which means like your United Nations, the Forum may unite to eliminate a common threat." Liam must have seen the growing discomfort among the group because he was quick to add, "It doesn't happen often, though. Even during Lukas's rise to power, my father attempted to gather the support of the Forum, to strike before Lukas solidified his movement. But they rejected his plea, instead opting for other measures."

"Like what?" Nolan asked.

"Sanctions," Allyn said.

"Something like that," Liam said. "First you have to understand that because our numbers are so few, our strength comes from remaining together. We learned after the Fracture that Families are stronger than individuals. The same can be said about the Forum. United Families are stronger than any single Family. To exist outside of that, to be an unrecognized Family, is akin to exile. Families who aren't recognized don't usually last very long, and often splinter to be assimilated into others.

"The arch mage refused to recognize Lukas's movement by not giving him a seat on the Forum, essentially declaring them an unrecognized Family. By doing so, Lukas couldn't petition the body, and had very little political influence. It also eliminated his access to the Forum's finances."

"But it didn't work," Allyn said. "It only made him desperate and quick to act."

Liam nodded solemnly. By not uniting to face down a common threat, the Forum had effectively left Graeme, Liam's father and grand mage of the McCollum Family, to contend with Lukas—something that ultimately claimed Graeme's life and the McCollum Manor.

Worse, the Forum had determined the McCollum Family's actions to be a violation of the Forum's declaration, and the Forum dissolved the Family's admission to the Forum. Had it not been for the Hyland Family splintering, as well, the McCollum Family would have been forced to splinter and assimilate into other Families. Jaxon's own parents, knowing of the Forum's decision, had ordered him to return to the Green Family—but Jaxon had refused. He'd made a vow to Allyn and Liam to see the McCollum Family reestablished before returning to his own Family.

"So my question remains," Nolan said. "Who's coming with the arch mage? Will the Forum come, as well? Because if they do, that means they have yet to vote, and there's still a chance we can sway their opinion. If not, then our fate might already be decided, and the arch mage is only coming to hand down judgment."

Jaxon stood at the front of their host. Leira was at his left shoulder, followed by Liam, Allyn, the other two machinists, and what was left of the McCollum Family. Grand Mage

Parke Hyland stood at his other shoulder, then Brandt, Juniette, and their son Devon, followed by the rest of the Hyland Family. Together, their two Families were less than one hundred in number, smaller than the greatest Families in the Order, but larger than average. Waiting in front of the estate, they formed a line, curving inward at the ends to form a very loose semicircle around the end of the driveway. Each wore their most decorative clothing. No compression armor or battle attire. This was a diplomatic meeting.

Or so I hope, Jaxon thought.

The welcoming host watched the driveway intently, holding their collective breath. Jaxon's sentries had spotted the arch mage's motorcade two miles away, giving him just enough time to have the Families form up. That had been ten minutes ago, and the extra time had done little to settle their Families' nerves.

Jaxon licked his lips, tasting the salty moisture that hung in their air like a fine mist. The sea spray was particularly thick today, making his skin and clothing damp. In his early days living at the Hyland Estate, Jaxon had expected to grow used to the smell of brine and sulfur, but it was just as oppressive today as ever. Compared to the clean mountain air of the Kaplan Cabin or the forest scents of the McCollum Manor, the Hyland Estate might as well have been a refrigerator full of spoiled fish.

A sudden wave of murmurs rose as the hood of a black sedan appeared around the bend of the driveway. Immaculately polished with blacked-out windows, the vehicle could have belonged to any world leader except that it lacked the patriotic window flags politicians liked to fly.

Jaxon stiffened as the lead car rolled toward them. Several others, all matching, appeared behind it. Half a dozen in all, they parked in a formation that would allow for a quick organized exit.

That must have taken practice.

Then again, in practiced unison, they shut off their engines. Car doors in all except the car at the center of the formation opened, and the broad-shouldered, bulky men of the arch mage's Elemental Guard emerged. Unlike the McCollum and Hyland Families, these men were dressed in black magi compression armor, though theirs were heavier, reinforced in the chest, back, and shoulders. The guards hesitated for a moment, surveying the magi in front of them, as a massive, seven-foot guard with shoulder-length brown hair made for the car in the center of the formation.

Jaxon immediately recognized the man as Rohn Agerland, Spark of the Elemental Guard—their leader and commander. With a barrel chest, powerful arms, and skin scarred red and purple by flame, he looked like something out of legend, like Canaan Severin, Varian Whitebrow, Galvin Oak, or any of the other legendary magi the young mages read about.

Rohn opened the rear door of the car, and a wiry man with salt-colored hair and a matching beard emerged. Arch Mage Westarra wasn't a physically imposing man, but his cold blue eyes could freeze steel and break stone.

Westarra stood with a grimace, likely uncomfortable after spending so many hours in the back of a car. His smile was all lips and no teeth as he strode toward the waiting Families. He was immediately flanked by Rohn and another of the Elemental Guard who had to be Myanna Makare, the only female magi in the elite squad. Her determined, take-no-flack expression reminded Jaxon of his mother, which meant Myanna was one of the few people in the world who could intimidate him.

Jaxon clasped his hands behind his back and brought his

heels together, bowing his head sharply to the arch mage. The two Families followed his lead, repeating the ancient salute.

"Be calm," Arch Mage Westarra said to his audience. "We are of One."

"We are of One," the two Families repeated.

Westarra nodded approvingly. "Jaxon Green," he said, his voice booming over their onlookers.

"Your Grace."

"You have assumed a great responsibility."

"We are of One, Your Grace."

The corners of Westarra's mouth rose a degree, and Jaxon couldn't tell if the man was proud or if he found the entire charade amusing. Without saying anything more, Westarra moved on down the line to stand between Liam and Leira.

"Leira," Westarra said. "Look at you—no longer a child. And you, Liam. You look more and more like your father every year. Though, I must say, I think you'll grow to be taller than he ever was."

Liam straightened at this; standing taller, chin high in the air. Being around him every day, Jaxon hadn't noticed. The change had come on gradually, but looking at him now, Jaxon was reminded that Liam must have grown another four to six inches in the past six months. His voice had even dropped another octave. He was still the same awkward adolescent struggling to grow into his body, but it was becoming easier to imagine him as something other than a boy.

"Your father was a great man," Westarra added. "We grieve with you."

"Thank you, Your Grace," Liam said.

Leira remained silent, her cool expression bordering on defiance. Jaxon eyed her, suddenly growing very nervous. Leira's body was coiled tight, her hands clenched tightly behind her back. Jaxon knew she didn't want Westarra's condolences. She didn't want the charade. The pomp. Leira believed Westarra had condemned them through inaction and was as responsible for her father's death and their Family's demise as Lukas was.

Hold it together, Leira. Just hold it together.

Getting nothing more out of her, Westarra smiled and moved on down the line, occasionally stopping to speak with other McCollum magi. Reaching the end, he turned and moved back up the line, slowing slightly to glance at Allyn and Nolan before continuing to the Hyland Family. The entire affair took ten or fifteen agonizing minutes, and by the end of it, Jaxon's nervous anticipation had reached its peak. When Westarra returned to the front of the group, Jaxon fought to keep his hands and knees from trembling. He hated facing challenges outside his control.

Westarra stopped in front of Jaxon, his lips near Jaxon's ear. "I think it's time you and I had a talk," he said. "Alone."

CHAPTER 4

JAXON LED ARCH MAGE WESTARRA to his study. He could feel the weight of the man's office behind him, hear it in the way his heavy footsteps echoed against the wainscoted walls of the hallway. Westarra hadn't come to socialize, to take afternoon tea and catch up with an old friend. No, he was here to remind the Order that he was their leader. Their superior. And that he should be treated as such. If Jaxon had any doubts about that, the four Elemental Guards trailing the arch mage quickly squashed them.

Jaxon opened the door to the study and waited as two members of the guard advanced into the room, securing it. Westarra didn't wait for their okay; instead he entered the room while the other two guards took up station outside the door. Jaxon followed Westarra inside and, at the arch mage's order, closed the door behind him.

"Have a seat," Westarra said, motioning to one of the armchairs. It was clear he meant to take Jaxon's seat behind the desk in what was yet another display of asserting his authority.

It rankled Jaxon. Westarra was taking the display too far. He wasn't only asserting his authority, he was rubbing

Jaxon's nose in it, taunting him. It was unnecessary. Jaxon wasn't an adversary. Why couldn't Westarra see that?

"Of course," Jaxon said, taking a seat. "How was your trip? Not too painful, I hope."

"Long." Westarra kept his back to Jaxon, gazing out the bay windows that overlooked the ocean. Even though the magi had painstakingly cleaned them earlier in the day, the windows were already muddied with sea mist and salt. Cleaning them had been a fool's errand.

"I can imagine. New England isn't too close to us out here." Jaxon wanted to wince at how artificial it sounded. He didn't know how to do small talk.

Westarra turned and pulled out his chair. "No it isn't," he said, sitting down. "And I wish I hadn't been forced to come."

"I hope we didn't force your hand, Your Grace."

"Don't give me that," Westarra said with a dismissive gesture. "It was your blind... *loyalty*"—he nearly spat the word—"that brought me out here, and you know it."

"Then I hope it wasn't too much trouble."

"Don't play games with me, Jaxon. You don't understand the game, and you aren't half the player your father is."

"I'm not half as experienced, either. Give it time. I will be."

"Just as confident though," Westarra added. "And likely just as stubborn. Which is, you might say, why I'm here." Westarra leaned back, studying Jaxon for a long moment.

Jaxon returned his gaze, unflinching. He refused to be intimidated in his own study.

"We have a problem, Jaxon," Westarra said. "I acted within my authority when I disbanded the McCollum Family. But in remaining with them, against your own Family's wishes, you've challenged me. Some are calling for me to burn you out, stamp the McCollum Family into the ashes, but I have others fighting to reinstate you. It puts us in a bit of a predicament, wouldn't you say?"

"I suppose, Your Grace."

"You see," Westarra continued, "if I enforce my original decree, I risk pitting the Families that support the McCollum Family against me. And if the recent past is any indication, we know where that could lead. The Order can absorb one splintered Family, even two, but a splinter of the Order itself..." Westarra pursed his lips. "We aren't strong enough for that."

Westarra paused again, and this time, Jaxon remained silent.

"On the other hand, if I do nothing, and I reinstate the McCollum Family, name you interim grand mage, what does that say about the Forum's authority? What does that say about the power of my office? Would the other Families see it as a sign of weakness? The Forum brought down by a single splintered Family? Or would they fall in line and respect the office—even though McCollum Family didn't?"

"It's difficult to understand how anyone will react, Your Grace."

"So you *do* understand," Westarra said.

"I've had to make difficult decisions myself."

"And yet, here you sit. With the weight of two Families at your back."

Jaxon nodded. "Loyalty is earned when your people believe you have their best interests at heart, Your Grace."

"And you don't believe I have your best interests in mind?"

"Pardon me, Your Grace, but no, I don't." Jaxon took a deep breath. "These two Families have been through more than you can possibly imagine, and in spite of Lukas, in spite of Darian, the McCollums and Hylands are united. I would think you'd want to promote that kind of resilience."

"You've done a remarkable job, Jaxon. For that, you have earned my respect. And despite what you might believe, I *do* have your best interests in mind. But I have to weigh those with the interests of our people as a whole."

"You sound as if you've already come to a decision."

"I have."

Jaxon shifted uncomfortably in his seat. "And?"

"And both choices are wrong."

"Excuse me?"

"There isn't a correct answer," Westarra repeated. "At least out of the two options I outlined. I can no sooner reinstate the Family as I can uphold my original decree. If the McCollum Family seeks to remain a part of the Order, and have a representative on the Forum, they're going to have to earn the Forum's favor."

Jaxon sat forward in his seat, suddenly encouraged. He'd expected a bigger fight than this. "How can we do that, Your Grace?"

"I have something in mind, but first, I have something to show you." Westarra motioned for one of the guards inside the room to come. The guard handed Westarra a tablet then returned to his post behind Jaxon at the door. "The Forum deliberately remained agnostic in the conflict between Graeme and Lukas. We considered it a private matter among the McCollum Family."

Jaxon disagreed, but he held his tongue.

"Imagine my surprise then," Westarra continued, "to see the conflict not only boil into other Families, but into the world at large."

Jaxon's blood ran cold. He knew what was coming before Westarra toggled the video on his tablet and slid it across the desk for Jaxon to see. It was the same video Nolan had posted online under the alias J.P. Niall. The grainy video taken from the dashcam of a squad car showed an injured Graeme battling one of Lukas's supporters in full magical glory. Shortly after Nolan posted the video, it had gone viral, accumulating over a million views in two days.

"You don't look surprised to see this," Westarra said.

"I'm not," Jaxon said, deciding not to hide from it. "We worked very hard to remove it but couldn't stop its spread."

"I see." Westarra's eyes narrowed, and the creases in the corners of his eyes deepened as he studied Jaxon.

He didn't expect me to know about the video. He doesn't know that Nolan was the one who uploaded it. Probably best to keep that detail a secret.

"Unfortunately," Westarra said, grabbing the tablet once more and holding it in the air for the guard to grab, "this video poses more danger than you can ever imagine."

"I don't understand."

"Of that, I have no doubt." Westarra clasped his hands together. "There are secrets among the magi leadership. Secrets that we've worked very hard to keep. What I'm about to tell you, Jaxon, I tell you because you've earned it. And because it's how the McCollum Family will earn the favor of my office and regain its seat among the Forum."

———————

The red coils of electricity made Allyn's arms tingle with energy. It was the only side effect of his ability—the coils didn't burn or emit any residual heat as they crawled from his shoulders to the tips of his fingers, crackling and sparking.

"Loose!" Allyn shouted.

Ren shot a blast of ice high into the sky, propelling it forward at incredible speed with a concussion of air. The blast soared in a gentle arc toward the tops of the evergreen trees on the east side of the Estate's grounds.

Allyn traced its trajectory, unleashing a static charge just as the translucent block of ice disappeared into the gray of the thick overcast sky. The static charge—nothing more than a series of coils wound into a tight flat disk—zipped toward the blast. Allyn rolled onto the balls of his feet, willing the charge forward, watching as it neared the blast and... missed.

Allyn blinked as the ice blast landed in the forested area to the distant sound of broken branches and squawking birds.

"It happens," Nolan said, slapping Allyn on the shoulder as he stepped up to take his place.

Kendyl offered him a shrug as he stepped away to give Nolan some space. Liam smiled but said nothing. He'd been stewing over something since the arch mage's arrival.

"Correct me if I'm wrong, Allyn," Nolan said, flashing a cocky grin, "but if I get this one, I take the lead, right?"

Allyn shook his head. Nolan *was* correct, but everything was a game to him. Jaxon was inside right now speaking to the arch mage, the same man who would determine the fate of their entire Family, and Nolan couldn't stop being his arrogant self for even one afternoon.

"No?" Nolan continued. "What's the score again, Liam?"

"You've each hit four out of six," Liam said. "Hit this one, and Allyn will have to hit his final shot to force a tiebreaker."

"That's what I thought," Nolan said. "Thank you, Liam. What do you say, Allyn? Want to put a wager on it?"

"I want to wipe that smile off your face."

Nolan laughed. "You're not the first, believe me. But that's not an answer. How about a little bet to make things a little more interesting?"

"What are you thinking?" Allyn asked. It was the only way to shut him up.

"If I hit this, you let me take your sister on a date."

"Excuse me?" Kendyl said, raising an eyebrow in apparent surprise.

She wasn't the only one caught off guard. Allyn opened his mouth to speak, but his words died on his tongue.

Nolan winked at her, making Allyn's blood boil. *That cocky son of a bitch.*

"I'm not a piece of property that can be won, bartered, or given away," Kendyl continued. Her voice had an edge to it that she usually reserved for Allyn.

"Oh, don't act like we haven't talked about it," Nolan said.

That stopped Kendyl's tirade in its tracks. Her face flushed, and she cast an uncomfortable look in Allyn's direction.

He's serious! Allyn had thought it was a joke, something meant to get under his skin and throw him off. Nolan had, after all, made a few similar offhanded comments over the last few weeks, but nothing so blatant. Nothing so public. Allyn had assumed it was guy talk. Joking about a man's sister, spouse, or even his mom was about as common among male circles as jokes could get. But no, the snarky comments before had only been to test him. Allyn could tell by the way Nolan's cocky smile slowly melted off his face as the silence between them stretched longer.

"Well?" Nolan asked. "What do you think?"

"Uh..." Allyn said, searching for words. *What do I think?*

Truth be told, he'd never given it any thought. He never would have expected Kendyl to be interested in Nolan. He wasn't her type. Not enough tattoos or piercings. Not artsy enough. And he worked for "the man." Nolan was about as far away from Kendyl's type as one could get. Then again, opposites attract, and it wasn't as though she had a lot of other options.

"What happens if you miss?" Allyn asked, deciding to go along with it.

Nolan shrugged. "Then I'll take *you* out, big guy."

Allyn barked a laugh—he couldn't help it. Nolan's easygoing attitude could be infectious.

"Either way, it's a win-win," Nolan said.

"Is this what you want?" Allyn asked Kendyl.

She blushed again, struggling to meet his eye. "He does have a nice smile," she said, then flashed one of her own toward Nolan.

How did I miss this? Allyn had been too consumed with Family politics, training, and managing their other struggles. *What else have I missed?*

"She's a big girl," Allyn said, attempting to keep his voice light and nonchalant. "If she wants to go out, that's up to her."

"Come on," Nolan said. "It's more fun this way."

"I will remind you, though," Allyn continued. "We're still on the run. Anywhere you go will have to be approved by Jaxon."

"I'm sure we can work something out," Nolan said. "You ready, Ren? I've got a beautiful woman's hand to win."

"Tell me when you're ready," Ren said without even a hint of amusement in her tone.

"Let's do this then." Nolan rocked his head from side to side, jumped up and down, and shook out his arms. "Loose!"

Nothing happened.

Nolan went through his routine again, this time waiting a few seconds longer before shouting, "Loose!"

Still nothing happened.

Allyn looked to Ren. Her eyes had drifted away from Nolan to Jaxon, who was striding across the grounds toward them. And he didn't look as if he wanted to challenge the victor.

"Hold on," Allyn said.

"What?" Nolan said. "Why?"

Allyn didn't answer him—he was too focused on Jaxon, who looked positively furious. *Not a good omen.*

"Where's Leira?" Jaxon asked as he approached.

"I'm not sure," Allyn said.

Jaxon looked over Allyn's shoulder. "Ren, find Leira and tell her to meet me here. We have a decision to make."

Ren rushed across the grounds to the Estate's eastern entrance without question, and an uneasy silence fell over the group. Allyn had a thousand questions, but he kept them to himself. If he'd learned one thing in the months he'd lived with Jaxon, it was that the man worked at his own pace. Nobody—not Liam, Leira, or his own father—could force Jaxon to do something he wasn't ready to do. So Allyn resigned himself to wait until Leira joined their group.

She arrived a few minutes later, the creases of worry deep in her face.

"Walk with me," Jaxon said, then led them down a narrow trail that paralleled the cliff. Allyn caught him cast more than one glance at the tree line to their left.

He's making sure we aren't being followed, Allyn thought, and then as the realization washed over him, he caught himself peering uneasily into the forest too.

Jaxon followed the trail to a small rise, the ocean to one side and a well-tended and manicured forest on the other. He stopped there, and the small group fell into a loose circle around him, waiting anxiously for him to speak. Between the wind whipping at their clothes and howling in their ears and the steady roar of waves crashing against the bluff below, there was enough noise to drown out their voices and prevent them from being overheard. Whatever Jaxon wanted to discuss, he wanted to do so privately, away from prying ears.

Leira pulled her wind-blown hair back and tied it into a knot. "You're starting to scare me, Jaxon."

He regarded her with an emotionless expression, the sea mist dotting his face like tiny tears. He shot a final look over Allyn's shoulder in the direction of the Estate, took a deep breath, and said, "What I'm about to tell you remains among us. No one else. Understood?"

They nodded.

"Arch Mage Westarra has given us a way to reestablish the McCollum Family," Jaxon said. He let the words linger. Sink in. "But he's asking for something in return."

"What?" Leira asked, taking the bait.

"Two days ago, the Ferdii Family was attacked, and their entire Family was wiped out. All except a single member."

"Who?" Liam asked.

"A girl," Jaxon said. "Not much younger than you."

"What happened?" Allyn asked.

"Other than that they were attacked," Jaxon said, "we don't know much."

"How did she escape?" Leira asked.

"We don't know."

"Maybe they let her go," Nolan offered.

"Perhaps."

"Who attacked them?" Liam asked.

"We don't know that, either."

"I've never heard of the Ferdii Family," Allyn said. "Are they local?"

"No." Jaxon shook his head. "They're an ancient Family, nestled deep in the Swiss Alps."

"Then with all due respect," Nolan said, "what does this have to do with us?"

"Westarra has tasked us to investigate the attack, discover who's behind it, and find out why."

"We're wanted men," Allyn said. "And Switzerland is halfway across the world. The moment we set foot in an airport, we're done—we'll be flagged by security and arrested—and say by some stroke of luck we're not, we'll never get back into the country."

"I didn't say it would be easy," Jaxon said.

The laugh slipped out before Allyn had a chance to wrestle it down. "There's a world of difference between difficult and impossible, Jaxon. You don't know how much information the feds have on us. One credit card purchase, one speeding ticket, one slipup of any kind, and it's all over."

"What do you think?" Jaxon asked, turning to Nolan.

Nolan glanced in Allyn's direction, undoubtedly uncomfortable with being pitted against him so blatantly.

"It's actually not as difficult as you might think," Nolan said. "There isn't a system solely dedicated to tracking all of these cases and connecting the dots, and there's very little collaboration between the Justice Department and other agencies. We're also fortunate because we were never apprehended and forced to give up our passports. To be honest, I think we're okay. We also still have the shadow user inside the FBI database. If you like, I can muck up their information to make it even more difficult."

"When will we know for sure?" Jaxon asked.

"Uh... when we land and we're not immediately arrested," Nolan said.

"That's the best you can do?"

"Unless you have a way of magically teleporting us there, then yeah, that's the best I can do. But like I said, I think we'll be all right."

"You're actually thinking about this," Allyn said. "After everything we've been through, you're ready to put the Family at risk again?"

"I'm exploring an option to make our Family whole again," Jaxon said. "Do you have another idea?"

He's challenging me by putting me on the spot. Allyn hated the tactic. It was something he used to do as a lawyer—when he didn't have an answer, he would often force the other party to supply him with one. It was a cheap strategy, petty even, but most of all, it was effective. And there was only one way to counter it.

"Why us?" Allyn asked, redirecting the conversation. "Why not let another Family investigate? Someone more local. Why not his Elemental Guard? If they have the expertise, why not let them use it?"

"Arch Mage Westarra knows we're desperate," Jaxon said. "And that will buy our discretion. As to the Elemental Guard, they're powerful warriors, but they don't have the expertise to lead such an investigation."

"I don't like it," Nolan said. "Something's off—there's too much secrecy. And what do we get for risking our lives?"

"We'll regain our seat on the Forum," Jaxon said. "Be re-legitimized as a Family."

"But what *exactly* does that get us?" Nolan asked.

Jaxon raised an eyebrow. "Everything. Power, money, influence. We are of One."

"How long did he give us to decide?" Allyn asked.

"He expects an answer before sundown."

"In other words," Allyn said, "we have to make a decision right now."

"Yes."

Allyn took in a sharp breath. He wasn't accustomed to making snap decisions and would much rather gather all the facts and formulate a plan. There was less room for error that way. Fewer chances someone would get hurt.

"Just to make sure I'm clear," Allyn said. "Westarra is asking us to risk detainment to fly halfway across the world, investigate an attack, and discover who was behind it so that we can regain something that should already be ours by rights."

"That's right," Jaxon said.

"And you think it's a good idea," Allyn said.

"I think it's our only option."

"You're the grand mage of this Family, Jaxon," Allyn said. "Whatever you decide, I'll support. But even you have to admit this sounds suspicious."

"I do," Jaxon agreed. "But you're wrong—I am not the grand mage of this Family. I'm asking for your council. Whatever we decide, we decide together. But before you do, there's one last piece of information you need to know."

"Of course there is," Nolan said.

"If we agree to this," Jaxon continued, "we won't be doing it alone. As you already pointed out, the Elemental Guard should play a role in this, and Westarra agrees. He will send two of his Guard to accompany us." He immediately held his hands up as if holding back their arguments. "I don't like it, either, but he has a good point. We've never been over there. We don't know the customs, and we don't know the terrain. His guards do. And we'll need their expertise."

"We'll need...?" Allyn repeated. "It sounds like you've already made your decision."

"I think I've been pretty clear about where I stand," Jaxon said. "This mission isn't without its risks. But it isn't without its rewards, either. Now where do you stand?"

Liam was the first to speak. "I'm in. As long as you agree that I'm part of the group that goes."

"That depends," Jaxon said.

"On what?"

"On Leira. A McCollum always needs to remain with the Family. If you go, she'll need to stay behind. And as the oldest member of this Family, I'll leave the decision in her hands."

All eyes turned to Leira. The loosely tied knot of hair had come undone, and dark strands blew in the wind, covering her face. "That's fine," she said. "I have no desire to risk imprisonment as an accomplice."

Liam grinned, perhaps surprised by his easy victory.

"Who will go?" Allyn asked, noting that the decision to go had already been made.

"I'll put together a team," Jaxon said. "But I was thinking you, Nolan, Nyla, Ren, and now Liam."

"You're not coming?" Allyn asked.

"I have other responsibilities," Jaxon said. "Ren will lead the team on my behalf."

"How do we know our chaperones won't attempt to take control?"

"The Elemental Guard is removed from the power of the arch mage's station," Jaxon said. "They don't have jurisdiction over this Family. They're only there to support you and see that the arch mage's wishes are being carried out. Now I can't say they won't attempt to influence your investigation, but if they do, I expect you to listen. Like I said, they have expertise we don't."

"I still don't like it," Allyn said.

"You don't have to like it. You just have to accept it."

Allyn blew out a breath. "Fine. I'm in."

Jaxon nodded, turning to Nolan.

"Seven," Nolan said. "Seven magi against an unknown force of unknown size. And all members of our Family."

"We can't risk a larger team," Jaxon said. "It will cause too much suspicion. There will be too many potential complications. And it has to be the McCollum Family. This is our fight. This is our redemption."

"All right," Nolan said.

Jaxon scanned the group, his gaze lingering on each of

them, silently probing for any additional voices of opposition. None came. They were in agreement—they would accept Westarra's offer.

"I'll let the arch mage know."

CHAPTER 5

"I'M NOT DOING THIS AGAIN," Kendyl said, setting her jaw defiantly. She sat in a black leather armchair under the window, watching as Allyn laid out his clothes on his bed. Multiple pairs of jeans, plain white t-shirts, and compression armor tops and bottoms.

"Doing what?" Allyn asked.

"I'm not saying goodbye as if it might be the last time."

Allyn gave her a thoughtful look, only slightly spoiled by his patronizing grin. She sometimes wondered if he even knew he was grinning like an asshole or if it was something that just came naturally.

"Kendyl," he said. "I think it's sweet you're concerned about me—I really do—but I'll be fine. I won't be alone. Nolan, Liam, Nyla, and Ren are going too—not to mention our two Elemental Guard babysitters. I don't think I could get into trouble if I tried."

He was being flippant and self-centered—making this about him instead of her, which aggravated her even more. And the Elemental Guard "babysitters," as Allyn had called them, were actually Myanna Makare, the only female member in the Guard and their second-in-command, and Braeburn

Carmala, a magi whose reputation outweighed his powerful frame. They were two of the most respected members of the Guard, and she wished Allyn would stop trying to disrespect them.

Kendyl stood and strode toward the door. "You misunderstand." She reached down to grab a bag that rested on the floor of the hallway then turned and threw it at Allyn's feet. "I'm not saying goodbye because I'm going too."

Allyn froze, looked down at the bag, then at her.

That got your attention, didn't it?

"Oh?" he asked. "Was this a new decision or something you came up with on your own?" He was referring to Jaxon's preliminary list, which hadn't included her.

"I won't be left behind again, Allyn," she said. "I can help."

"I'm not the one who made the decision."

"But you have Jaxon's ear. You can convince him I should go."

Allyn began stuffing his clothes into the duffel bag beside the stacks. "What if I don't want you there?"

"What if I don't care what you want?" Kendyl said. Now he was *definitely* trying to be an asshole. "I get the whole big-brother routine—I really do—but I'm tired of it. And I'm sick of always being the person who stays behind."

"Everyone's going for a reason, Kendyl. Ren is leading the mission, Nolan understands how investigations work, Nyla in case shit goes sideways, and our two Guards because Westarra wants to keep an eye on the operation."

"What about Liam?" She felt sick for asking the question. She liked the kid, and it was cute how he failed so hard to hide the crush he had on her. But he was a teenager, with even less experience in the world than she had, and she found it insulting that he'd been included and she hadn't.

"Liam's an invaluable member of the team," Allyn said.

"And he needs experience in the field if he's ever going to grow into his father's old position." He held up a hand, cutting her off before she had a chance to respond. "And before you ask, *I'm* going because I was asked to."

"I am an *empath*," Kendyl said. "The only one that Leira knows of in the entire Order. I may not be able to summon lightning like you, or heal the wounded like Nyla, but I have a unique set of abilities too. Use them."

That seemed to give Allyn pause.

"Just talk to Jaxon," she pressed. "If you don't, I will."

"All right."

Kendyl crossed her arms. "I can tell when someone is lying, Allyn."

"I thought you were still developing that ability?"

"I am," she said. "But I don't need to use it to read you."

Allyn smiled like a toddler who just got caught sneaking candy. "Fair enough. I'll talk to Jaxon."

"Thank you," she said. "And let him know I'm already packed. It should save him an objection."

"I must say," Arch Mage Westarra said, frowning, "I didn't expect it to take so long for you to come to a decision."

Jaxon remained silent. He had his reasons for consulting the Family before making a decision, but those reasons were his, and his alone. Arch Mage Westarra didn't need to become involved in intra-Family politics. Besides, the arch mage would never understand his reasoning. He was like Jaxon's father, Wesley Green—he made a decision and demanded the rest follow. Derision and defiance was met with a firm hand at best, a fist or cudgel at worst. Opposing ideas weren't sought out or encouraged.

That wasn't Jaxon's leadership style—he meant to be

more collaborative, more democratic, especially while he held the interim title.

"I thought it was more than a fair proposition," Westarra continued. "Bring the McCollum Family back into the fold and allow it to reclaim its rightful position."

If you truly believed it was our rightful position, Jaxon thought, *we wouldn't have to earn it back.*

They were inside one of the large sitting rooms within the Estate. A pair of designer chairs occupied the center of the room, evenly spaced around a short coffee table, while a puffier, and no doubt more comfortable, couch lined the wall under the ocean-side window. The floor-to-ceiling drapes had been thrown open, and gray daylight streamed in, catching the dust particles that floated in the air like tiny snowflakes. Two guards, backs stiff and jaws set, watched from the corners. Jaxon had found Westarra here, thankful the arch mage hadn't taken up residence within his office.

"I don't know what you want to hear, Your Grace," Jaxon said. "We agreed to your terms within your deadline. I don't know what else there is to say."

"You're right," Westarra said, though it was clear he didn't approve. "Might I ask who you selected for this sensitive mission?"

"The mission will be led by Ren, one of our most experienced magi," Jaxon said. "Joining her will be Allyn, Liam, Nolan, and Nyla."

Westarra froze, his face plainly displaying his displeasure.

"You don't approve," Jaxon said.

"You're putting a lot of faith in these so-called Machinists," Westarra said.

"I am."

"Surely there are more experienced, more qualified members of your Family?"

"Perhaps," Jaxon said. "But the machinists have a certain set of advantages the others don't."

"Pardon me for my skepticism," Westarra said. "But—"

"You're pardoned, Your Grace," Jaxon interrupted. "But we're bowing to your ask and allowing your Elemental Guard join us. As you pointed out, they're experts with the terrain. Allyn and Nolan are experts too, and will help us to blend in while traveling. More importantly, you haven't seen their abilities, and you don't know what they're capable of. I have, and I do. And I think they perfectly mirror the sensitive nature of this mission."

"Can I ask how?"

"No," Jaxon said matter-of-factly. Having become privy to a few of the secrets the Forum held so dear, Jaxon had a level of confidence he hadn't felt in his first meeting with Westarra. The arch mage could certainly have him captured, detained, or possibly even imprisoned, but Jaxon was making the bet that the mission Westarra was sending them on would greatly outweigh any slight the arch mage felt from him. Besides, if Westarra were truly skeptical, nothing Jaxon could say would put the elder magi at ease. "But I am willing to show you."

Westarra's expression turned thoughtful, if not mildly surprised. He nodded, little more than a slight incline of his head. "Bring them."

It took longer than Jaxon would have liked, but he was able to find and assemble the Machinists in Westarra's sitting room. Westarra, perhaps feeling threatened, was surrounded by a larger complement of his Elemental Guard. The first two guards remained in the corners of the room, but Myanna Makare and Braeburn Carmala, the same two magi who would be joining the McCollum host on the mission, flanked Westarra, and a third, Rohn Agerland, Spark of the Elemental Guard, stood directly behind Jaxon, ready to intervene should the demonstration take a violent turn.

Jaxon lined up his machinists shoulder to shoulder in front of Westarra as if they were a military regiment. Westarra looked them up and down, measuring them. The whole display gave Jaxon the impression Westarra was purchasing cattle. It was as if the arch mage didn't see people in front of him. He saw tools. Solutions to a problem.

"I brought you here," Jaxon said, "because the arch mage needs to see your abilities before he trusts you can be representatives of his office." He turned back to Westarra. "Some of their abilities are easily seen. Allyn and Nolan, for example."

Jaxon nodded at the two men, and on command, they wielded. Red coils of electricity manifested around Allyn's arms, writhing in constant motion, rolling up and down, twisting around his wrists and forearms. There were no patterns, the movements all random. And as the coils collided, they snapped and hissed, sending off tiny sparks that disappeared in the air.

Nolan's power manifested differently. The balls of white light started out as roughly the size of a quarter, then grew to the size of a baseball, filling the inside of his palms. Unlike the chaotic nature of Allyn's coils, the balls of energy glowed steadily, almost as if Nolan held two circular LED lights. Interestingly, they didn't create any residual heat, though they did fill the room with a slight hum, like the resonance of a deep bass note, and distort the air around their circular edges like a vapor rising from a hot asphalt road.

Westarra took a sudden step back as the two men's power manifested. His eyes opened wide, his mouth agape.

"It's true," he whispered, then shot a look at Jaxon and collected himself. "How does it... what... where does the power originate?"

Westarra was referring to the magi's source of power. As they all well knew, a magi's power was directly proportionate to the elements within his or her body. Traditional magi wielding water, air, or fire used the elements within their own bodies. Use too much, and they could dehydrate or asphyxiate themselves, and in the case of fire, draw too much heat from their bodies and die from severe hypothermia.

The machinists' abilities were different, but should, as far as Jaxon was concerned, operate under the same rules. After all, all magic had a cost.

"So far," Jaxon said, "each of their abilities has been unique, so each of their sources are unique, as well. Allyn's, we think, is directly connected to the electrical system of his heart. Like fire, once the spark occurs, it can grow exponentially without him having to wield more. But increase the voltage or draw too much, and it will disrupt his body's electrical system. If he's not careful, he could send himself into cardiac arrest."

"Magnificent," Westarra said. "Truly magnificent." He turned to Nolan. "And this one?"

"Nolan isn't all that different," Jaxon continued. "Where Allyn feeds off the electrical current within his heart, we believe Nolan feeds off the ambient energy stored in his body."

"Elaborate," Westarra said.

"Put simply," Jaxon said, "his power draws off his stored energy."

"Think body heat, motion, or even blood pressure," Liam offered.

Westarra turned to him, the corner of his mouth rising in apparent amusement.

Liam flushed, likely a little embarrassed for jumping in unprompted. "Some people have invented ways to charge cell phone batteries or other small electronics using ambient energy. This is just our version of that."

"Thank you, Liam," Westarra said.

"Unlike Allyn," Jaxon said, "Nolan's power's growth rate isn't exponential. Once he's burned all of his body's ambient energy, he pulls energy used by his body's other basic functions."

"So if he wields too much," Westarra said, "his organs will shut down."

"That's what we believe," Jaxon said. "Allyn has suffered from moderate arrhythmia after wielding too much, and that gave us clues about the source of his power. We haven't had the same direct evidence with Nolan. But he feels fatigued after wielding. Hungry even. So this is our best guess right now."

"That still doesn't account for the amount of energy I just saw," Westarra said.

Jaxon grimaced. "You're right. But as Liam said, a property of ambient energy is heat. We think in addition to the energy he's converting, he's also absorbing it from his surroundings. That would account for the air distortion around the balls of light. It's not emitting heat; it's absorbing it."

"Interesting. Very interesting." Westarra shuffled down another step to stand in front of Liam, beaming like a proud father and taking the younger magi by the shoulders. "And Liam?"

"Liam was the first we discovered," Jaxon said. "But unlike the others, his ability is more difficult to understand."

"Okay?" Westarra said. "Explain."

"I can interface with computers," Liam said.

"Excuse me?"

Jaxon bit the inside of his cheeks to keep from smiling. He imagined he had likely looked similar when Allyn and Liam originally came to him with their discovery. Watching Westarra, the man who'd dismissed the machinists as nothing more than a desperate Family's ploy for an audience, struggle with Liam's words was nearly as fulfilling as Jaxon had imagined it would be.

"Human computer interaction," Liam said, clearly expecting it to erase any of Westarra's confusion.

"Liam... uh..." Westarra barked a nervous laugh.

Jaxon let the awkward moment stretch as long as possible before he jumped in. "You and I need a mouse or keyboard to interact with a computer. Liam can do it with his mind."

"That's..." Westarra rubbed his forehead. "I'm having a difficult time understanding that."

Jaxon couldn't bite back his smile any longer. He let it swallow his face, so big it hurt. "You and me both. But it makes sense to Liam, and when it comes to the technological realm, I make it a point to listen to him."

"Spoken like a true leader." Westarra smiled and took a step back to observe the squad as a whole. "Are there any more?"

"Not that we've found," Jaxon lied. He'd purposely left Canary out of the little showcase, wanting to keep her abilities a secret. He still didn't fully trust the arch mage's intentions, and if they were less than pure, she could provide Jaxon with an edge. "But we expect there are."

Westarra nodded. "Then they will have to do. Be back in an hour for your instructions. Your team leaves first thing tomorrow."

Allyn was waiting for Jaxon as he exited Westarra's study.

Jaxon had lingered behind to answer the arch mage's many remaining questions. For almost an hour, Westarra had quizzed Jaxon from how they had discovered Liam's abilities to how they'd used the machinists' powers in combination with one another. It was exactly the type of conversation Jaxon had wanted to have with the magi leadership for months. So whatever was on Allyn's mind must have been important. That made Jaxon wary. He didn't need another complication. If the Family hadn't been under a microscope before, they certainly were now.

Jaxon kept moving, turning to walk down the hallway toward his own study. Allyn fell into step with him.

"Everything okay?" Allyn asked.

"So far," Jaxon said. "It seems we have the arch mage's attention."

"That's good." Then when Jaxon didn't immediately respond, he added, "Isn't it?"

"Better than being ignored."

A group of five or six young magi raced around the corner in front of them, in the middle of a make-believe magi battle. They nimbly changed course, paying Jaxon and Allyn little heed as they barreled past them down the hall. One child tripped on the corner of the hallway runner, careening into a table displaying decorative glass vases and flowers. The vases rattled and wobbled but didn't topple, and before Jaxon could blink, the boy was on his feet again, racing down the hall in pursuit.

Jaxon suppressed a grin. It was good to see children of the McCollum and Hyland Families playing together. After everything that had happened between their two Families, it was a sign that the damage wasn't irreversible.

"We're short on time," Jaxon said, slipping around the

same corner the children had just rounded. "What's on your mind?"

"I have a favor to ask," Allyn said.

"I don't like the sound of that."

"Kendyl isn't happy about being left behind."

"No," Jaxon said, then instantly regretted it. Making snap decisions rarely left one with options, and if he'd learned anything in the short time he'd been grand mage, it was that leadership required flexibility.

"Hear me out," Allyn pressed. Jaxon took a deep breath, which Allyn must have seen as a positive sign, because he added, "She has a point."

"I'm not going to..." Jaxon trailed off as Allyn's words finally registered. "Wait. You agree with her?"

"I said she has a point."

"Which means you agree with her."

"It means I understand where she's coming from," Allyn said. "She's tired of not being included. Of being little more than a bystander. She just wants to help."

"I understand."

"Then I can tell her she's a part of the trip?"

"No."

"Jaxon—"

"I won't risk the Family's future because your sister has hurt feelings. Nearly every other member of this Family is remaining behind too. Like them, she can find other ways to be useful." With that, Jaxon started down the hallway again.

Allyn lingered behind, visibly shaken by Jaxon's abruptness. It wasn't that Jaxon didn't understand—he did—but the risk was too high. The mission was too important.

"You're right," Allyn said.

Jaxon stopped but didn't turn.

"I do want her to come."

"Why?"

"Call it a hunch," Allyn said. "I don't know why or where it's coming from, but I can't shake this feeling that we'll need her."

Jaxon turned, met Allyn's eye, and to his surprise, saw complete honesty. Allyn believed what he was saying was true, down to his very core, and Jaxon was beginning to learn that he couldn't argue with belief like that.

"I'll think about it," Jaxon said.

"When can I expect an answer?"

"When I come up with one."

CHAPTER 6

ALLYN ASSEMBLED WITH THE REST of the squad in the driveway of the Hyland Estate. It was early morning with dawn little more than an eventuality, and the darkness made deeper by a thick blanket of clouds that obscured the moon and stars. The magi waited silently, listening to the soft rumble of the running engine of the car that would take them to the airport. Nobody waited with them, no large group to give blessing or see them off. Theirs was, after all, a secret mission.

Word had come down from Westarra late the night before. Ren's squad, accompanied by Myanna and Braeburn of the Elemental Guard, would fly out on the first flight from Portland, and after a short layover in Atlanta, they would cross the Atlantic for Zurich, where someone from the Klausner Family would be waiting for them. The Klausner Family, Allyn had learned, was the nearest Family to the Ferdii Family, and they were caring for the sole survivor of the attack.

Allyn took a deep breath, filling his lungs with the cool oceanic air. Despite the early hour and a restless night of sleep plagued by dreams of cops, handcuffs, and squad cars, Allyn was alert and ready, if also growing increasingly anxious. He was dressed in black magi compression armor hidden under a pair of inconspicuous denim jeans and a loose button-down shirt. A duffel bag packed with spare clothes and other travel necessities rested at his feet.

Liam waited beside him, his young eyes showing none of the fatigue some of the others displayed.

"What's it like?" he asked.

"What's what like?" Allyn asked.

"Flying. Is it fun? Can you tell you're moving that fast?"

"It's not that much different from riding in a car," Allyn said. "Except you have less room."

"Oh," Liam said, disappointed. "Is it scary? Being that high up? Going that fast?"

"I really try not to think about it."

Truth be told, Allyn wasn't the world's greatest flier. Traveling by plane was simply a necessary evil made easier by ensuring he was three or four drinks deep before boarding—a luxury he didn't expect to have on this trip.

"But I'll put it this way," Allyn continued. "We'll be flying thirty thousand feet in the air at five hundred miles per hour in a pressurized metal tube made by the cheapest bidder."

Liam blanched at that.

"And then comes the turbulence."

"What's that?"

"It's when the plane hits rough pockets of air and bumps or shakes or falls a couple hundred feet out of the air."

"Falls out of the air?" Liam said, his voice going up in pitch.

"Yeah."

"How often does that happen?"

Allyn bit the insides of his cheeks to keep from smiling. Liam sounded properly terrified now.

"All the time."

Liam's mouth hung open, the remaining color in his face disappearing. Before Allyn could tell Liam he was joking—or at least only partially kidding—the double doors to the front of the Hyland Estate opened.

Arch Mage Westarra, wearing a grim expression and escorted by four of his Elemental Guard, strode into the early morning darkness. Behind him was Jaxon and, to Allyn's surprise, Kendyl. Allyn hadn't heard anything from Jaxon regarding his sister, and he'd taken that as a bad sign. However, Kendyl's step was light and bouncy, damn near giddy, and she smiled when she saw him.

Allyn knew that walk too well. It was the self-satisfied walk of victory, and Allyn wasn't the least bit surprised when Jaxon informed the group that Kendyl would be joining them.

"Thank you," she whispered, taking her position at Allyn's shoulder.

"You're welcome."

The squad shifted into a loose semicircle around Arch Mage Westarra, and it might have been Allyn's imagination, but Westarra's gaze seemed to linger a little longer on him and Kendyl than it did on the others.

He thinks I'm to blame for her coming.

If the mission went sour, especially if it involved Kendyl, Allyn knew he would somehow bear the responsibility. The idea sent a chill down his spine. It wasn't a big issue, but it was yet another wrinkle. Another complication. Another piece on the board he'd have to be aware of.

"Thank you for your service," Westarra said, pulling Allyn from his thoughts. "What we do, we do in secret. But rest assured our mission is of the utmost importance, and if the Families knew what you faced, what was at stake, they would be here with you. Be safe. Be victorious. And keep the secret. We are of One."

"We are of One," the group repeated.

And with that, Westarra bid them farewell.

Nolan proved to be correct, and their flight from the States was met without incident. Not that it was easy—spending fourteen hours in a plane or airport wasn't something Allyn considered fun—but to his surprise, he wasn't flagged or pulled aside by TSA security while in the States or detained by customs upon landing in Zurich.

He wasn't sure what he had been expecting from the Zurich International Airport, but he couldn't escape the feeling of being underwhelmed. The immense structure was an impressive sight, made of curved glass and shaped like a boomerang, but it felt *familiar.* Sure, the walkways, skyways, and even stairwells were crafted with a modern aesthetic that reminded Allyn of something out of a science fiction TV show, but for all of its glass and grace, it was still an airport. Travelers still carried bags and rolled luggage. Pilots and flight attendants still walked the terminals, smiling and waving at gawking children. Shops and restaurants continued to attract bored travelers. And security roamed corridors and made announcements over the terminal-wide PA system.

It all felt so normal. Where was the old-world charm? The old-world flair? Why didn't it feel more European?

The main entrance prominently displayed the words *Flughafen Zurich* in big bold letters, and signs were predominantly written in Swiss, but everywhere he looked, he saw English and the echoes of American culture. There was even a McDonald's in the food court, and two separate Starbucks in the main terminal.

Where Allyn couldn't help but feel jaded and underwhelmed, Liam was bright-eyed and awestruck, looking at everything with a perpetual grin. On more than one occasion, he fell behind the group, getting lost in the large crowds milling through the concourse.

In his defense, the rest of the magi weren't much better. Though instead of awe and wonder, they looked at everything with an awkward discontent. Fortunately, Kendyl moved through the airport with expert precision and quickly led them to their baggage claim, and then out of the terminal to where their envoy was waiting.

The emissary from the Klausner Family was pushing his middle years and balding, with hard eyes and harder features. Dressed in a thin, nondescript black jacket and a pair of surprisingly well-fitting jeans, he stood with a number of other hired drivers and chauffeurs, holding a sign that read *McCollum*.

"Sten?" Allyn asked, approaching the man.

"Yes," Sten answered in a heavily accented voice.

Allyn offered him his hand. "Allyn McCollum."

"Nice to meet you," Sten said, accepting Allyn's hand and looking over the rest of their party. "This everyone?"

Allyn quickly counted, making sure they hadn't lost anyone in the crowd. Seeing everyone was accounted for, he nodded.

"This way then." Sten led them through the throng of people toward the exit. "How was your flight?" he asked over his shoulder.

"Long," Allyn said.

Sten chuckled softly. "I'm sure. I wish I could say it would get better."

"Why wouldn't it?" Allyn asked. The prospect of another long trip made him irritable.

"The manor," Sten said, "it's not close."

"I was under the impression we would begin at..." Allyn trailed off. Sten might not have known of the attack and the McCollum Family's true purpose for coming. "I didn't realize we would be going to the manor first."

Sten shrugged. "I am just a driver. Those are my orders."

Allyn pursed his lips. He couldn't tell if Sten was being truthful, or if this was the first sign that the Klausner Family wouldn't be as helpful as Westarra had originally suggested. Allyn quickly dismissed the idea. He didn't see what the Family stood to gain by being obstructionists.

"How far are we talking?" Nolan asked.

"Hmmm?"

"To the manor," Nolan said. "How far is it to the Klausner Manor?"

"About an hour," Sten said. "Give or take."

Nolan looked at Allyn then Ren, shaking his head. An hour's delay wouldn't make or break their investigation, and allowing Sten to take them to the Klausner Manor might prove to be a shorter delay than forcing otherwise. Not that Allyn was looking forward to another hour of travel, but whether Sten took them to the manor or to the scene of the attack, more travel was a necessity.

"To the Klausner Manor, then," Allyn said, hoping his tone of resignation wasn't as clear to the others as it was to himself.

———————•••————————

If Allyn had been disappointed with the Zurich Airport, he was absolutely in awe of the Klausner Manor. Located in the Canton of Schwyz at the base of the Alps, the landscape was something out of a fairy tale. Towering snowcapped peaks dwarfed the manor. The stunning blue of the sky was a stark contrast to the slate gray of the mountain range and its pristine-white snow. Winter wildflowers of every shade of blue, purple, red, and yellow mixed with thick tufts of emerald-colored grass and extended for as far as the eye could see.

The town itself was something of a wonder. Instead of the urban, industrial sprawl Allyn had grown accustomed to, whitewashed homes with timber-colored roofs dotted the landscape, like an extension of the Earth instead of being built from it. Window shutters and church steeples were painted the same colors as the wildflowers, and even the paved and cobbled roads mirrored the slate gray of the natural rock. Livestock grazed inside the town proper, penned in by simple fences and buildings alike. At home, human development was at war with nature, but Schwyz was a model of symbiosis.

The manor was a four-story structure, wider than it was deep, that overlooked the canton.

Natural rock adorned the corners of its whitewashed walls, and wood shutters and crisscrossing timber beams further embellished the idyllic structure. A single Swiss flag flew above it, flapping in the strong mountain gusts.

The cultivated manor grounds had a subtle wildness to them. Trees, shrubs, and flowers grew with little direction in a natural order that felt *right*—so much so that the cobbled driveway in which they parked felt like a violation.

"Remind me again," Nolan said as the car came to a rest, "where the hell all of your money comes from."

The quip snapped Allyn out of his reverie, and he laughed, thinking of the countless times he had asked the same question. Liam and Jaxon had explained it to him, of course—the compounding interest, land grabs, and other investments the Forum had made behind the veil of an international corporation named the First Family. Unlike the

McCollum Family, who operated under extreme isolation, the Forum managed shrewd, sometimes bullish global venture capitalist endeavors.

How the Forum had made that initial investment remained a mystery to Allyn, but he supposed the old saying "to make money, you first have to have money" was at play. The Families, working together, had been able to cobble together their collective homes, property, possessions, and liquid wealth into a single fortune, which had grown exponentially over the centuries. Unlike their existence, their fortune was hidden in plain sight.

"Follow me," Sten said, stepping out of the vehicle.

Allyn's legs trembled under his weight as he exited the midsized SUV, but it felt good to stand. Save for the quick walk from the airport to Sten's vehicle, he hadn't been on his feet since their connecting flight in Atlanta.

The crisp air was colder than he'd expected, and it brought goose bumps to the backs of his arms.

"Beautiful," Kendyl said, stepping up beside him, viewing the town below.

Allyn nodded. Kendyl had been to many places like this before, and she was fond of prodding Allyn about it, telling him that he didn't know what he was missing. That he needed to get out of the States and see the world. He would never admit it to her, but in this moment he knew she'd been right.

He also realized for the first time that unlike the McCollum Manor, which had been roughly twenty miles outside of Portland, and the Hyland Estate, which was even more secluded, the Klausner Manor was nearly *in* town. He couldn't put a finger on why exactly, but somewhere inside, he knew it was a profound differentiation between the Families.

"This way," Sten said, beckoning them toward a small stone path that led to the north side of the manor.

Allyn brought up the rear and felt Ren fall into step beside him. She leaned in close and spoke in a deep whisper. "We cannot remain here long. They won't remain content."

Allyn followed her gaze to the two Elemental Guards. "I know. We'll be away from here as quickly as possible."

Sten led them around the back of the manor to one of the rear entrances and opened a door before ushering them inside. Once the McCollum magi were inside, Sten closed the door behind him, and Allyn watched through the room's windows as Sten made his way back up the path toward the front of the manor.

"I wonder where he's going," Nolan said.

"I don't know," Allyn said. "Maybe they don't want the Family to know we're here."

"Why not?" Liam asked.

"Hard to say," Allyn said. "But I imagine they're already on edge, and there's no need to stoke their fears any more than necessary."

Allyn turned away to appraise the room. They had entered a small sitting room with aged maple floors and wainscoted walls painted a light cream. At its center, armchairs and small couches surrounded a knee-high coffee table resting on an elegant, hand-woven rug. Fire crackled in a tiled fireplace, but the focal point of the room was the wall to Allyn's left, where a series of paintings hung in intricate, hand-carved frames.

The first depicted a lone male figure inside a dark space. Dwarfed by the darkness, the man occupied less than a quarter of the painting and was relegated to the bottom right-hand corner of the canvas. The artist, with only a few precise brushstrokes of conflicting colors, had captured the man's despair.

Cold, wet, and dying, the desperate man held his hands

before him, marveling at the fire they held. His face showed the conflicting emotions of surprise, terror, and relief, and Allyn got the distinct impression the man in the painting understood that the fire offered refuge from the darkness, staved off the cold, and promised to preserve his life.

Magi lore said that in the first days there weren't magi and man. There was only man, and as man evolved, human needs evolved, as well. To create fire, man used rocks and timber; to hunt, men developed staves and crude knives of rock and obsidian; to treat wounds and sickness, man developed rudimentary methods of medicine using local vegetation for poultices and sedatives. But another branch of man discovered different ways of achieving the same goals.

Magi men and women learned to use their bodies, drawing on their own body heat to create fire. For weapons, they learned to project that fire, wielding deadly creations that could be launched at game or would-be attackers. Instead of medicine, they used their bodies to heal one another. Where man turned to technology, the magi turned to magic. The portrait was clearly a representation of one of the first magi.

What are the other three then?

A strange voice provided Allyn with his answer. "The four ages of magi."

Allyn turned to find a regal man standing in the hallway that connected the room with the rest of the manor. Straight backed with a strong jaw, dark eyes, and thick gray hair, the man carried with him an air of influence.

The man started across the room, pointing at the portrait Allyn had just been looking at. "The Age of Discovery." Then pointing toward the next two in succession, he said, "The Age of Prosperity and the Age of Despair."

"And this one?" Allyn gestured to the fourth painting.

"The fourth age?" the man asked, stopping beside him.

"I suppose that would depend on who you speak with. I've heard it called many things: the Age of Rebellion, the Age of Reckoning. I prefer to think of it as the Age of Rebirth. But, then again, I've always been something of an optimist." He gave Allyn a wry smile and extended his hand. "Grand Mage Harold Klausner."

Allyn took the man's hand in his and studied his expression. There was something behind his smile, something knowing. He had called the fourth age, the age they currently lived in, the Age of Rebirth. It felt a little too close to their reality for comfort—had Westarra told him of the machinists?

"It's a pleasure, Grand Mage," Allyn said. "We appreciate your hospitality."

Klausner waved a dismissive hand. "It's nothing." He gestured toward the sitting area at the center of the room. "Please sit. All of you."

"We've been siting for a long time, Grand Mage," Allyn said. "And... my apologies, but none of us expected to arrive here until after we'd had a chance to visit the scene."

"I understand," Klausner said. "And your apologies are unnecessary. I only assumed you would want to speak to the survivor prior to going to the scene."

"She's still here?" Allyn asked.

"Where else would she go?" Klausner asked, appearing genuinely confused.

Allyn stammered, struggling to provide Grand Mage Klausner with an answer. Thankfully, Kendyl spoke up, letting him off the hook.

"How is she doing?" she asked.

"About as well as you can imagine," Klausner said. "We're doing our best, but she's been through a rather traumatic experience, and these last few days have been difficult for her."

"What has she said about the attack?" Nolan asked.

Klausner sighed. "Not much. Only that she and another young magi were playing a game when men dressed in full tactical armor and carrying rifles arrived and opened fire."

"Without provocation?" Nolan asked.

"It appears that way."

"Did they take any hostages?"

"We don't know."

"What about anything from the site?" Allyn asked. "Why were they there?"

"We don't know that, either."

"How about—" Nolan started.

"Like I said before," Klausner cut in, "the girl has been through a very traumatic couple days and hasn't been very forthcoming about her ordeal. We've done what we can, but we don't want to press. I'm sure you understand—she's been through enough already."

"She is also our only witness," Nolan said. "If it's okay with you, I'd like to speak with her myself. I have experience with this kind of thing."

"Of course," Klausner said. "As I said, I assumed you would want to. I just wanted to preface it by ensuring you understood her emotional state."

"I'll be gentle," Nolan said.

"I'd like to go with you," Kendyl said.

"I'm not sure that's a good idea," Nolan said. "We need to make her comfortable, establish trust, and that's hard to do with too many people in the room."

"I agree," Kendyl said. "It should only be the two of us."

"Kendyl—"

"I can help her feel better," Kendyl said. "Help her open up. And when she does, I can read her in ways you can't."

The room went quiet. Nolan, for all his worth, seemed to be contemplating Kendyl's words.

"What is she talking about?" Klausner asked.

Allyn didn't see any reason to keep Kendyl's abilities a secret. Unlike machinists, empaths had been around for centuries. There just hadn't been one to Jaxon's or Leira's knowledge in at least a century.

"Kendyl is an empath," Allyn said.

Klausner's eyebrows rose in surprise. "Really? Well, that does change things."

"Yes, it does," Allyn agreed. "Talk to her. See what you can discover, but don't press. If we push too hard, she might shut down forever." He turned to Klausner. "How far away is the scene?"

"Two hours," Klausner said. "Two and a half at most."

"Good," Allyn said. He met Nolan's and Kendyl's eyes. "You have an hour. After that, we move for the Ferdii Village."

CHAPTER 7

EMELINA'S ROOM WAS IN THE northeastern corner of the manor. The top-floor room, likely one of the largest in the manor, was dark—the two small windows hidden behind drawn floor-to-ceiling curtains. The fire had gone out too, the wood and timber little more than glowing embers, offering little warmth and even less light.

The canopied, four-post bed at the center of the room stood vacant, its cotton bedding untouched. The chairs spaced evenly around the front of the fireplace were empty as well, as was the chair to the writing table on the other side of the room.

"Emelina?" Kendyl asked, stepping deeper into the room.

Nolan closed the door behind them, shutting out the little light that had been in the room before. Kendyl stopped, waiting for her eyes to adjust to the new darkness.

"Emelina? My name is Kendyl. Can you tell me where you are, honey? I brought you some hot chocolate."

She waited, and when no response came, she began to wonder if the young girl understood her at all. Grand Mage Klausner hadn't warned them of a language barrier, and he and Sten had spoken fluent English, but both of them were much older than Emelina and from a different Family. Surely if it had been a potential issue, Klausner would have said something.

"Emelina," Kendyl said again. "I'm coming into the room, okay? My friend Nolan is with me; please don't be afraid."

"Hi, Emelina," Nolan said, his voice surprisingly soft.

When Emelina didn't answer, Kendyl set the hot chocolate on a coffee table and began to search the room. She knew Emelina was in here—the magi posted outside her door would have known if she had left, and neither of the windows was open. The young girl was simply doing what many children did when they were scared and had nobody to turn to—she'd hidden.

On the other side of the room, Nolan mirrored Kendyl's efforts, and after a quick search turned up nothing, he held his arms up as if to say, *I don't know.*

Kendyl pursed her lips. While the room was large, there weren't many places to hide. She briefly thought about turning on the light, but she knew that would be a mistake. Emelina bathed in the safety of the darkness, found refuge in its strange comfort, and turning on the light would violate that safety.

"Emelina, honey," Kendyl said, "please come out. We just want to make sure you're all right."

Still not getting any answer, Kendyl sighed and closed her eyes. Stilling her breath, she focused on her surroundings. The wind had picked up outside, howling through the trees and rock, causing the manor to creak and groan. Somewhere among it, she thought she heard a soft rustling coming from behind the curtains.

Of course, Kendyl thought. She grabbed the hot chocolate and made her way toward the source of the sound. She stopped a few feet away from the window and took a seat in a nearby chair.

"Emelina, I know you're behind the curtains, honey. Can you come out please?"

The curtains rustled slightly, but Emelina didn't emerge.

"My friend Nolan and I want to ask you a few questions. I know you don't want to come out, but can you talk to us?"

Silence.

"Emelina? Please?"

The curtains suddenly shifted, and a young girl who couldn't have been any older than eight or nine emerged.

Kendyl nearly gasped. Klausner had said Emelina had been taken care of, but she didn't look anything of the sort. Sunken, hollow eyes peered out from a pale face as the girl shuffled forward on her bare feet. Her raven-colored hair was unkempt, her clothes tattered and dirty. Why hadn't she been bathed? Why hadn't her clothing been changed?

"Oh, honey," Kendyl said. "Are you cold?"

Emelina nodded.

"Come here, then. Let's get you warm." Kendyl offered the girl her hand, and to her surprise, Emelina took it.

As their fingers touched, Kendyl inhaled sharply and yanked her hand away. She was on her feet a moment later, staggering backward until she tripped over a coffee table and crashed to the ground, slamming the back of her head against the bare hardwood floors. When she finally regained her bearings, Nolan was standing over her, concerned.

"Don't move," he said.

"I'm fine." Kendyl sat up, but the world warped, and she found herself on the floor again.

"Easy," Nolan said. "Give it a moment."

Kendyl didn't fight him. She let herself relax, focusing

on the coolness of the floor to ease her nausea. After several breaths, she felt ready to try again. "Okay."

"Easy now." Nolan reached for her hand.

"No." She pushed his hand away. "I've got it."

"Okay," Nolan said, his voice thick with a mix of concern and confusion.

Kendyl sat up, exhaling deeply. She scanned the room. Emelina had disappeared again.

"What the hell happened?" Nolan asked.

"That poor girl," Kendyl said. "That poor, poor girl."

"Kendyl—"

"I wasn't ready for... her emotions, Nolan. They're so... *raw*. I haven't felt anything like that in a long time."

"I don't—"

"I can feel them, Nolan. All of them. She's dejected, crestfallen, confused, terrified. I don't... oh, Nolan, that poor girl." Kendyl stood, using the back of a nearby chair for support.

"Are you sure you're all right?"

"I should have known better."

Like Kendyl, Emelina had lost her parents, one of the most traumatizing things a child could go through, but unlike her, Emelina hadn't had any forewarning and had seen the violence firsthand. Kendyl's pain, as deep as it was, as life altering as it had been, was nothing compared to this young girl's.

"Come on. Let's get back to it," Kendyl said.

"I'm not sure that's a great idea."

"We don't have a choice," Kendyl said. "We're running out of time."

Kendyl found Emelina back in her original hiding place within the curtains. The girl trembled, her bottom lip quivering, dark eyes bloodshot and wary. She reminded

Kendyl of an abused pet who had recently been adopted into a new family—tentative and terrified, her old wounds too deep to overcome. But buried deeper than her fear was something else.

Kendyl struggled to put a word to it. Loss and abandonment came to mind, but they only scratched at the surface. It was the despair of being anchorless—Emelina was paint without a palette or canvas. Not only had she lost her family and loved ones, she'd also lost her home—everything that made her who she was had been taken away.

Emelina might have had different color hair and eyes. She might have had a different upbringing. Her emotions might run deeper than Kendyl's had. But in those feeling of loss and abandonment, despair and confusion, they were the same, and fortunately, Emelina had someone who could make a difference. Someone who could make all those feelings go away—even if it was only for a short time.

Kendyl knelt in front of the girl, keeping her hands on the ground for support, not yet ready to re-establish her connection with Emelina. The girl recoiled, turning away to bury her face in the curtains. Kendyl readied herself, focusing on the pool of emotions buried inside herself and was surprised by what she found. Buried deeper than her surface-level emotions, Kendyl found desire, determination, and contentment mixed with frustration, fear, and jealousy. The latter of which surprised her, but they were there, shallow pools that swirled with the rest to make up Kendyl's current emotional state.

She hadn't taken the time to think about how removing one emotion or strengthening another would affect her own overall state. The last time she had done something of this magnitude was when she had given Allyn the confidence and courage to face down Special Agent Richard Maddox after securing the McCollum Library's prized contents.

That had left her completely drained, emotionless, an empty husk of a person. Emelina's emotions ran much deeper than Allyn's had; changing her emotional state was a larger task and would take even more out of Kendyl. But she was committed now. Emelina's pain was too deep, and alleviating that was too important to be concerned with any temporary side effects.

Kendyl pooled her contentment and separated it from the rest of her emotions, knowing that it alone wouldn't be enough—Emelina's grief was too deep, too complex to be subdued with a single contradictory feeling. Emelina wouldn't trust it. She would, at least on a primal level, see through the manipulation and rebel against it. So Kendyl found a reservoir of understanding, another of reassurance, and pulled them aside too, mixing them with her contentment. She was like a chef devising a new dish, and with a pinch of hope and a dash of support, Kendyl was ready.

She snapped out, taking Emelina by the arm and re-establishing her connection. Before the girl could pull away, Kendyl wielded, projecting her emotional concoction into Emelina. The wave of emotion hit the girl like an electrical charge. Emelina froze, her body growing rigid, back arching, eyes and mouth wide with shock. The torrent of emotion flowed out of Kendyl in an instant, leaving a void in its wake. She had a vague memory of the emotion, but like the memory of a dream, the harder she thought about it, the more it faded.

Her emotion spent, Kendyl staggered, but held onto Emelina, both for support and to keep their connection alive. Nolan was there in an instant, but she shook him off.

Emelina looked at Kendyl's hand on her arm then up at her face.

"I'm sorry," Kendyl said, breathless. "I didn't mean to scare you."

"What did you do to me?" Emelina's voice made her sound even younger than she appeared.

"I'm trying to help," Kendyl said. "Would you sit with me? We want to talk." Kendyl felt Emelina's skepticism before she saw it, and since their connection was still active, she countered it with a mix of honesty and trust. Then when that wasn't enough, she added a hint of encouragement.

Blending emotion was an inexact science, but finally, Kendyl found a mix that worked, and Emelina nodded and moved past Kendyl to climb into one of the armchairs. She sat with her knees tucked beneath her, arms crossed, eyes distant and stuck on the floor.

Seeing the girl swallowed by the oversized chair, Kendyl felt as though she truly saw Emelina for the first time. Beneath the dirt and grime, under the tangled mess of thick hair and tattered clothing was a child. A nine-year-old girl. The very embodiment of innocence.

Kendyl sat on the arm of her chair and placed her hand on Emelina's shoulder. She meant it as a calming gesture, but it also reconnected their bond. When the girl didn't relapse, Kendyl nodded for Nolan to join them.

Nolan pulled a small footrest in front of Emelina's chair and took a seat. Then looking up at her, he said in a surprisingly compassionate voice, "Hi, Emelina. My name is Nolan, and I want you to know that I think you're very brave. I know answering questions can be scary."

Kendyl felt a wave of fear pulse through Emelina, but she left it uncountered. They were in Nolan's territory now.

She would help where she could, but she didn't want to risk getting in his way.

"I am a police officer," Nolan continued. "Do you know what that means?"

Emelina shook her head.

"It means it's my job to protect you. To find bad people who have done bad things so they don't hurt anyone else. Does that make sense?"

"Yes," Emelina whispered.

Nolan offered her a small, reassuring smile. "Good. Right now, I'm trying to find the bad people who hurt you. Do you think you can help me?"

Emelina's hand found Kendyl's, and she grasped it tightly.

"It's okay," Kendyl said, squeezing back.

"He smiled at me," Emelina said.

Nolan cocked his head to the side as if in question. "He smiled at you? Who smiled at you?"

"The man in the black shell."

"One of the bad men?"

Emelina nodded.

Nolan's smile faltered. Whether it was because he didn't want the girl to draw any parallels between him and her attacker or because it was an unconscious reaction to what the girl had said, Kendyl didn't know.

"He saw you?" Nolan asked.

Emelina nodded again.

"Where did he see you at?"

"In the tower."

"He saw you in the tower?"

"Uh-huh."

"What were you doing in there?"

"Looking."

"For the bad men?"

Emelina shook her head.

"No?" Nolan asked. "Who were you looking for?"

"Marcellus."

"Marcellus," Nolan repeated. There was a cadence to his questioning. Repeating what Emelina told him, clarifying, but using it to frame his next question. "Who's Marcellus?"

Tears welled in Emelina's eyes, and she clutched at Kendyl's hand as if it were a lifeline. The emotion building in Emelina was almost enough to push Kendyl over the edge. She marveled at the girl's strength, not knowing how someone so young held herself together.

"They killed him," Emelina said.

Nolan shifted in his seat. His eyes flicked to Kendyl then back to Emelina.

"They killed him," Emelina repeated. "And he smiled at me."

For the first time in the conversation, Nolan seemed at a loss for words. He studied Emelina as if questioning how far he could push her—or at least how far he *wanted* to push her. He bit the inside of his lip, then as quickly as the indecision had hit, he was shifting tack and moving forward again.

"Can you tell me what he looked like?"

Emelina closed her eyes. She shook her head, slowly at first, then faster and faster violently.

She's trying to hide, Kendyl thought. *We're losing her.* Refusing to accept failure, Kendyl dug through her own emotion. She found courage and gave it to Emelina. The young girl stopped shaking, but she didn't open her eyes. It wasn't enough.

He smiled at me.

Emelina's words echoed in Kendyl's mind, bringing with them an image of a monster. Sharp teeth, claws instead of fingers, black armor that looked like a carapace.

This is what she sees. This is what she faced.

And in the eyes of the monster was a burning intensity—something visceral, almost tangible. A seething hatred reserved for the lowest of the low. And it was directed at Kendyl. At Emelina. Kendyl didn't understand the root of it, but she wilted under its intensity, feeling less than human. She was a parasite. Something that didn't deserve to live. Something that needed to be killed. Eradicated. Exterminated.

She's not scared, Kendyl realized. *She's crumbling under that hatred.*

Kendyl knew what she had to do—there was only one counter to hatred. She dug through her feelings of love and affection, choosing the most powerful—her love of her family—and beginning with a trickle, she shared it with Emelina. Almost instantly, Kendyl could feel the girl's body loosen. Her iron grip on Kendyl's hand slackened as the rush of negative emotion was soothed. She didn't open her eyes, but Kendyl knew she was ready to talk.

"What did he look like?" Kendyl asked.

"Tall." Emelina sounded almost as if she were in a trance. "Taller than everyone but Elder Ulrich. Pale skin, like yours."

"What about his hair?" Kendyl asked.

"Dark."

"Was it long or short like Nolan's?"

"Shorter."

"And he wore armor," Kendyl said.

"Yes."

"Anything else?" Kendyl asked. "Anything you hadn't seen before."

"He had a gun. They had lots of guns."

"Guns?" Nolan asked. "Big guns or little guns?"

"Both," Emelina said. "They sounded like thunder."

"You saw more than one person?" Kendyl asked.

"Yes."

"How many did you see?" Kendyl asked.

"Three," Emelina said. "But there were more."

Nolan and Kendyl exchanged a look. More than three. Men wielding guns. It didn't sound like magi Families warring with each other.

"Did they say anything?" Nolan asked.

"They were arguing."

"About what?"

"About what to do with Marcellus," Emelina said. "I don't think Squareface wanted to kill him, but the other man did."

"Squareface?" Nolan said. "Who is he?"

"The man who smiled at me," Emelina said. "He smiled at me when him and the other men left."

"Did he say anything to you?"

Emelina shook her head. "He put his finger to his lips."

"He told you to be quiet," Kendyl said.

"Yes." Emelina's voice quivered.

"What were you doing in the tower, Emelina?" Nolan asked.

"Playing hunters with Marcellus."

"Marcellus is another boy in your Family?"

Emelina nodded.

"What happened after the bad man smiled at you?" Nolan asked.

"They left."

"Left the tower or left the Family?" Nolan asked.

"The tower."

"Where did they go?"

"They killed them."

Nolan took a deep breath. "How long did you hide in the tower?"

Emelina didn't answer.

Nolan repeated the question.

"I don't know," Emelina said. "They were gone when I came out."

"What happened next?"

"I..." Emelina faltered. "They were all gone. Laid out in the courtyard. I didn't want to see anymore."

A heavy silence filled the room. Kendyl waited, not wanting to be the person who violated its sanctity.

"I didn't want to see it anymore." Emelina opened her eyes and peered into Kendyl's. "I don't want to see it anymore. Please, I don't want to do it anymore."

Nolan met Kendyl's eye and nodded. He was finished.

"You don't have to," Kendyl said, and then again, more softly, "You don't have to."

CHAPTER 8

"I DON'T UNDERSTAND," ALLYN SAID, LOOKING over the group in the sitting room. "Why would the man smile at her and then tell her to be quiet?"

"I don't understand it, either," Nolan said. He stood next to Kendyl, who sat in an armchair near the fire on the opposite end of the room from Allyn. The rest of their squad and the two Elemental Guards occupied the space between them, sitting in the various chairs and couches in the center of the room. Grand Mage Klausner leaned against the desk under the window to Allyn's left, a silent observer.

"At first," Nolan continued, "I thought it was because the man had taken pleasure in the killing, but now I'm not so sure. If he had enjoyed it, why not kill her too? What stopped him?"

"That's exactly what I'm getting at," Allyn said.

"They might have wanted a survivor," Ren said. "Someone to spread the word of the attack."

"I thought about that too," Nolan said. "But then why tell her to be quiet? He could have just as easily drug her out of her hiding space and given her instructions. The way Emelina made it sound it was as if the man was telling her to be quiet so she wouldn't be found. So she wouldn't be killed too."

"You're giving a murderer a lot of credit," Nyla said. "He killed the boy, after all."

"I'm just telling you what it sounds like to me," Nolan said.

Allyn watched Kendyl through the exchange. She had been silent and largely absent for most of the conversation.

"What do you think, Kendyl?" Allyn asked.

Kendyl looked up from the ground, meeting his eye, and Allyn faltered a bit. Something had happened to Kendyl during her time with Emelina. She had gone in the girl's room confident and eager to help, but had come out frail and haunted, almost as if she were in shock. Her face had gone pale, her eyes cold and lifeless. Even her movements were lethargic.

"I agree," she said, her voice soft and pained. "Something isn't right, but that's what she said. I don't know why the man did it, but I can tell you she didn't find it comforting."

"Of course she didn't," Ren said. "She had just watched her friend murdered."

"What are you getting at?" Allyn asked.

"I'm saying that as tragic as it is, the girl's feelings are irrelevant. What matters is what happened and what we can learn from her."

"How can you—" Kendyl started.

"She's right," Nolan interrupted. "As ineloquent as that was, Ren is right."

Kendyl's mouth dangled open for a second before snapping shut. She shot Nolan an irritated look and then slid farther back in her chair and returned her eyes to the floor.

"Let's go back over it then," Allyn said. "From the top."

At Allyn's prompting, Nolan began his retelling of

their conversation with Emelina. He had, by his own admission, reorganized her story so that he was able to tell it chronologically, and since they'd already been through it twice, the retelling went quickly.

"You're sure they didn't ask her or the boy about anything in particular?" Klausner asked, entering the conversation for the first time.

"I'm positive," Nolan said. "I asked her that point blank."

Klausner shrugged. "Maybe she didn't want to answer."

"No." Nolan shook his head. "That was after Kendyl..." He looked down at her. "No, at that point, Emelina was answering quickly and freely. Either they never asked the boy anything, or she didn't hear it when they did. And nobody spoke to Emelina."

"That doesn't give us much to go on," Ren said.

"No, it doesn't," Allyn agreed. "We still may not know who it was or why they were there, but Emelina *did* answer one thing for us."

"What's that?" Nolan asked.

"The people behind the attack weren't magi."

"Because they used guns?" Nolan asked.

Allyn nodded.

"I thought the same thing, Allyn," Nolan said. "But I'm not ready to rule magi out yet."

"Magi don't carry guns," Ren said.

But Nolan wasn't ready to back down—he met Ren's challenging eye. "You're sure of that?" he asked. "You know every magi in every Family? Because from the little I've seen, there isn't a lot of commonality among you." He looked over the magi in the room. "This is an investigation, and we cannot let our personal feelings or expectations influence our thinking. We have to keep our options open and trust the process."

"Magi *don't* use guns," Ren repeated with finality.

"No. The magi *you* know don't use guns. There is a difference." Nolan held up a hand, buying himself another moment. "Do I need to remind you that I'm a part of this mission because of my experience running investigations?"

Grand Mage Klausner interjected before Ren could respond. "We recognize your expertise, Nolan. And we respect your process. But you're new to our way of life, and there are factors you simply don't understand. Ren is right. It's highly unlikely a magi Family has resorted to guns. We have been on the receiving end of their violence too many times before."

Nolan didn't look successfully quelled, but after a glance at both Ren and Grand Mage Klausner, he seemingly realized he was outnumbered and let it be.

"I suppose the question is then," Allyn said, "who would attack a magi Family?"

All eyes turned to the grand mage.

"The answer to that," Klausner said, "is so long and complicated that it won't be of any help."

"Anything you can offer would be useful," Nolan said.

Klausner took a deep breath. "The magi have had dozens of enemies throughout the centuries. Kings, queens, emperors, religious leaders, and rogue organizations, but since the Fracture, we've gone to ground, and many of our enemies have lost their battle with time."

"So you're saying they're all dead?" Nolan asked.

"No," Klausner said, shaking his head. "I'm certainly not saying that. Our plight is still very real, but every enemy we still have suffers from the same foundational problem—they don't know where to find us."

"Someone did," Allyn said.

"Yes they did," Klausner agreed. "So the question becomes

not a question of who, but how. And once you can answer that, discovering the who should be easy."

A sudden question came to Allyn. Arch Mage Westarra had said that the Ferdii Family was one of the oldest in the Order. Suffering from the despair and violence in the days preceding the Fracture, the First Families had isolated themselves from the world as much as possible. Seclusion meant safety. If the Ferdii Family was indeed one of the oldest, it stood to reason that they were also among the most withdrawn.

"Where is the Ferdii Family located?" Allyn asked. It was such a basic question he was almost embarrassed to have to ask it.

"Deep in the mountains," Klausner said.

"Secluded?"

"Very much so."

"Could it be we're dealing with one of the magi's oldest enemies then?" Allyn asked. "I mean, why else attack one of the most secluded Families in the Order? Is it possible they're the only Family they knew where to find?"

Grand Mage Klausner took on a contemplative look, rubbing his chin and bottom lip. "It's possible."

"Would that narrow your list?" Nolan asked hopefully.

"Considerably," Klausner said. "But I'm afraid of saying too much more. You haven't been to the scene yet, and to your previous point, I don't want to influence the way you see it."

He's got a point. There came a time when more discussion wouldn't equal more answers—and they were quickly reaching that point.

"Fair enough." Allyn turned to Nolan. "Thank you for speaking with Emelina. The information has been helpful, and I'm sure it'll prove more so as we get deeper into this thing. But we've waited long enough. Ren, it's your call, but I think it's time we moved out."

"Agreed," Ren said.

"Do you mind if I join you?" Klausner asked.

The question didn't surprise Allyn. Of course Klausner would want to go. The real question was: what would the arch mage say? He had made it abundantly clear that the investigation was to remain a secret, but Grand Mage Klausner already knew of the attack, had been helpful, and held a wealth of knowledge that the McCollum Family lacked. What did Westarra care more about? Secrecy or answers?

Allyn found himself looking at Myanna and Braeburn, who were watching Ren. Both remained expressionless, giving no hint as to what the arch mage would deem correct.

Klausner seemed confused as to who was leading the mission and saw the look on Allyn's face, taking it as a negative. "I'm sorry for asking," he said. "It was presumptuous of me."

"No," Ren said, interjecting before Allyn could respond. "We'd welcome your help. And your secrecy. I only ask that all information and conversations go through me first, and that I'm the only one to speak with the arch mage."

"Understood," Klausner said.

"Good," Ren said. "Let's prepare to move then. I don't want to be rushed by nightfall."

The team adjourned, many running quick errands to prepare themselves for another lengthy journey. Kendyl stopped Allyn before he could do the same.

"I'm going to stay behind," she said.

"What?" Allyn said. "Why?"

"My time with Emelina took a lot out of me."

"It was that bad, huh? You look..." A little voice in his head told him not to finish the sentence.

Kendyl smiled knowingly, but the expression held little warmth. It wasn't that she was angry, just... hollow. "We'll talk about it when you get back."

"Okay," he said. "Do what you think is best."

"Be safe."

"Always."

She gave him another empty smile and turned away, making for Nolan. Allyn watched as she neared him, growing increasingly uncomfortable.

She's hiding something from me, he thought. And Kendyl never hid anything from him.

When Ren had said she didn't want to compete with the coming darkness, Allyn had assumed she didn't want their investigation cut short by nightfall. But two hours into their drive, that statement took on a different meaning.

The road was little more than a narrow ledge cut into the cliffside—a sheer rock wall on one side and a straight drop on the other. No shoulder. No guardrails. No safety features of any kind. It was just them and a lonely, snow-covered mountain pass that was eroding by the day. Their squad was split between two vehicles. Allyn, Grand Mage Klausner, Nyla, and Liam rode with Sten in the lead vehicle. Nolan, Ren, Myanna, and Braeburn occupied the other, which was driven by Loic, another member of the Klausner Family.

It was slow going. Sten kept their speed under thirty kilometers an hour for most of the drive, only opening their SUV up when the pass widened or provided a lengthy straightaway. And even then Allyn found himself white knuckled and holding his breath. He'd thought flying was bad, but that at least offered the illusion of safety. This was just insane. The prospect of having to drive back at night was nearly enough to give him a panic attack.

Allyn was thankful for the second vehicle. Not only did it mean fewer people could see him sweating or closing his eyes in fear, but it also meant one vehicle could go for help if the other fell from the treacherous pass. More importantly, it also gave him time away from Nolan. He'd seen the looks Nolan gave Kendyl. He'd suffered the sarcastic comments. He'd even watched as the two spent more and more time together. One could suppose it was something of an inevitability—romantic options weren't particularly plentiful, after all—but it still left him stunned. This was Kendyl. And *Nolan*. They didn't have anything in common. He just didn't like it.

Allyn pinched the bridge of his nose with his thumb and index finger and closed his eyes. It wasn't that he disliked the guy—quite the opposite actually. Nolan was a good guy, and Allyn considered him a friend—but this was Kendyl he was talking about. His *sister*. And real friends didn't date their friends' sisters. It was as simple as that.

Allyn would have to talk to them. Tell them he didn't agree. Tell them to call it off. Tell them it was just *wrong*. They would understand.

Then as quickly as the thought came, he dismissed it. Kendyl wouldn't give two shits about what he had to say. She never did. "This is my life," she would say, and tell him to stop trying to protect her. *Get on board or stand aside, and whatever you do, don't get in my way.* She was a little too much like him in that respect. When they wanted something, they went after it, repercussions and reputations be damned.

No, he couldn't *tell* them anything—they would never listen. And besides, *telling* only caused contempt. He would have to find another way. He would have to—

What does it matter? a little voice inside asked, almost as if Kendyl had planted it there. *Why does it matter? Because she's my sister! And because... bah! Are we there yet?*

Allyn opened his eyes just as they came around a wide corner and the valley opened up to them. He took in a sharp breath. There it was. Buried deep in a valley that would soon be thick with grass was the Ferdii Family's home. Less a manor or Estate, this was more like a small village with dozens of modest dwellings. One large building that reminded Allyn of a medieval fortress was built directly into the mountainside, and stood above the rest.

And it was all in ruin.

CHAPTER 9

THE FERDII VILLAGE WAS BUILT along the base of the mountains in a crescent shape, with layers of huts climbing the elevating terrain until they met a single stone structure built directly into the rocky mountainside. Multiple stories high, the fortress-like structure stood above the entire village, overlooking the huts like a king from his throne.

The elevating terrain provided natural roadways behind each hut, as well as, Allyn assumed, natural protection against the snowy winters. But more than anything, it created a highly defensible position, offering multiple fallback positions and choke points. Since each row of huts stood above the one in front of it, the retreating Ferdii Magi would have always had the high ground against an advancing enemy. It was becoming more and more clear that whoever had conducted the assault hadn't been amateurs.

They parked on the outskirts of the village, maybe twenty yards from the outer layer of huts, where the terrain was most even. The air was crisp and cold, smelling of wood smoke and blood.

Allyn surveyed their surroundings. The village was still

and silent, like the land around them, but there were plenty of places an enemy could hide. Something in the air didn't feel right. It might have been the ruins that looked like ancient watchtowers on the ridge above, but Allyn couldn't shake the feeling that someone was watching them.

Ren must have felt the same unease. "Sten," she said, turning to the driver. "You can wield?"

The driver nodded.

"Good. Remain here with the cars and stay alert. There's something bad in the air."

The man glanced at Grand Mage Klausner, a clear sign that the McCollum Family's authority didn't extend to the Klausner Family members. The grand mage nodded, however, and the Klausner magi settled in to defend the two vehicles.

"What are those?" Nolan asked, pointing to the ruins that watched over the valley.

"The Eyes of Ferdii," Grand Mage Klausner said. "Watch-towers. When our enemies were more plentiful, the towers watched over this valley."

"They're unmanned?"

"Yes."

"Emelina said she saw the attackers in a tower," Nolan said. "I assume those are them?"

"Yes," Klausner said again.

Nolan turned his attention to Allyn and Ren. "We'll want to search those before we leave."

"Agreed," Allyn said. "What's first, Ren?"

"We'll divide into three squads," she said. "One for either side of the village, and a third for the middle. We'll work our way up toward the top, meeting outside that stone fortress. Take your time and search the huts. We can't let a clue go unseen or another survivor unfound."

Or let an enemy slip behind us.

"Do you really expect to find another survivor?" Liam asked.

"I don't know what we're going to find," Ren said. "That's why we're here."

The plan in place, Ren organized their remaining members into three squads, placing Allyn in charge of Nolan and Nyla. The other two groups made for the edges of the village, leaving their squad alone.

"What do you sense?" Allyn asked.

Nyla closed her eyes and held her hand before her in the direction of the village, attempting to scan for other signs of life. After a series of breaths, she opened her eyes again, letting her hand drop to her side.

"Nothing," she said.

"Nothing?" Allyn repeated.

"Nothing."

Allyn shivered. He swallowed his rising fear and turned to watch as the other two squads got into position.

"Let's go," he said.

The huts were of a simple design, two stories tall, and constructed with light-colored stone bricks. The windows were nothing more than open squares in the stone walls, complete with hinged wooden shutters. Overlapping flat rocks made up the roof, rising ten to fifteen layers high, to form the roof's peak. Allyn had never seen anything like it, but he supposed that under the weight of winter snow, the Family would need roofs stronger than timber or thatch could provide. But why not upgrade to a more modern design? Why not replace the shuttered windows with glass? Sometimes the magi way remained a mystery to him.

Allyn approached the nearest hut and found a doorless entryway that opened to the bottom level. The shutters on the ground-level windows had been closed, leaving the room in darkness. Allyn stepped inside, wielding, letting his red coils cast the room in a bloody light. The room extended the length of the hut and was broken into various pens made up of stone half-walls, and inside each of the pens were straw beds and animal droppings.

"A barn?" Nolan asked from the doorway.

"A stable," Nyla corrected. "It looks like the Family's animals slept here."

"Why not a separate barn?"

"It helps keep the house warm."

"Doesn't do much for the smell," Nolan said, covering his nose. "Are they all like this?"

"Probably," Nyla said. "The Family doesn't look like it has much contact with the outside world and would need to be self-sustained. That means a large number of livestock."

"Then where are they?" Allyn asked, thinking back on the village. He hadn't seen or heard a stray animal anywhere.

"Killed too?" Nolan suggested.

"Maybe," Allyn said. "But we haven't seen any sign of that."

"We haven't seen any sign of anything," Nolan corrected.

"Let's keep looking then."

Allyn exited the stable and ventured up the hillside toward the front of the hut. The ground rose sharper than he'd expected, and was slick with snow and ice. A bitter wind whipped through the valley, making the climb even more difficult, and Allyn had to lay a hand on the side of the stone for support.

He froze. A red splotch, eye level and only a few inches in diameter, stained the pale brick. At its center was a chip that could have been made from a bullet impact.

Allyn ran his finger along the chip. *Is this where it started?*

The outer layer of dwellings *would* have been among the

first hit. He took a step away from the hut, inspecting the ground. The top layer of snow was undisturbed. Using his boot, he scrubbed the top layer aside, uncovering crimson ice below.

"So much for not finding anything," Nolan said.

"Don't." Nyla's voice cut as sharply as the bitter wind.

"What?" Nolan asked.

"What happened here was a tragedy," Nyla said. "Don't make light of it."

"I wasn't trying..." Nolan's face contorted in shame as he trailed off. "You're right. I'm sorry."

If Nyla said anything in return, Allyn didn't hear it. He was already moving again, rounding the corner of the hut. The open door swung in the breeze. Unlike the bottom level, the second-floor windows were open, revealing a single large room filled with sparse furniture and a stone hearth. The ceiling was low enough that Allyn felt as though he had to stoop, and he quickly realized why. Extending up the wall at the back of the hut and through a hole in the ceiling was a ladder.

The bedroom, Allyn thought. He made for the ladder and climbed up until he could see the second room. Blankets and pillows covered a thin mattress, but the area was otherwise vacant.

Allyn climbed back down and left the hut, and his group searched three more before splitting up and venturing into the remaining dwellings. Each one was empty, but the closer they came to the central building of the village, the more signs of struggle they found. Bullet casings. Blood. Torn clothing. Scorch marks. Still no bodies.

"Allyn!"

Allyn exited the home he was in, finding Ren standing outside another hut. "Here," he said.

She turned to him, her face hard, body coiled almost as if she were prepared for a fight.

"We found something."

Allyn's insides twisted. This was it, the moment where it all came to a head. He followed Ren toward the fortress, apprehension growing with every step. It wouldn't be as bad as he imagined, he told himself. *Imagination is always worse, right?*

The hill leveled out into a flat shelf extending from the fortress. The members of the Ferdii Family were laid out there, crumpled in unnatural positions amid a pool of frozen blood. Spent shell casings littered the ground. Men, women, and... a sudden wave of nausea hit Allyn, and he almost emptied his stomach. He became hot, despite the freezing landscape, and his body trembled. The feeling was short-lived, however, and was quickly replaced by hot, unbridled anger.

Allyn knelt beside the body of a young boy who couldn't have been any older than seven or eight. His smooth face was slack, expressionless despite the bullet holes that had mangled his body. *Who could have done something like this? What could have been so important that it warranted killing children?*

"Is this everyone?" Allyn asked, silently hoping others like Emelina had escaped.

"Far as we can tell," Klausner said. "They number what we believe was in the Family."

"You don't know how many were in the Family?"

"We didn't have much interaction with them."

Allyn found himself thinking of Emelina. The poor girl had witnessed the massacre—the murder of her friends and family, everyone she'd ever known.

"There's no way the people who committed this atrocity

walked away unscathed," Allyn said. "Did anyone find anything else?"

Nobody spoke up.

"*Nothing*?" Allyn said, exasperated. "No bodies? No weapons? No boot prints? *Nothing*?"

The group wilted under his angry gaze. They looked at the ground, the bodies, their surroundings—anything to keep from meeting his eye.

They are struggling with this too. It shouldn't have come as a surprise. As good as the magi were about controlling their emotions, that didn't mean they didn't feel them. And the more he studied their body language, the more he realized their façade was close to crumbling.

"They took their dead with them," Ren said.

Allyn agreed. It was the only explanation he could think of. The Ferdii Family were a hard people, made that way by their treacherous environment, and even caught unaware, there was no way they hadn't inflicted their own damage and taken a few of the enemy bastards with them.

Allyn studied the scene, noting the way the Ferdii bodies were laid out. At first, he'd believed it had been a mass shooting, something like a firing squad, but the bodies were laid out too meticulously. It was too intentional. Too *staged*. There was a pattern to them; he was just having a hard time figuring it out.

"Why bring them up here?" Allyn asked, thinking aloud. "Why not leave them where they fell?"

A few magi offered suggestions, but it was Ren who hit on what he was feeling. "They're trying to tell us something."

"I agree," Allyn said. "But what?" He turned to the large structure built into the mountainside. "Has that been secured?"

"Only the closest chambers."

"Good enough." Allyn circled the fallen magi, making for the entrance to the multi-story structure.

Nolan fell into step with him. "What are you doing?"

"Looking for another perspective," Allyn said. "The bodies are too organized to be accidental. We're missing something."

A pair of enormous wooden doors marked the entrance to the stronghold. Standing at least ten feet high, the timber was dry and cracked, weathered by decades or even centuries of exposure. What once would have been a majestic entrance was ravaged by the attack. The wood was scorched and littered with bullet holes, and one of the doors hung perilously by a single hinge, creating a crack between the two doors, large enough to walk through.

Allyn stepped between the doors, immediately entering total darkness. Unlike the huts outside, which used shuttered windows for light, the stronghold was lined with unlit braziers and torches. He wielded, illuminating a large chamber. Hallways, little more than holes carved into the stone, ran deeper into the mountain, eventually falling away into darkness. Rugs, skins, and furs covered the cold floors and walls, adding small amounts of warmth and decoration.

Nolan passed Allyn, stepping deeper into the chamber. He was wielding too. Ren and Klausner followed them, and each spread throughout the room, wielding fire and lighting the torches. Slowly, the dark room took on a warmer quality, and Allyn let the coils dissipate.

"This way," he said, making his way toward the edge of the room, where a staircase rose to the second and third levels. "We need to get some height."

The third level was much like the first, except better illuminated by small windows, murder holes, and arrow slits that broke up the exterior wall. A moment later, Allyn found what he was looking for, and he quickly stepped through a doorless entryway that led out onto a narrow rampart overlooking the Ferdii Village.

Stepping back into the cold mountain air, Allyn could see the village as a whole and the ledge below. His breath caught in his throat. The bodies *were* laid out intentionally, but it wasn't a design or code—it was a message, each magi body making up part of a letter.

The Accord has been violated, it read.

"It can't be," Grand Mage Klausner said quietly.

"I don't understand," Allyn said, turning to the grand mage. "What is the Accord?"

Klausner met his eye, and to Allyn's surprise, the man failed to hide his terror.

"What is the Accord?" Allyn asked again, more forcefully.

But before Klausner could speak, Nolan pointed at something in the distance. "What is that?"

Allyn followed his gaze.

And that's when the first shot rang out.

CHAPTER 10

SEVERAL THINGS HAPPENED AT ONCE. Ren, Nolan, and Grand Mage Klausner dropped behind the safety of the stone rampart's parapet as the sound of high-caliber rounds echoed off the face of the mountain. Bullets cut the air, hitting the wall. Rock chips peppered Allyn's face like shrapnel. Below him, the remaining magi scattered, rushing toward the nearby huts for cover. But not everyone made it.

Frozen and seemingly unable to move, Allyn watched as two magi were gunned down, blood splattering across the gray landscape. Their screams were the only sign they weren't dead. It all felt surreal. Distant. As if hidden behind a screen and far away. And Allyn was powerless to stop it. Worse, even if he could do something, he didn't know what.

Gunfire continued to rain down throughout the valley from what sounded like dozens of locations.

Yelling.

Someone was yelling. Allyn blinked, struggling to emerge from his fog. Somewhere deep inside, he knew if he didn't move, he would be dead. Gunned down like the magi below. But he felt so heavy. Slow. As if he were waking from a potent anesthesia.

More yelling. Then grabbing. Pulling.

Allyn stumbled, yanked to the ground beside Ren. She had a hold of his arm. Her dark eyes were large, intense, and demanding his attention.

"Allyn!" Ren shouted. "Allyn! Snap out of it!"

He stared at her blankly.

Ren cursed, turning away from him to the other magi on the rampart. "On my mark, spread out and give our people cover. We need to get them inside these walls."

"Where?" Nolan shouted over the gunfire. "Where are they?"

"Use your ears." Ren wielded, ice blasts filling her hands. "Go!"

Without waiting for further acknowledgment, Ren leaped to her feet and unleashed a barrage of attacks. Ice cut through the air, propelled forward by simultaneous concussions of air. Nolan, who had rushed to the other end of the parapet, unleashed his own attacks, but Klausner appeared to have frozen like Allyn. Still, it might have been Allyn's imagination, but the gunfire seemed to subside.

"To me!" Ren shouted over the sounds of battle. "To me!" She continued her counterattack, upping its intensity. Ice. Fire. Fire. Ice. She alternated between attacks, finding a rhythm that allowed for maximum efficiency. "Allyn! Get in the fight! Klausner, you too!"

Allyn shook his head sharply, shaking away his lingering sluggishness. The shock was wearing off, replaced by dread and fear, but those were feelings he had experienced before. Those he could fight. He stood and took a couple steps away from Ren, giving her space to operate, and then wielded, using the tingle of the electric coils to further enhance his focus. He studied Ren, following her gaze and attacks, attempting to decipher the whereabouts of the enemy.

Use your ears, she had said. It was easier said than done. Gunshots repeated in an unrelenting cacophony, difficult to track due to the echo from the mountainside. It was like trying to isolate a single voice among a choir. Impossible. And Ren's seemingly random attacks didn't offer any clues.

This is useless, he thought. *I can't...*

Except some of the gunfire *did* sound different. Maybe he couldn't isolate a single voice among the choir, but he *could* isolate a different tenor.

There!

He turned toward the south just as Ren did the same, launching another lance of ice in that direction.

His confidence growing, Allyn isolated another burst of gunfire. He snapped his head around, sighting a dark mass against the gray stone. He threw a static charge, then another a couple moments later. The figure disappeared behind a rock outcropping just before the first charge neared, then reappeared after it struck harmlessly against the rock. The second charge took the enemy soldier directly in the helmet. The figure crumpled, dropping their gun, and shook violently on the ground.

"Good!" Ren shouted at him.

But Allyn didn't answer. Falling into a deep focus, he isolated another burst of gunfire, and without thinking turned and hurled a second volley of attacks toward it. He didn't wait to see if they struck, and instead turned to unleash a third burst toward yet another attacker. He fell into a steady rhythm, mimicking that which Ren had been in. The attacks came smoothly, effortlessly, as if he knew where to turn before he even heard the gunfire.

A bullet struck the wall in front of him, sending shards of broken stone into the air, snapping him out of his rhythm.

I'm drawing their attention, he thought as he ducked behind the parapet for cover.

He surveyed their surroundings in his mind's eye. Their attackers had them boxed in, using both the terrain below and the natural cover of the mountainside above. If that wasn't enough, they had the magi outnumbered by at least three or four to one. The longer the battle raged, the lower their chances of victory were.

Beside him, Ren seemed to come to the same conclusion. She halted her attack, turning to him, not bothering to duck behind the parapet.

"Get down there," she commanded. "Get our people inside."

Allyn nodded, stood, blasted another series of static charges, and withdrew into the safety of the fortress. He hit the bottom of the stone stairs at a run then sprinted across the fortress toward the door—toward the battle. It quickly became apparent that the battle felt different at ground level. It was more brutal. More chaotic. With the height advantage and the protection the fortress offered, he and the others had enjoyed relative safety from the onslaught, but below, there were no such advantages.

Enemy forces advanced through the village, sandwiching the magi outside between them and the enemy snipers who occupied the high ground. Making matters worse, the magi had scattered, breaking from the courtyard for the temporary safety provided by the huts.

Braeburn and Loic were on the ground nearest him, each wounded and struggling toward the fortress. Allyn couldn't see the rest. They would likely be on their own—alone and ripe for the picking.

Taking two sharp breaths, Allyn cleared his mind and darted outside, hurrying toward the nearest fallen magi.

Braeburn was on his stomach, a small slick of warm blood streaked behind him as he crawled toward the fortress. He looked to have cauterized his own wound to slow the bleeding.

Allyn took his hand and pulled with everything he had until the large man was back in the safety of the fortress.

"You going to be okay?" Allyn asked.

"Go," Braeburn said.

"I'll be back," Allyn said, then darted back outside.

Crack!

A bullet shattered stone in front of him. Allyn stumbled, hesitated, and then after making eye contact with the other fallen magi, he pushed forward.

Loic cradled the gunshot wound in his stomach. Unlike Braeburn, he hadn't cauterized the wound, and if his pale skin was any indication, he was dying because of it. Allyn pried away Loic's hand, taking it as he had Braeburn's, and pulled. But Loic's bloody hands were too slick, and Allyn fell just as another gunshot cracked.

The fall likely saved his life. The bullet hissed through the air in front of his face right where his head had been. Scrambling back to his feet, Allyn took hold of Loic's arm with both hands and started again. More gunshots followed. Allyn flinched, expecting sudden pain, but when it didn't come, he pulled harder, gaining speed and momentum. The fortress was close. Allyn stepped through the doorway when another gunshot rang.

Loic's body lurched, and it wasn't until they were safe in the fortress that Allyn saw the fresh hole in Loic's chest.

"No!" Allyn shouted, slumping to the ground.

Loic's lifeless eyes stared at Allyn accusingly. *You failed.*

"No," Allyn repeated, quieter this time, almost a whisper. They'd been so close. He rubbed his eyes with blood-slicked hands, knowing more would die if he didn't hurry. If he didn't get back in the fight.

"Help me to my feet," Braeburn said. "I can cover you."

"No," Allyn said, rising back to his feet.

"Do as I say, boy," Braeburn said. "I can help you."

Allyn sighed but moved toward the man. "If you die, it's not my fault."

"If you live, it might be mine."

Taking the magi's hand, Allyn heaved him to his feet. Then with one arm thrown around his neck, Allyn positioned him by the door.

The battle had taken on yet another pitch. The gunfire seemed closer, somehow more targeted, as if the enemy were nearly upon them. And the magi weren't fighting back with as much vigor. Exhausted, depleted, or simply hopeless, he couldn't tell. In either case, the battle's end was nearly at hand. He was running out of time.

He spotted Nyla with her back to a nearby hut.

"Nyla!" Her head snapped toward him, and he waved her forward frantically. "Inside! Come on!"

"Give her cover," Braeburn said.

With Braeburn half hidden behind the door, Allyn stepped beyond the doorway, and together, they provided magical cover fire against the advancing enemy.

Nyla darted from the hut, streaking toward them, her silver hair streaming like a ribbon behind.

Gunshots followed immediately, bullets striking the courtyard and ricocheting with odd whistling sounds. One even cut through the extra folds of her pants, narrowly missing her leg. Allyn stepped aside, and Nyla ducked around the corner, positioning herself so the thick wall was between her and the onslaught outside. She met his eye, breathing heavily.

"It's a bloodbath out there," she said between breaths.

"I know," Allyn said. "We need to get everyone inside."

Nyla closed her eyes and took a couple deep breaths. "Who's left?"

"Ren, Nolan, and Klausner are on the rampart," Allyn said. "That leaves Liam and Myanna."

"And the drivers."

Allyn shook his head, glancing toward the dark shape of Loic's fallen body resting a few feet away. "Loic's dead. Sten is too—he would have been the first to go."

"Both drivers are dead?"

Allyn nodded.

Nyla cursed. "They hit our escape first then. They knew we'd come."

"I was thinking the same thing."

"Have you seen the other two?"

"No," Allyn said. "I think Myanna is fighting back, but Liam... he's probably inside one of the huts."

Nyla risked a glance outside, surveying the battlefield. "I'll go for Myanna; you find Liam. He'll need your help."

Allyn nodded and turned to Braeburn. "Same plan?"

Braeburn hadn't moved except to slide behind the wall for protection, and in a silent response, he readjusted his position so he could again provide cover fire.

An eerie silence had fallen over the battlefield, interrupted only by the intermittent sounds of assault rifle magazines being reloaded, bullets chambered, and the click of heavy boots on stone.

"They're advancing," Allyn said. "We need—"

Another burst of gunfire cut him off, followed almost immediately by balls of fire and lances of ice. Myanna was still fighting back. Above them, Ren and Nolan re-engaged, focusing their return fire on Myanna's position, providing her with additional support.

"Go!" Allyn commanded, then raced across the open courtyard. Nyla was close behind before veering toward Myanna's position.

Allyn pushed for the nearest hut, arriving unharmed only a couple of breaths later. "Liam?"

No answer.

Allyn ducked his head into the hut, quickly surveying its innards. Empty. He moved on, making for the next hut in the line. Also empty. Did he dare call out and risk drawing attention to himself?

No. Too risky.

Stepping back outside, he positioned himself so his back was to the hut and he had a clear view of Ren, Nolan, and Klausner atop the rampart. He needed their attention, but they were focused on Myanna. Not knowing what else to do, he jumped up and down, waving his arms above his head, hoping one of them would see his movement out of the corner of their eye.

It worked.

Too well.

Ren snapped around, an ice blast already in her hands. In a blink, it was racing toward him. Allyn didn't have time to curse. He didn't have time to move. It would pierce his chest in an instant. Fortunately, Ren was faster than he was.

No sooner was it out of her hand than she realized her mistake and corrected it with another concussion of air, sending the blast careening off its original trajectory to shatter against the wall of a hut only a few feet away. She glared at him, an unspoken question on her lips.

With her attention now focused squarely on him, Allyn

struggled to find a way to communicate. "Where is Liam?" he mouthed.

Ren tilted her head to the side, confused.

"Liam," he mouthed again, this time exaggerating the movements. But the distance was too great. Ren couldn't make it out, so accepting the risk, he shouted Liam's name.

Ren visibly relaxed—she understood—and her eyes broke away from his to scan the village. Several seconds went by before she looked back at Allyn and shook her head.

Allyn's mouth went dry. He couldn't lose Liam too. Not Liam. He stepped away from the hut, making himself more visible, and screamed with everything he had.

"Liam!" Allyn's voice carried over the battle. Over gunfire, fireballs, and ice blasts. "Liam!" He was a beacon amid a storm. A single light in true darkness. The sound of a friend to someone who had no one. "Liam! To me! To me! Liam!"

A moment later, the young machinist emerged from a hut in the second layer, a look of pure terror on his face. He stopped when he saw Allyn, almost as if he didn't believe it was truly him.

A smile began to make its way across Allyn's face just as a dark figure appeared behind his younger friend.

No!

Time slowed. Gun already raised, the enemy advanced. With amazing clarity, Allyn watched as the man's finger tightened against the trigger. He couldn't shout. Couldn't warn Liam. Doing so would only cause him to turn around and face his attacker.

Moving on instinct, Allyn wielded, projecting a weakened static charge into Liam's midsection. Liam doubled over just as the shot rang out, causing it to go high. Then, in a single fluid motion, Allyn brought up his other hand, his electric coils cracking with violent anticipation.

He didn't send another static charge. Missing meant death. Instead, Allyn *reached* for their attacker, projecting his coils along an imaginary line traced between himself and the man. They streaked forward in a continuous tendril, hitting the armed man and enveloping him in a brutal web of electricity that melted his boots to the ground and sent the rest of his body into violent convulsions. When Allyn finally cut power to the coils, the man was on the ground, steam rising from his broken body.

Allyn rushed toward Liam. Tenderly wrapping an arm around the boy's shoulders, he helped Liam stand up straight. Liam held his midsection with both arms, wincing against the motion.

"Are you all right?" Allyn asked.

"You shot me," Liam said.

"Yeah. I'm sorry about—"

"Thank you."

"Anytime," Allyn said, stifling a laugh. "Come on, let's get you inside before more of those assholes find us."

With Liam leaning against him for support, Allyn rushed back to the fortress, and once inside, he helped Liam to a comfortable corner out of harm's way. The young magi sat with a grimace, still holding his stomach.

"Are you sure you're okay?" Allyn asked, dropping to a crouch so he was eye level.

Liam nodded. "Was I the last one?"

"No." Allyn looked back at the doorway. "Nyla was out getting Myanna."

"Is she back?"

"I don't think so."

"Then go get her," Liam said. "I'll be fine."

"Okay. Hold yourself together until I get back."

Allyn jogged to the citadel's entrance, stopping near

Braeburn. The broad-shouldered magi didn't pay him any heed. Instead, his face had the look of intense focus, and he hobbled outside. Beyond him, Nyla and Myanna were making for the citadel. Nyla led the charge; Myanna was only a half step behind, running backward, fire ready in her hands.

It took several agonizing seconds for Nyla and Myanna to cross the last couple dozen feet. Allyn watched, helpless. The gunfire had ceased, and no more of their attackers showed themselves, but he knew they were spread across the mountainside. All it would take was one well-placed bullet.

But the shot never came.

Nyla and Myanna stormed into the citadel a moment later, and once inside, Allyn helped Braeburn close one door and align the other so that it blocked most of the doorway.

Footsteps echoed above them as Ren, Nolan, and Klausner descended the stairwell.

"Keep away from the doors and find cover," Ren said, her voice firm and unwavering. "We need to be prepared when they come."

"You think they'll come for us in here?" Liam asked. He sounded weak by comparison, his voice quivering with fear and apprehension.

"Yes. Find something to barricade the doors. We need time to think."

They did as commanded. Those who could stand and walk unaided filtered throughout the chamber and into nearby rooms, searching for anything that could be used as a barricade.

Once that was done, and after Nyla had a chance to tend to the wounded, Klausner found Ren and pulled her aside.

"We're not prepared for a standoff," he said, nearly out of Allyn's hearing. "We don't have food, water, or supplies for nightfall. We'll freeze to death if we don't move quickly."

"I know," Ren said. "But we can't fight, either. Not in our present condition."

"There might be another way," Klausner said. "This citadel is built directly into the mountain for protection. It may look like it only has one entrance, but that's not our way. I assure you, it will have another."

"Do you know where?"

"No, but these chambers only go in one direction. Given enough time, I'm sure I could find it."

"It's a good idea," Ren said. "But I need you here. We need all the magi we have in case they strike."

An embarrassed expression crossed Klausner's face, and it might have been the orange glow from the flickering torches, but he seemed to flush. "I won't be much help in a fight. I'm a cleric."

"Oh," Ren said, visibly surprised. "I didn't realize... then above..."

"That's why I couldn't attack," Klausner said.

Things seemed to click in Ren's mind, but she quickly moved on. "In either case, we'll still need you here. I can't have you running off—it wouldn't be good for morale, and besides, if you can keep even one magi on their feet and fighting back, that's not a resource we can let slip away."

"Who are you thinking then?"

Ren shot a glance at Liam, who was sitting at the base of the stairs, watching the entrance, his foot tapping with concern.

"The boy?" Klausner asked. "Surely—"

"He's stronger than you think. More importantly, he's got a great mind. If anyone can find this hidden exit of yours, it'll be him."

Klausner looked skeptical but nodded.

"Liam," Ren said. "Come here."

Liam stood and jogged over to Ren.

"Grand Mage Klausner has told me of a secret exit from the citadel," Ren said. "Unfortunately, he doesn't know where it is. I need you to find it."

"Me?" he asked.

"I need someone uninjured, with a sharp mind, and who's familiar with magi architecture. That's you."

"Okay," Liam said, his voice lacking the confidence he tried so hard to display.

"Talk with Grand Mage Klausner," she continued. "Between the two of you, I think you'll be able to think of a few places to check first." She turned from him, speaking to the larger group who, like Allyn, were eavesdropping. "The rest of you follow me. It's time we organized our battle plan."

CHAPTER 11

L IAM HADN'T BEEN OUT OF sight for more than a couple minutes before the standoff took an unexpected turn. Their defensive magi force formed a loose semicircle around the entrance, with Myanna and Braeburn resting against the wall on opposite sides of the doors. Allyn, Ren, and Nolan stood fifteen or so paces away, directly in front of the citadel's entrance, but spread out from each other and hidden behind individual battlements made up of overturned tables and other furniture they'd found in nearby chambers. The two clerics, Nyla and Klausner, were with Ren and Nolan on either side of Allyn. Either of them could rush to his aid if needed.

Ren hadn't divulged Klausner's secret—if one could call it that—and had instead offered no explanation as to why he shared a battlement with her. If the other magi questioned it at all, they likely believed it was for his protection. He was, after all, the senior-ranking magi among them—even if Ren was acting commander of the operation.

Allyn crouched behind his cover, watching the entrance. His heart thundered in his chest, and despite the cold, sweat beaded along his forehead and ran down his back. In his limited experience, he'd found that the anticipation of battle was worse than the battle itself. In the heat of the moment, there wasn't time for thought or fear. Only time for action. But it was in this period of waiting when one's dark thoughts crept into consciousness.

"Hello in there," a male voice called out, in an accent Allyn didn't recognize. It had a gravelly quality, as if its bearer had spent his years smoking, screaming, or both. "It seems we have ourselves a little standoff."

Allyn and Ren met each other's gaze. Ren shook her head. *Don't take the bait*, she seemed to say.

"I've had my men stow their weapons," the man said. "I'd appreciate it if you did the same. Maybe we can have a quick chat like more *civilized* men."

Allyn found himself shaking his head. He imagined the man outside; clad in dark body armor with an assault rifle in hand, smiling as if this were some game or he'd made a bad joke. It wasn't funny to Allyn. Sten and Loic were dead, Braeburn was injured, and the rest were terrified and on edge. Then there was Emelina, who was back at the Klausner Manor and might never recover from her emotional wounds. There was no humor in this, gallows or otherwise.

"Come now," the man continued. "I don't appreciate talking to myself. I don't keep that good of company. Join me."

Ren remained silent, her eyes fixed on the entrance.

"Very well, then," the man said when it became apparent no one would answer him. "I'll take your silence as an invitation to join you inside."

Allyn gritted his teeth, and with his peripheral vision, he saw Ren wield ice. She looked at him and nodded for him to do the same. Following her lead, he channeled the energy filling the deep void hidden in the recesses of his body and projected it outward. As always, the energy manifested as red coils of electricity that writhed around his arms, causing his skin to tingle as if they had fallen asleep.

The rest of the magi inside the chamber did the same—Myanna and Braeburn wielded ice, and Nolan, his orbs of energy. He and Allyn hid their creations behind their battlements, careful their light didn't give away their positions.

Outside, there was a ruffling sound and clicking. Then thick boots scraped over solid ground. Allyn held his breath as the sounds neared the doorway, and then, when the sounds couldn't get any closer, they were replaced by silence. It stretched out long enough to be discomforting.

Allyn exhaled, unable to hold his breath any longer. Only a few paces away, Ren remained steady, her own breathing slow and measured.

Something bounced, clinking to a stop against one of the table legs that made up the base of the door's barricade, and almost immediately, the footsteps outside rushed *away*. Allyn's eyes narrowed in confusion.

Why would—

Then realization.

"Down!" Allyn screamed. "Everyone—"

The grenade exploded. Shrapnel blasted through the chamber, bouncing off walls and cutting into their battlements, ravaging their hastily built fortifications.

Allyn found himself on the ground, his vision blurred, ears ringing. He blinked, shook his head, and tried to pop his ears, but the only cure for his disorientation was the one thing he didn't have. Time. He staggered to his feet. Smoke filled the room, but through its thin veneer, he could see the entrance. And it was open. Their door's barricade was destroyed, cast through the room like debris after a tornado.

The door that had hung awkwardly now lay on the ground, and the other swung loosely as if it too would soon fall.

Through the smoke, the first man appeared. Covered in full body armor, he rushed through the doorway. He was dressed for war, a helmet obscuring his face, carrying a thick metal shield that protected his armor-clad body from knees to chin. Protruding from a narrow slit in the upper half of the shield was the black barrel of a gun. Directly on his heels, but forming a tight V formation were two more soldiers, dressed in the same fashion with shields and guns at the ready.

Allyn caught a glimpse of at least two more immediately behind them when the first lance of ice struck the leader's shield. It shattered, leaving little more than a harmless wet streak that disappeared as quickly as it had materialized. Two more ice blasts, these from Myanna and Braeburn, struck the next soldiers in line, but neither was any more effective than the first.

Standing tall and emerging from the safety of the remains of his battlement, Allyn threw a static charge at the nearest soldier. It struck the shield directly in its center, and tendrils of electricity spread across its metal surface like spiderwebbing cracks in glass. The soldier recoiled as if he'd touched a hot surface, his shield dipping, exposing his head and chest.

Ren capitalized on the opening, launching a fireball at the soldier. He recovered just in time, raising the shield over his face as the fireball struck, exploding in a wash of fire that cascaded over the shield like a torrent of water around a boulder. The explosion slowed him, but he and the others appeared unharmed. Another fireball crashed against the shield, this time even less effective, but Allyn saw another opening.

"Again!" he shouted.

Ren didn't ask why. She didn't even spare him a glance before launching a third fireball.

Allyn was ready. After taking an extra half breath to focus on his aim, he threw a series of static charges that trailed behind Ren's fireball, angled downward toward the soldier's feet. As the fireball raced toward the soldier, he braced, raising the shield so that it once again covered his face. The movement exposed his boots, and the barrage of static charges knocked his feet out from under him, sending him crashing to the ground, breaking the formation.

"At will!" Ren ordered. "At will!"

But the enemy soldiers were already adjusting into a diamond-shaped formation, and they easily repelled the magi's stream of attacks. Gunfire echoed off the vaulted ceiling of the entrance, so loud Allyn thought his eardrums would burst.

"Nolan!" Ren shouted over the cacophony. "Now!"

Nolan had been waiting for this order—his attacks, unlike the other magi's, were less directional, less controlled, more dangerous to everyone, including the magi. The first energy blast targeted the solider second in line. He was ready and angled his shield so that it would block the blast, but he didn't understand the difference between Nolan's energy blasts and Ren's fireballs.

The white orb exploded in a brilliant flash of light, temporarily blinding anyone who had been watching, and threw the soldier and the one behind him backward into the door. The blast also sent a shockwave in all directions, hitting Myanna's position nearly as hard as it had hit the soldiers. The Elemental Guard was ready for it, however, avoiding the worst of it behind what was left of her battlement.

The shockwave kicked up dust as it raced toward Allyn, and he ducked behind his battlement, but by the time the shockwave struck his fortification it had weakened significantly and didn't do any additional damage. Allyn rose from his battlement just in time to see the enemy soldiers reforming into their formation. He readied another attack, but the soldiers retreated, obviously wary and unprepared for the new weapon.

The magi force pressed them farther, attacking relentlessly, driving the retreating force back through the entrance, not stopping until they disappeared from view. Silence again filled the space, as thick as the smoke left behind by the fireballs and exploded grenade.

"Report!" Ren called out, and one by one, Myanna, Braeburn, Allyn, Nolan, and the two clerics responded. No one down. No one injured. They had won—for the moment.

Allyn made for Ren's battlement, thinking of how quickly the grenade had nullified their barricade. He kept his voice quiet enough that only she could hear him.

"What now?"

"Now we rearrange our positions," Ren said. "They know how many of us are here and how we're placed. We can't change our numbers, but we can make it so they don't know what to expect the next time they enter."

"It won't be only five that come for us next time," Allyn said. "The chamber's too big, and we're too spread out. Why not retreat deeper into the citadel where the hallways narrow? Bottle them up, use their numbers against them?"

Ren shook her head. "That only works if there *is* another exit. If there isn't, then the narrow corridors will work against us. Besides, we need to be here when Liam returns. If we're not... I don't want his blood on my hands." Her face became more resolute. "We remain here."

Finding no flaw in her reasoning, Allyn nodded and turned

to move back to his battlement, ready to dismantle what was left and rebuild it elsewhere.

"Allyn," Ren said, grabbing his arm and stopping him. "In either case, we must hold out until nightfall. There's too many of them for us to slip away unseen. We'll need darkness and..."

"Luck?" Allyn offered.

Ren flashed him a rare smile. In most cases, it would have unnerved him—a viper would sooner smile than Ren, but in their increasingly dire circumstances, the gesture filled him with fondness for the other magi. It was a simple thing, but it reminded him that she was more than the stern leader he'd grown accustomed to, and even resented at times. He returned her smile with one of his own.

"Luck," she agreed.

"That's good, then. We have an overabundance of that."

"And it's been all bad," Ren said.

"True, but that just means we're getting all of the bad luck out of the way now so we'll have nothing but good from here."

"Do you really believe that?" Ren's smile faltered a bit as worry flashed in her eyes. Through Ren's cracking façade, Allyn saw a sliver of who she truly was—vulnerable, complete with contradicting emotions and her own hopes and dreams. Oddly, he found himself wanting to know more.

"I don't have a choice," Allyn said. "It's either that or..."

"Despair," Ren finished for him.

"Exactly."

"Better this way then."

"Better this way." He smiled again, driving the point home.

She smiled back, sharing the moment with him.

The enemy leader outside cut it short. "Well, well, well—I wasn't out here talking to myself after all."

Allyn's and Ren's eyes left each other, turning to the doorway instead. With the one door completely fallen, they had a clear view into the space beyond. It was vacant for the time being, but Allyn knew that was only an illusion. Their enemy would be hidden just out of sight.

"He knows we're in here now," Allyn said. "What do you say we get a look at who's pulling these strings?"

"I think it's time." Ren turned, calling out to their remaining squad one by one, and then pointed to where she wanted them to reassemble. She pulled Myanna and Braeburn away from the door to accompany Nolan and Nyla behind the battlements that had taken on the least damage. They would lose their proximity with the door, but they would be able to retreat directly into the nearest chamber if needed.

"Allyn, Grand Mage Klausner," Ren said. "With me."

Ren led their group up the stairs and out onto the rampart. Face hard and hiding the fragility Allyn had seen only moments before, she strode up to the crenelated wall, flanked by Allyn and Grand Mage Klausner, to survey the scene.

As Allyn had expected, the enemy force was split into two groups, one on either side of the entrance. Maybe twenty in all, they were clad in the same black body armor, black military-style boots, and black helmets that hid their faces. Their leader stood apart from the rest, a couple paces nearer the door. He had removed his helmet, holding it under his arm, while his other hand lingered near a pistol strapped to his hip. Middle-aged, with a full head of short gray hair, the man held himself as if he were half his years.

One of the men below saw them atop the rampart and called out. The leader snapped his head up, and seeing them, smiled. Where the same expression had warmed Ren's demeanor, this did the opposite to the man's. Allyn wanted to turn away. Retreat. Hide. The man wasn't smiling because he wanted them to feel comfortable. He was doing it because he knew he had them.

"Ah, that's more like it," the man said. "I feel we got off on the wrong foot. My name is Sedric Lang, and you could say I control these parts. How about you tell me who you are, and what it is you're doing here."

"I'm not playing your game," Ren said. "We know what you did here."

"See," Sedric said. "Where I come from, if you want something, there's a certain protocol you go through to get it. And manners are one of those protocols. So how about you give me your name and try again."

"Ren McCollum," she said. "And we're here investigating the murder of this Family."

Sedric beamed. "Doesn't that feel better? Did you see that, men? A little hospitality can be taught even deep in these godforsaken mountains—and to a witch, no less. But did you hear her? She's accusing us of murder. Of *murder*. As if they hadn't violated their own sacred contract." He turned back to Ren. "No, Ren McCollum, what we did here wasn't murder. It was justice."

"Justice?" Ren asked, incredulous. "The murder of innocent men, women, and children is justice?"

"There are no innocents in war, Ren McCollum. Especially among your kind."

"Who are you?"

"The Hammer of God who's been unleashed to cleanse your existence from this world."

"I don't understand."

"Then ask the man beside you. He is one of your so-called grand mages, isn't he?"

Ren and Allyn turned to Grand Mage Klausner. He had taken a step back, fear etched deeply into his face.

"No," Klausner said.

"What's going on, Grand Mage?" Allyn asked. "Who are they?"

"A legend," Klausner whispered.

"You'll have to be more specific than that."

Klausner's wide eyes met his, frantic. "The war begins anew."

"What are you talking about? What war?"

"They come again."

"Who comes again?" Allyn grabbed the grand mage by the shoulders. "What is going on?"

"They're going to kill us all."

Allyn followed Klausner's gaze, looking over the armed men below.

Sedric watched with an amused expression. "Family secrets?" he asked, raising an eyebrow. "That's unfortunate. Ignorance isn't a defense. Still, I haven't the stomach for this much bloodshed. There's no doubt if we storm your fortress, we'll be able to tear it from your grasp and kill all of you in the process, but at what cost? You've already killed some of my men today—men with wives and children of their own—so what do you say we save the widow making for another day and negotiate a ceasefire?"

"What do you propose?" Ren asked.

"We let you walk," Sedric said. "Fight another day."

"Under what conditions?"

"Now that's the question, isn't it?" Sedric asked. "How do we make this agreeable for both parties?"

"You want something in return."

"That is the foundation of all negotiations."

"I expect you already know what you want?"

"I wouldn't be very good at these things if I didn't." Sedric pointed at Grand Mage Klausner. "I want him. I want your grand mage."

No! Allyn opened his mouth to speak, but Ren beat him to it.

"What assurances do I get that you'll hold up your end of the agreement?" she asked.

"What are you doing?" Klausner hissed.

Ren ignored him.

She's not actually thinking about doing this, is she?

"I suppose my word isn't good enough?" Sedric asked.

"Ren?" Klausner pleaded. "What are you doing?"

"Quiet," she commanded under her breath. Then to Sedric, she said, "No."

"I thought not," Sedric said. "Let's try this then. Parade your grand mage out that front gate of yours, and we'll flee these parts and let you do the same."

"Just like that?" Ren said. "We deliver the grand mage, and you ride off into the sunset?"

"That's what I'm proposing."

"Can we have time to talk it over?"

"Of course," Sedric said, as if they were negotiating the purchase of a car. "But I can't give you too long." He looked to the darkening sky. "Nightfall isn't too far off, and we'd best be on our way before it arrives. You have twenty minutes."

Ren withdrew from the rampart without further discussion.

"We're not really doing this, are we?" Allyn asked as they reentered the citadel.

"Of course not," Ren said. "But we need more time, and he just gave it to us. The question is, will it be enough?"

Liam was lost. Not because the citadel housed a maze of

rooms or was overly large, but because of the darkness. He'd brought a torch from the front chamber, and while it provided enough light that he didn't walk into a table or trip over a rug, it was little more than a single dim star in the vastness of the night's sky.

Making matters worse, he hadn't thought to light any of the unlit torches that lined the walls deeper in the complex. If he'd been thinking, he would have lit every torch and brazier so he could have seen each room in its full glory, leaving no corner unlit, no possibility uncovered. As it were, he occasionally entered a new room or tunnel and had the vague feeling he'd been there before. Those mistakes had cost him time, and he had long since begun to sweat.

He wasn't sure how he felt about the mission. Ren had obviously been looking for a reason to get rid of him. Find a secret entrance inside a centuries-old citadel? Liam wanted to laugh. If there was such a thing, his chances of finding it were slim at best. Especially when he considered how little time he had left. No, Ren had sent him on yet another fool's errand meant to get him out of harm's way and out from underfoot. He was tired of being a liability in battle, and even more tired of agreeing with the sentiment.

You're many things, Liam, he told himself. *But a warrior isn't one of them.*

But even as he told himself this, something inside him wanted to prove them wrong. Hadn't he demonstrated his worth during the battle for the McCollum Manor? Mason may have led the assault, but it had been Liam who'd broken orders and carried out a rescue operation that had saved the lives of several magi. He had also overridden the pressure-sealed doors in the McCollum Library when he, Allyn, Kendyl, and Nolan had been trapped, freeing his friends and turning the tide of the battle in the process.

No, he wasn't a liability; he was just inexperienced and untrained. Unless Ren, Allyn, or Jaxon let him take part, he would never become more confident. More importantly, he would never earn the trust of the Family he was supposed to eventually lead.

But what would you have done? he asked himself, reentering what he'd deemed the Grand Hall, a particularly large chamber with exposed stone walls and a vaulted ceiling. *It wasn't as if there were any rescue missions to organize or remote doors to override. Not in this place.*

Liam circled the chamber, lighting the sconces that lined the wall at even intervals. The flickering firelight slowly brought the chamber back to life. It was the largest chamber he'd been in yet. The exposed stone made the space feel organic, almost as if it had been built within a natural cave, and the vaulted ceiling allowed Liam to stand straight for the first time in a while. Stretching the tense muscles in his neck and upper back, he finally felt as if the mountain weren't pressing down on him.

He passed rows of benches as he approached an elevated dais at the head of the chamber. He'd never been in a throne room, but this is what he'd imagined one might look like. Grand. Organized. Decadent. Tapestries more than twice his height, with ancient magi symbols for fire, water, air, and health, hung from the walls, providing warmth and decoration. Between them were portraits depicting different arch mages from magi history. They weren't all represented, not like in the halls of Ukiah, the Order's capital. These portraits were only of the most respected. The most legendary.

Liam continued to circle the chamber, his heart sinking with every step, with every lit torch. Nearly every chamber had emptied into another, every hallway and tunnel leading deeper into the mountain. And while the citadel wasn't overly large, it had held enough rooms to keep hope alive for a spell, but within this last chamber, that hope was coming to a bitter end.

He stopped exactly halfway around the circular room, directly behind the dais. *What's the point in finishing?* If there was a second exit, it wasn't in the Grand Hall. Completely contained, it had only one entrance and exit, just like the citadel itself.

But I don't know where else to look.

Liam pinched his forehand with his off hand and found himself staggering toward the dais. Unlike a throne room, where a single throne would occupy the dais and preside over a large audience, this dais held five separate seats around a table that ran the length of the dais. The middle seat was taller than the rest, and its wooden frame was accented with faded paint.

The grand mage's seat, Liam thought.

The other four confused him. Every Family had its own grand mage, its own leader, and while largely autonomous, the Families had to operate within the will of the Forum and arch mage. Beyond that, the magi had no governing bodies, no councils. Each grand mage had complete and absolute control over his or her Family. Unlike Liam's father, who was the last true grand mage of the McCollum Family, Jaxon governed with the aid of an inner circle. It might have been a byproduct of knowing his time as grand mage was limited, or it might have been the way Jaxon planned to lead in the future. In either case, it was his prerogative—even if it was unconventional. But even Jaxon's inner circle didn't have public seats of prestige above the rest of the Family, and Liam had never heard of a Family who operated like that. What then, were the other four seats for?

Liam ascended the stairs to the dais, tracing the backs of

the chairs as he walked past. He stopped at the grand mage's chair and took a seat on its worn cushion. The table was of a strange design, with a second layer of wood that ran its length, only inches above the floor.

A place for my feet? Or just an interesting design choice?

Liam sat straight, tapping his nails on the table's lacquered top, imagining the room filled with magi. As he did, a distant memory bubbled up from the deep recesses of his brain. Something about the room felt familiar. Not the familiarity of having been in the hall before, or even the déjà vu of having been in one like it. This was different—almost as if he'd seen pictures of it, heard about it from a story, or read about it.

A cold shiver crept down his spine as the pieces fell into place. An ancient Family, the watchtowers above, the very chamber he was in. He doubted many locations fit all the criteria, and if he was right, he'd read about all of them in the dusty book he'd found in the Hyland Library all those months ago. If he was right, then he knew what Arch Mage Westarra and his enemies were after, and he understood why it had been hidden and kept secret for more than a thousand years.

He pushed himself away from the table, ready to rush back to Ren and Allyn to tell them about his discovery, but as he did, something strange happened. The sudden force shoved the table away first, not his chair, and below it, something caught his eye.

He looked closer. There wasn't a door or latch. There was nothing. Darkness. In a room half-filled with light, the floor under the bottom layer of the table was black.

CHAPTER 12

"T HIS WAY," LIAM SAID SOFTLY, waving for the rest of the group to follow. "Come on."

Allyn followed a few paces behind, he and the rest of their squad laboring under the weight of the injured and fallen—the latter carried by Nolan and helped along by Grand Mage Klausner. The order to carry Loic's body hadn't come from anyone in particular; it was just unanimously accepted as the right thing to do. Once they were able to recover Sten's remains, both magi would be returned home to the Klausner Manor where they would be given a proper magi burial under the watchful care of their family.

"How far is it?" Ren asked, glancing back through the narrow corridor, toward the entrance.

"All the way at the end," Liam said. "But the citadel isn't that big. We'll be there soon."

"Good," Ren said.

Allyn thought he heard more unspoken words on her lips. *I'm not sure how much time we have left.* Sedric's twenty-minute time limit would expire at any moment, and once he and his squad stormed the citadel and found the front chamber empty, it would be a race to see if Ren's magi squad could navigate the secret corridor and second exit and return to the cars unseen before the enemy force found them or realized what they were doing.

As they passed through the various chambers, Ren fell behind the group, snuffing the torches Liam had lit during his search.

"Darkness is our friend," Ren said when she caught Allyn looking at her. "When they find the front chamber empty, they'll expect we bunkered down in a more strategic spot, not knowing we learned of the second exit. The darkness will slow them, buy us more time."

Allyn hoped she was right, but something gnawed about Sedric at him.

The man knows more about us than we do him.

Would he know the citadel had a second outlet? It wasn't, after all, such an abstract concept. And foreseeing this, would he pull back and go for the vehicles rather than pursue them through the citadel? Their plan was shaky under closer scrutiny, but Allyn didn't have a better one, so he kept his thoughts to himself.

Liam led them through chamber after chamber until finally, they reached what Liam had called the Grand Hall. A circular room with a vaulted ceiling and rows of pews extending from a dais at the head of the room, it was easily the largest in the citadel.

Why didn't the magi live within the citadel itself?

Until recently, the winter conditions and wildlife would have been their biggest threat. Had they lived in the village during the spring and summer months, when the conditions were more hospitable, and then in the citadel during the colder fall and winter seasons? It hadn't appeared that way. What then was the citadel's purpose?

What am I missing?

Once inside the Grand Hall, Liam rushed down a long hand-woven runner that split the pews into two sections, making for the dais. Allyn followed, his confusion building. Where was the exit? The walls were solid stone, and save for the doorway they had just entered through, he didn't see another. Again, he kept quiet, trusting Liam, and his patience was rewarded when they topped the dais. The long table resting atop it had been pushed aside, exposing a hole in the floor.

Liam knelt, waving his torch in the hole, illuminating a single steep stairwell that descended into an unlit corridor. "It goes all the way through the mountain," he said. "Opening east of the village. It'll be a straight shot to the cars from there."

"You went through it?" Allyn asked.

"I had to know if it was what we were looking for."

"Good work, Liam," Ren said. "How heavy is the table?"

"It's not light. Why?"

"We'll need to slide it back in place once we're all below," Ren said. "The exit won't be much of an advantage if Sedric is able to find it quickly."

"Right," Liam said. "I'm the smallest one here, so once everyone is inside, I can slide the table back part of the way and wiggle in. Once I'm inside, we can slide it the rest of the way. If it's too heavy, at least it'll be partially covered."

"Good," Ren said. "Let's go, then. Injured first."

Braeburn limped forward, his arm wrapped around Klausner's neck for support. The bandage on his leg was soaked with blood, and his face was losing color. If he didn't get medical attention soon—magical or otherwise—Allyn wasn't sure how much longer he had left. At the lip of the hole, Klausner ducked out from under Braeburn's arm and started down the stairs, and then halfway down, he turned and helped the Elemental Guardsman navigate the steps until they disappeared into the darkness below.

Ren circled the hall and snuffed out the remaining torches as Nolan entered the passageway, carrying Loic's limp body. The others followed, leaving Liam alone in the Grand Hall.

The corridor was tight, its walls barely wider than Allyn's shoulders, and the ceiling hung low enough that the taller magi had to stoop. He wasn't sure what he had expected—maybe a damp corridor with mold and lichen covering the walls or something overcome with spiders and cobwebs like in an Indiana Jones movie. Instead, it was dark, dry, and cold, much like the rest of the citadel had been.

Above him, the table scratched against the hall's floor, groaning as Liam slid it back into place. When the hole was more than half covered, Liam slipped his legs into the hole and wiggled into the tunnel. Once inside, Allyn helped him move the table the rest of the way. They had no way of knowing if it was back in alignment with the dais, but the hole was covered, and that would have to be good enough.

"How far from here?" Ren asked.

"The entire tunnel is a few hundred feet," Liam said. "But halfway through, it forks, one passage leading to the exit, another to some sort of chamber."

"Chamber?" Myanna asked. "Was there anything inside?"

"Not really," Liam said.

"No," Myanna pressed. "Or not really?"

"I don't know," Liam confessed. "I didn't spend a lot of time in it."

"What does it matter?" Allyn asked.

"It doesn't," Myanna said.

There was something in her tone that Allyn didn't trust, and as soon as they were safe, he would have to ask her about it.

"Is there a door or wall at the exit?" Allyn asked. "Something to conceal it?"

"No," Liam said. "From the outside, it just looks like a narrow cave, and it blends in with the rest of the mountainside, so it's impossible to spot unless you know exactly where to look."

"It's getting dark," Ren said. "We'll have to leave the torches behind."

"There's a bend just after the corridor forks," Liam said. "We can leave them there."

"Okay," Ren said. "Lead the way then."

Liam did as commanded, leading the rest of their squad down the dark tunnel, and just as Liam said there would be, they came to a fork after a couple hundred feet. Liam didn't hesitate, though, taking the left fork that, by Allyn's best guess, would lead them away from the main entrance to the citadel.

"This is as far as we can go with the torches," Liam said, once they were just past the fork.

"Good work, Liam," Ren said. "Myanna, make for the mouth of the cave and scout the area. I want to know what we're stepping into. We'll meet you there in five minutes. If anything is amiss, you need to meet us back here before we move forward and stumble into it."

"Understood," Myanna said, disappearing down the passage.

"I thought we were going to wait until dark before we moved?" Allyn asked.

"We can't afford to wait that long," Ren said.

"What's our plan for getting to the cars unseen then?"

"That'll depend on what Myanna finds."

She expects to fight, Allyn realized. He wasn't surprised, but he had hoped to avoid another battle.

152

Together, they waited. Nobody talked, and in the dark confines of the tunnel, there was nothing to mark the passing of time, so when Myanna returned, it felt both as if she'd been gone for hours *and* had just left.

"Liam was right," she said. "The mouth of the cave is well hidden, and they haven't spotted it. Without knowing how large their force is, I can't tell for sure, but it appears most of them remain at the citadel's entrance."

"They haven't entered yet?" Allyn asked.

"It doesn't look like it," Myanna said. "But like I said, I can't know for sure. The ones I spotted might only be a rear guard."

"What about the cars?" Ren asked. "Anyone guarding those?"

"Yes," Myanna said. "A cursory guard. Four men. And we'll have natural cover most of the way. We can take them."

Ren nodded. "We move forward then. Allyn, up here." She beckoned him forward with a snap of her head.

Allyn complied and pushed past the other magi, falling in beside her and Myanna.

"It's up to us," she said softly. "We'll move forward, neutralize the guards, and clear the way for the others. This has to be done silently—we can't afford to have the entire force come down on us. Understood?"

Allyn nodded, but Myanna wielded. Ice formed in her hands, cylindrical and roughly a foot in length, ending in jagged points.

Daggers, Allyn realized. *Myanna just wielded ice daggers.*

The woman grinned as if she could read his mind, and for once, Allyn was happy the Elemental Guard was on their side.

"Good," Ren continued. "Myanna, you take point. Get us as close as you can. The rest of you follow, but wait for us at the mouth of the tunnel until this is done. Understood?" Then when she didn't get any questions, she added, "Let's go."

Myanna led them away from their previous position, toward a sliver of gray light a couple hundred feet in front of them. When they came upon it, Allyn had to squint. Not that it was bright exactly—the sky had become a dark gray—but compared to the darkness of the tunnel, twilight felt like midday.

The wind howled, bringing with it a blistering-cold chill that seemed to blow *through* him. So sudden and unexpected, it took Allyn's breath away. He struggled to breathe, his lungs squeezed in winter's cold clutches. If he hadn't understood what Ren had meant when she'd said they couldn't remain in the mountains for the night, he did now. They could, quite literally, freeze to death.

Allyn followed Myanna away from the mouth of the tunnel, mimicking her and Ren by keeping his head low, moving on the balls of his feet. They'd come out on the east side of the village, and since it had been built inside a hollow of the mountainous valley, that meant the village was behind them and that they were nearer the cars.

The four guards were plainly visible, forming a loose rectangle around the cars. Assault rifles in hand, fingers near the trigger, they scanned the surroundings, heads on a swivel. These weren't disillusioned magi fighting a half-baked rebellion. They were professionals.

Once they got as close as they were going to get without exposing themselves, Myanna stopped, crouching behind a series of large boulders. With one of her ice daggers, she quickly drew a rough sketch of the guards' formation in a patch of snow.

"We're coming at them from here," Myanna said, drawing

an arrow that represented their angle of approach, "which means their formation is slightly askew, putting this soldier nearest us." She pointed at a circle at the head of the rectangle. "But they have us outnumbered, so we need to move on from him before any of the others can raise the alarm. Ren, can you hit him on your way to neutralize this one?"

"Yes."

"Good. I'll take this one, which means Allyn you have—"

Allyn crossed out one of the circles on Myanna's crude map. "This one."

"Exactly," Myanna said. "Clear?"

"Clear," Allyn and Ren said in unison.

"Good," Myanna said. "Then on my mark." She stood, surveyed the soon-to-be battlefield, and upon another sudden wind gust, she said, "Go!"

Myanna raced forward, Allyn and Ren a step behind and fanning out to give each other space to operate in. They wielded—Ren ice blasts and Allyn static charges—ready for what came next. Halfway across the terrain, the lead guard spotted them. His alarm went up, followed by his assault rifle half a second later, his finger already sliding to the trigger.

I'm running toward *a gun*, Allyn realized, horrified. He'd battled other magi, even killed a few, but something was different about this. Something about the gun. It was perhaps a cultural bias of having seen so many terrible news stories about murder and mass shootings, but the black weapon pointed at him terrified him more than anything he'd ever seen before.

Worse, they weren't going to make it before the guard fired his first shot.

Ren must have done the math too, because she fired an ice blast. The shard of ice buried itself in the guard's chest, but not before he could fire his weapon. The shot *cracked*, echoing through the valley and hollow alike.

Allyn flinched, but the shot went wide. He exhaled, relieved, but it was only a temporary feeling, as the three other guards stepped forward, their own weapons at the ready. By then the magi were passing the fallen guard, and without slowing their advance, Ren drove another ice blast into the fallen guard's chest, ensuring he wouldn't rise again.

Eyes locked on his own target, Allyn wiped his mind clear, focusing on the weapon moving into position instead of the man behind it. He couldn't think about the soldier as a living, breathing human being. Couldn't worry if he had a wife or child at home. He was a murderer hell-bent on killing Allyn's Family and destroying everything he held dear. He was an object, less than human. And he deserved the justice Allyn sought.

Allyn shot three static charges in rapid succession. Two missed, striking the car behind the guard and sending sparks into the air, but the third took him in the shoulder. Another shot *cracked* as the guard stumbled, bouncing off the back of the vehicle before dropping to a knee.

Shaking off the effects of the static charge, he brought the gun up again, but not before Allyn unleashed another barrage. The guard was ready for them and rolled to safety before they could strike.

From the corner of his eye, Allyn saw Ren and Myanna quickly dispatch their targets. His guard was the last.

Before the guard could raise his gun again, Allyn closed the remaining distance and took the man's helmet in his hands. The electric coils leaped from his hands as if alive, wrapping around the guard's head like the tendrils of a great beast, strangling the life from him. The guard fell limp, his supercharged armor glowing red. Allyn wasn't sure if the man was dead or not—he didn't want to think about it, didn't want to know—but it was plain he wouldn't be getting up anytime soon, and that was good enough.

It wasn't until the immediateness of the battle fell behind him that Allyn realized they'd failed. The guards had fired off not one shot, but *two*.

"They're mobilizing," Ren said, looking toward the citadel, where Myanna had said the majority of the enemy force still remained. From their low vantage, they didn't have a great view, but dark figures were moving in their direction. "Allyn, go! Now! Get the others; we'll hold them back."

"But—"

"Move!" Her tone left no room for questions.

He dashed across the battlefield as fast as his legs would take him and entered the mouth of the tunnel where the remaining magi waited.

"What happened?" Nyla asked. "We heard gunshots."

"We took down their guards, but not before they could open fire."

"What does that mean?" Liam asked.

"It means we have to hurry," Allyn said. "They know we're running. Let's go!"

"We can't," Nyla said. "Braeburn is still inside."

"Still in—" Allyn started. "Where?"

"Down the other passage."

Allyn cursed. "Get to the cars, now. I'll find him."

"But—"

"Go!" Allyn shouted.

Without argument, Nyla and the remaining magi moved beyond the mouth of the cave, hurrying to where Ren and Myanna waited.

Allyn rushed into the darkness, keeping a hand on the wall for guidance. Gunfire erupted outside, and Allyn did his best to avoid worrying about his friends. He hadn't taken more than ten or fifteen steps before Braeburn appeared, holding a torch.

"Allyn?" Braeburn said, looking surprised.

"What are you doing?" Allyn asked, his eyes falling onto the object in Braeburn's other hand. Several feet in length, but little more than an inch or two in diameter, it looked like a rod of some kind with an intricate head that Allyn couldn't make out. "What is that?"

"Nothing," Braeburn said. "Where are the rest?"

"Gone," Allyn said. "We need to go."

"Let's go then."

Allyn gritted his teeth then led Braeburn back down the corridor. Stopping at the mouth of the cave, they took a moment to catch their breath and survey the scene.

The enemy poured through the village like an avalanche, the closest soldiers already emerging from the outer layer of huts. Ren and Myanna had fallen in behind the cars, providing return fire and cover while the rest climbed into the cars.

We're not going to make it in time, Allyn realized. *Not with Braeburn's injury.* They would have to fight through the advancing enemy soldiers to make it to the cars.

"Come on!" Braeburn shouted, breaking from the cave as fast as his injured leg would allow.

Allyn followed, quickly catching up, then slowed so they moved at the same pace.

The enemy forces, focused on Ren and Myanna, didn't see Allyn and Braeburn closing in on their flank. Allyn cut down the first line of enemy soldiers with a series of static charges. Braeburn followed with a massive fireball that hit the second line half a beat later, throwing the closest enemy soldiers into the air and creating a break in their line large enough for him and Allyn to advance through.

"Let's go," Ren shouted as they neared. "Let's go, let's go, let's go!"

Ren and Myanna continued their onslaught as Allyn and Braeburn dove into the vehicles—Allyn into the driver's seat. Then, with the final two members of their squad inside, Ren and Myanna jumped in too.

Allyn fired up the engine and punched the gas, speeding off as the entire enemy force opened fire. The magi dropped their heads between their knees and covered themselves with their arms as windows shattered and bullets punched through the thin metal skins of the doors. The magi shouted and cursed in fear, but one voice cut above the rest.

Allyn turned quickly to see Ren grab her side, blood already soaking her black compression armor.

"No!" he yelled. "Nyla, Klausner, do something." But the two clerics were in the other vehicle. "Someone do something!"

"Don't stop," Ren said between clenched teeth. "Keep going."

Cursing, Allyn slammed on the gas, throwing up dust and rock behind them. By now they were out of sight of the village, but there was no way of knowing how quickly they would be pursued.

Up the narrow mountain road, they raced, the two cars screaming perilously around blind corners. The steering wheel was moist under Allyn's sweaty palms, but he didn't slow. He couldn't. Ren was growing paler by the minute. Myanna had ripped off a section of her own compression armor and was using it to apply pressure and slow the bleeding.

Hold on, Ren. Just hold on.

Night had fallen by the time they arrived back at the Klausner Manor. They'd completed the trip in half the time it had taken them on their way out—but Allyn wasn't sure if it would be enough.

His car skidded to a halt, and he was out the door a second later, rushing to check on Ren. Myanna had laid her across the backseat, stroking her face while talking to her in an attempt to keep her conscious. Her face was ghostly white under the light of the winter moon, her breathing soft and shallow.

Nyla was at his side a moment later, her body tense with concern. "What happened?" she asked.

"She was shot," Allyn said. "Leaving the village."

"Leaving the village? Why didn't you stop? We could have helped."

"We couldn't risk it. And I think the bullet is still inside—there's not much you could have done."

"I could have tried." Nyla pushed past him and placed a bare hand on the exposed skin of Ren's stomach. White light blossomed at her touch, sending ripples of light through Ren's body. They extended up Ren's torso and down her legs, all the way to the top of her head and the tips of her toes, before returning back to Nyla's hand, where they'd begun. With each returning ripple, Nyla would understand more of Ren's condition.

"She's hemorrhaging," Nyla said. "This is beyond me—we need to build a *chain*."

"A what?" Allyn asked.

But Nyla didn't answer; she was already moving. "Grand Mage Klausner," she said, rushing toward the grand mage. "I need six of your best clerics. It's her only chance."

The grand mage's eyes slid to Ren's lifeless body, then back to Nyla. "Of course. Follow me."

At his command, Myanna pulled Ren out of the vehicle, holding her as if she were a child being carried to bed. Ren groaned, but didn't open her eyes, as Myanna followed Grand Mage Klausner and Nyla into the manor.

"She's going to be all right," Nolan said, laying a hand on Allyn's shoulder.

"How do you know that?"

"I just do."

"I hope you're right." Allyn exhaled. "Liam, get Jaxon on the phone. It's time we got some fucking answers."

But Liam didn't answer.

Allyn scanned the manor grounds, searching for the young magi. The only other person he saw was Braeburn, who sat in the passenger seat of the second vehicle, adjusting the bandage on his wounded leg.

"Did he go inside?" Nolan asked.

Allyn snapped his head back to the manor, catching a final glimpse of Grand Mage Klausner, Nyla, Myanna, and Ren. But no Liam.

Allyn closed his eyes, replaying their escape in his mind. He'd seen Nyla, Nolan, and Grand Mage Klausner make it to the cars, and had assumed Liam was already inside.

"Allyn?"

"Tell me he was in the vehicle with you."

"No," Nolan said slowly, stretching the word out into three syllables. "I thought he was with you."

It was more than Allyn could handle. He fell to his knees, eyes burning from tears of anger, despair, and failure.

"He's not here," Allyn said. "We left him behind."

CHAPTER 13

JAXON GATHERED IN HIS STUDY with Leira, Arch Mage Westarra, and two members of the Elemental Guard. The thick oak door was closed, as were the windows behind him, limiting the risk that someone might overhear their conversation.

"What do we know?" Arch Mage Westarra asked as Jaxon worked with his laptop to bring up the teleconferencing window. Allyn had called a few minutes before, and Jaxon had asked him to call back once he'd assembled the larger squad.

"Only that they made contact," Jaxon said.

"With those behind the attack?" Westarra asked.

"Yes."

Arch Mage Westarra stirred in his seat as the teleconferencing window opened, showing a grainy image of what Jaxon assumed was the interior of the Klausner Manor. In a sitting room with formal furniture, wainscoted walls, and a fire burning in a brick hearth, Allyn sat with Nolan, Nyla, Kendyl, Myanna, Braeburn, and a man Jaxon had never seen before. Stiff backed and with his shoulders pulled back in perfect posture, the man had to be Grand Mage Klausner.

Jaxon stepped back and took a seat in the open armchair

between Arch Mage Westarra and Leira. "We can see you," he said. "Can you see us?"

"Yes." The grainy picture made it difficult to tell who had answered.

"Good," Jaxon said. "I'll let you get us started then. Tell us what happened. Start from the beginning."

Nolan recounted the early stages of their mission with the efficiency and clarity of someone who had given dozens of such reports. He explained their arrival in Schwyz and of Kendyl's initial interaction with Emelina, but when his report got to the Ferdii Village, his tone took on a different tenor. Instead of the cold, methodical nature he'd used before, his voice had an edge to it.

Jaxon found himself sitting forward in his seat, hands clasped together as he listened to Nolan.

"The Accord has been violated," Nolan recounted.

Jaxon watched Arch Mage Westarra intently, hoping for a reaction, anything that would clue him in to the arch mage's thoughts. But the magi leader remained stoic, giving up nothing.

"You sent us here to determine why this Family was mutilated," Allyn said, standing and stepping forward. Even in the grainy image, Jaxon could see the fury radiating from his body language. "This is why. The Accord. And it's time you told us why magi are dying because of it."

Arch Mage Westarra stared at Allyn's image, refusing to look away, as if the two of them were engaged in a battle of wills. The moment stretched on for several uncomfortable seconds, but Allyn, and those with him, remained firm. Arch Mage Westarra was outnumbered and backed into a corner. As far as Jaxon could see it, there were only two ways out— tell Allyn what he wanted to hear or kill the feed and end the discussion. But he couldn't do the latter without appearing to run away, and doing so would ruin his chances to have Allyn and the rest cooperate any further.

"I'd have Jaxon leave the room," Arch Mage Westarra said, relenting, "if I didn't already know you'd tell him behind my back. As it were, know that what I'm about to tell you is known only to the Forum and myself. And I expect it to stay that way. Can we agree on that?"

"For now," Allyn said.

Arch Mage Westarra set his jaw, and for a moment, Jaxon thought Allyn's outburst might be enough to prevent Westarra from sharing anything more, but the arch mage exhaled softly and continued.

"To understand the Accord, you first have to understand its necessity. You've been told of the events leading up to the Fracture, but you don't understand the true horror our brethren went through or how close we were to being extinguished from this earth. Behind the riots and witch hunts, behind the murders and abductions, were the Knights of Rakkar, a secret group of assassins whose sole purpose was the destruction of the magi race. We were fighting an invisible war against a well-trained, well-armed army who believed to their very soul that their cause was righteous. And we were losing." Westarra paused, his eyes growing distant. This likely wasn't a topic he explained often.

Jaxon watched him intently, studying his face, a torrent of conflicting thoughts and emotions warring inside him. It wasn't that what he'd grown up believing was wrong or a lie—it was just incomplete. And every grand mage, every leader he'd ever known or looked up to, knew what the arch mage was telling them now. More so, the arch mage had conveniently left this information out when he'd asked Jaxon to investigate the attack. The arch mage had done more than violate their trust, he'd taken advantage of them.

"But," Arch Mage Westarra continued, "as I said before, this was an invisible war, and no matter how well-trained or well-armed the Knights of Rakkar were, they were still limited in number. It's important to know the Church, who at this time knew of our existence, went to great lengths to discredit it among the populace. This means they couldn't openly fight our existence, because doing so would admit at the highest level that their God wasn't the only being capable of doing what the Church deemed supernatural. And because the Knights reached into every country under the faith, their number was stretched thin. It's for this reason, and likely this reason alone, that we're still around today. The Knights of Rakkar simply didn't have the numbers to wage the war completely.

"Still, our early brethren were fighting a losing battle. When the Knights uncovered our people, they were incredibly *effective*, rooting out entire magi lines and using kids and loved ones as bait or for more information. I can't tell you how long the war went on, because we honestly don't know when it began. We do know, however, that when word finally spread that magi were being targeted, those in the open quickly went underground, and the Knights' progress slowed. It was then we realized who and what we were up against. The war raged for over a century, and you've no doubt seen it depicted in much of the magi art displayed among the manors and estates of the Order. But it isn't discussed. Because of what's known as 'the Accord,' nobody beyond the Forum knows of the existence of the Knights of Rakkar.

"That's because," Westarra continued, "secrecy is the main pillar of the Accord. Our existence, the existence of the Knights of Rakkar, the war—all of it was to remain secret. To violate that secrecy is to violate the Accord—which is exactly, it seems, what they're saying we have done."

"You're saying," Allyn said, "the men we faced today are some modern-day version of these Knights of Rakkar?"

"It would appear that way," Westarra said. "Other than the Forum, there are only two organizations who know of the Accord: the Knights and their founders. If it wasn't the Knights you faced today, then whom?"

Nobody answered.

"Let me ask you this," Westarra asked. "Did you speak with any of them?"

"Yes," Allyn said. "Their leader. He said his name was Sedric Lang."

"And did this Sedric Lang quote any scripture to you?"

"No," Allyn said, then hesitated. "Though he did say he was the Hammer of God who would wipe us from existence."

Arch Mage Westarra nodded. "The Knights were fond of leaving quotes of scripture behind, often written in the blood of the fallen. 'You shall not permit a sorceress to live,' Exodus 22:18, was the most popular, though there were others. We cannot know for sure if these men are today's version of the Knights of Rakkar, but there are enough parallels that we can't discount it, either."

Those in the Klausner Manor exchanged a series of looks, but nobody spoke up in disagreement.

"You didn't explain what the Accord was," Jaxon said.

The arch mage turned to him. "It was an agreement, a treaty of sorts, between Arch Mage Oran Anderwood and Jakob Connolly, the Knight Commander of the Knights of Rakkar."

"If they were winning," Allyn said, "why would they sign a truce?"

"When the magi went underground and formed the First Families, the war slowed, battles occurring less and less often. And when they did happen, the Knights found a unified force fighting at a time and place of their choosing. They no longer had the same advantages they'd enjoyed before, and the magi Families began turning the tide of the war. Struggling to regain their early momentum, the Knights dug in, no doubt hoping time would finish what they were unable to.

"And it nearly has," Westarra continued. "Our numbers today are a fraction of what they were then. For the First Families, the Accord provided a much-needed respite to regroup, consolidate fortunes and possessions, and begin a new way of life, hidden beyond the watchful eyes of the Knights, the Church, and the common man. We've been living by the agreement ever since."

Answers to many of Jaxon's questions began to take shape. So many times he'd questioned his people's lack of desire to venture out and live among the populace, to take the first step into the larger world. There was so much to learn, so much to see. And living so secluded, so separate from everything had stagnated their growth as a people—not only in numbers, but in innovation, in creative thinking, and other pillars of community and culture. Stagnation equaled death. Sometimes a slow death, but death nonetheless.

But if Westarra's story was true, then their entire way of life was carefully orchestrated. Controlled. And likely wouldn't change anytime soon.

"What about Lukas?" Jaxon asked. "Or Darian Hyland? Their entire movement was predicated on living beyond our walls. If that violated the Accord, then why didn't the Forum intervene?"

"Are you familiar with the steam engine, Jaxon?" Westarra asked.

It was a ridiculous question, and judging by the arch mage's expression, he knew it.

"What you have to understand," Westarra said, "is that the steam engine relies on heat and pressure to operate. Water is heated within a boiler to create steam. That steam is then piped through the boiler into a cylinder, where it pushes a piston up and down and moves the machine. Early steam engines, however, were prone to exploding because the pressure within the boiler grew too strong. So early engineers designed a pressure-release valve that would release excess steam and relieve pressure, preventing the entire mechanism from blowing up.

"For all the illusions of autonomy, Jaxon, we still live in a very rigid existence. If we don't allow young, idealistic magi the room to blow off steam, the entire system would explode."

"Instead, nearly an entire Family was eliminated," Jaxon said, feeling his blood pressure rise. "And one of your most respected grand mages was murdered."

"What happened to Grand Mage McCollum was a tragedy," Arch Mage Westarra said, "but we're still here and able to talk about it."

"Except it didn't work," Jaxon said. "We contained Lukas's threat, but it didn't end there. Even before Darian Hyland picked up Lukas's mantle, Lukas had used our own need for secrecy against us and called the police to investigate the disappearance of the very woman he kidnapped. That led to the dashcam videos that eventually made their way to the Internet and..." The realization suddenly came to him. "That's what this is all about, isn't it? The videos! That's what violated the Accord."

Westarra nodded.

"And you knew!" Jaxon said, his voice booming. "You showed me the video before they left. You knew what they were stepping into."

"I had to know for sure."

"Why didn't you tell us this before?" Jaxon asked. "You could have prepared us."

"I couldn't run that risk," Westarra said. "If it hadn't been the Knights, I would have divulged one of the oldest secrets among the magi leadership, and in doing so, jeopardized the Accord myself. It had to be done this way, Jaxon. I tried to warn you as best I could. Don't forget, an entire Family was massacred. It wasn't as if your team was entirely ignorant of what they were facing."

"This isn't—"

"How many are there?" Allyn asked, interrupting what was quickly becoming a private argument.

Arch Mage Westarra pried his eyes away from Jaxon, looking back at the screen. "How many are in the Knights of Rakkar?" he asked. "I have no way of knowing the answer to that question. Until very recently, we had assumed they'd been disbanded, but at their peak, it was estimated they numbered close to one thousand, and they usually operated in platoons of fifty. If they are indeed still around, or have been re-founded, I imagine their number to be smaller than that, but there's no way to know for sure."

"And do we know where they operated out of?" Allyn asked.

"No."

Allyn cursed and stormed aside, disappearing out of the webcam's view. Kendyl immediately followed.

What in the First Families was that about?

"Something still isn't making sense," Nolan said. "You said part of the reason the Knights signed the Accord was because they struggled to find the remaining magi. If that's the case, then how did they find the Ferdii Family?"

"The Accord was signed within the Ferdii Village," Westarra said. "Inside the very citadel you escaped from."

"What else do we know about them?" Nolan asked.

"Not much," Westarra said. "And much of what we believe we know is rumor or conjecture, and tainted by a thousand years of misinformation."

"Then what happens now?" Nyla asked, entering the conversation for the first time.

"We get you on the next flight home," Westarra said. "So we can begin preparing for what comes next."

"And what's that?"

"War," Westarra said. "They massacred an entire Family. Men. Women. And children. There has to be retribution for what they've done. There must be justice."

Allyn reappeared a moment later. If he'd been angry before, he was absolutely livid now. "No," he growled. "We are *not* returning yet. Leave us. Let us find them."

"I've already said we don't know where they're headquartered."

"Then we'll make them come to us," Allyn said.

"Why the sudden interest in fighting for me, Allyn? Ten minutes ago, you looked ready to reach through that screen and rip out my throat."

"It's not for you, arch mage. It's for..."

Something clicked in the back of Jaxon's mind, and he immediately began taking count of those with Allyn. He felt like he was in free fall, his stomach rising into his throat as he realized they were a couple members short.

"Where's Liam?" Jaxon asked.

Allyn looked away from the screen to the floor. Kendyl laid a hand on his shoulder while the others in the room watched.

"He..." Allyn's voice was thick with emotion. "We... *I* left him behind."

As soon as the words had left Allyn's mouth, Jaxon wished he had never asked the question. He didn't know what to say.

Didn't know what to do. He found himself looking not at the screen but at Leira.

"You left him behind?" she asked. Her tone was soft, and she wore a mask of strength, but Jaxon could feel the torrent of fury and grief boiling inside her—he would have been able to even if they hadn't developed an *echo*. As it were, he felt her emotions as if they were his own, and it cut to the very heart of him. His eyes burned as he struggled to breathe and force the rising lump in his throat down. He had to keep himself together. Not for the Family, or even those two thousand miles away, but for Leira. She didn't need to carry the weight of his emotions along with her own.

Allyn nodded.

"Where?" Leira asked.

"The Village," Allyn said.

"How could you let that happen?" she asked, her voice taking on a sharp edge.

"We thought he was with us," Allyn said. "It was chaos. People were everywhere. We thought he was with us. We thought he was in the other car."

Leira shook her head as if trying to shake away the bad news. Then, suddenly overcome with emotion, she rushed out of the room.

Jaxon stood to follow. Leira would need him as much as he needed her.

"Jaxon," Allyn said, stopping him. "I'll get him back. I promise. I *will* get him back."

CHAPTER 14

ARKNESS BECAME LIAM'S NEW REALITY. First, it had been the dark thoughts and feelings that had consumed him as he'd watched Nyla, Nolan, and the rest of his group leave him behind, oblivious to the fact that he'd fallen. Something, likely a bullet, had grazed his leg and rendered it useless. He'd sought cover after that, hiding in a nearby rock outcropping, and had missed it when Allyn and Braeburn emerged from the tunnel. Once he realized his mistake, he shouted to them and had even attempted to follow, but the barrage of bullets drowned out his shouts and forced him back to the cover.

The darkness of nightfall came next as he desperately attempted to find a more permanent shelter. He'd thought, hoped, and prayed that if he could find somewhere to hide, maybe make it back to the tunnel, that Allyn and Ren would come back for him. But the pain in his leg quickly grew worse, and he hadn't made it far. Making matters worse, his wound left a trail of blood that led his attackers directly to him.

That was when the third stage of darkness overtook him. Fear paralyzed him as the armor-clad men swooped in, guns raised as if they anticipated more resistance. But Liam continued to crawl away, all the while expecting to be riddled with bullets and enter the forever dark. Instead, someone shouted, and several more men quickly arrived. One pulled up Liam's pant leg, inspecting the wound, and then after barking a laugh, the man tore away part of the cloth and tied it around the wound.

Liam gasped in pain, but the cloth slowed the blood loss. He rebuked himself, frustrated that he hadn't done something similar. If he had, the blood trail might not have been as noticeable and the men might never have found him.

"Come on," the man had said in a heavy accent. "On your feet. You can walk."

Without waiting for Liam to comply, the man pulled him to his feet. Liam's leg flared with pain, and the world spun. The burning taste of bile crept up the back of his throat, but he didn't fall.

"Let's go," the man said. "The Knight Commander will want to speak with you."

The man was completely useless as he and Liam scaled the terrain on their way back to the first row of huts, where Sedric awaited. Anytime Liam fell or cried out in pain, the man laughed, chiding him with insults that cut deeper than Liam wanted to admit.

When they found Sedric, the Knight Commander looked to be taking an inventory of his losses, looking over fallen bodies as if he were reviewing shipping reports of coffee or tea imports. There was no humility in his eyes. No remorse. Just the cold demeanor of someone whose plan had gone awry.

"Knight Commander," the man said, saluting. "We found a straggler."

Sedric looked up, and seeing Liam for the first time, he cocked his head to the side, weighing Liam with his eyes.

There was no fear there. No concern or apprehension for magi abilities or Liam's potential to fight back. Sedric was in control, and he knew it.

"Good work," Sedric said, then quickly dismissed the man, ordering him to assist the others who were combing over the Village.

They're searching for something, Liam realized. *They weren't here to murder the Ferdii Family—they were here for something else. But what?*

Sedric's heavy gaze brought Liam from his thoughts, and for the first time since he'd laid eyes on Liam, his expression showed a spark of interest.

"Who are you, little devil?" Sedric asked.

Mustering his courage, Liam clenched his mouth shut, defiantly raising his chin into the air.

"Got a little spirit, do you?" Sedric said, sounding amused. "That's good. You'll need it. Tell me, though. Do you know who I am?"

Liam may have known the man's name, but he didn't know anything beyond that, so he shook his head.

"Good. That's good. We'll have a lot to talk about then." Sedric laid a hand on Liam's shoulder. It wasn't a compassionate gesture meant to make him feel at more ease. No, this was Sedric asserting his dominance, showing Liam that he was firmly under his control. "Come now, let's become more acquainted. I've got a couple questions I think you can help with."

Allyn wandered the halls of the Klausner Manor, his mind distant and preoccupied. If he'd been paying attention, he might have realized its interior greatly resembled the McCollum Manor before it had been lost to the fire. The walls were wainscoted and chair-railed with two-tone paint colors, while the windows and doors were framed with cherry-colored wooden moldings. Many rooms had vaulted ceilings, some with exposed wooden beams that matched the moldings. Large hand-woven rugs of deep maroon and gold, with ivory stitching stretched between traditional furniture and ran the lengths of hallways, while solid wood built-ins proudly displayed books, small sculptures, vases, and other magi art.

But Allyn barely recognized any of it. Had he been thinking about it, he might have noted the strange sense of déjà vu tickling the back of his mind. During a similar night, while Kendyl had still been in Lukas's clutches, Allyn had roamed the halls of McCollum Manor, searching for answers and running from guilt.

That night, he'd come across Nyla, legs draped over the side of an armchair and silver hair pulled over her shoulder, gazing out the floor-to-ceiling windows, lost in thought. He could remember being intimidated by her—Nyla had been mourning the loss of her lover and silently recovering from the effects of the echo she'd shared with him. Allyn and Nyla had become friends that night and discovered why Lukas had been after Allyn and Kendyl in the first place.

He didn't find Nyla tonight. He didn't find anyone. The halls of the Klausner Manor were empty. Cold, despite the burning fires spread throughout the manor. Lonely, despite the dozens of Klausner Family members sleeping just a few rooms away.

Allyn found himself in a grand dining room, sitting alone at a table made for sixteen. Somehow, despite the ornate twelve-foot ceilings and glowing embers in the fireplace, the room felt like a cave.

Allyn was tracing his finger along an embroidered

tablecloth, deep in thought, when a shadow stepped into the room.

"I wondered where I would find you," Nolan said.

Allyn looked up then back at the table. There wasn't anything to say, so he didn't say anything at all.

Nolan circled the room and took a seat across the table from Allyn. "What are you doing in here?"

Allyn shrugged.

"Did you eat?"

Allyn shook his head.

"You should," Nolan said. "I can get you something."

"I'm fine."

"Are you? Because you don't look fine."

"I said I'm fine."

"Okay." Nolan tapped the table with his fingernail. "I spoke with Ren and Nyla. We're in this together. We'll get him back."

Allyn bit his lip in frustration, shaking his head. He had wandered the halls, hidden within this very room so he wouldn't have to have this conversation. So he wouldn't have to face the others. Part of him wondered where the old Allyn had gone. The Allyn Kaplan, first-year associate at a prestigious Portland law firm, who laughed at stress and never gave up. That man had believed he was capable of anything.

That man is dead now, he thought. *I left him behind months ago.*

Instead, he was Allyn McCollum, machinist within the McCollum Family, trusted advisor, and part of Jaxon's inner circle. Achievements he was beginning to question.

"Liam made me part of the McCollum Family," Allyn said softly. "Did I ever tell you that? Made me and Kendyl fake IDs and everything."

"Yeah," Nolan said. "I knew that."

Of course Nolan knew that. He'd been the one to advise against using the new IDs during their travel as to not create any potential new problems.

"He's a good kid," Nolan continued. "And he really looks up to you."

"And look how I repaid him."

"Don't."

"Don't what?"

"Don't do that," Nolan said. "Don't beat yourself up. It won't help."

"What am I supposed to do, Nolan? He's just a kid, and he was put under my protection. You said it yourself, he looks up to me, and I embraced that. I want to help him, you know? Teach him things. Guide him. All the stuff he needs since his dad..."

Allyn couldn't bring himself to finish the sentence. In his sour state, the last thing he wanted to do was unearth old demons. He would be crushed under the weight of old guilt. He had never been able to shake the feeling that he'd been responsible for what happened to Graeme and the rest of the McCollum Family. It was part of the reason he'd stayed and taken on additional responsibilities. He owed it to them.

"He's not looking for a father figure, Allyn. He's looking for a friend. And you've been a good one. I didn't know Liam before all of this, but everything I've heard says he's grown a lot over the last year. And if it hadn't been for you two, none of this would have happened."

Allyn looked up sharply.

"That came out wrong." Nolan held his hands in front of him in a placating gesture. "I mean, you two discovered the machinists. You two found me. And you've given hope to all those who have flocked to our Family. For all the bad you want to lay at your own feet, there's also been a lot of good. I can tell you that."

The tension inside Allyn lessened a bit. "You're a good man, Nolan."

Nolan gave him a halfhearted smile. "It's about time you realized that."

Allyn didn't want to, but he smiled back.

Nolan's expression faltered a bit, and he looked away. "Allyn, there's something I've been meaning to tell you. And I know this isn't the right time, but, well, there's no such thing as the right time, and I can't hold it in any longer."

"If it's about my sister, you should probably wait."

"It's not about Kendyl."

Allyn stirred in his seat, unsure if he wanted to hear what would come next.

"When I was working with Special Agent Maddox we... well, you'd disappeared. Gone off the grid. And normal investigative procedure is to build a network of known friends, family, and associates—anyone who might help aid and abet. It also helps us build a profile, begin to understand the fugitive and their thought process as a way to predict their next moves. This meant we spoke with everyone who was even tangentially associated with you—friends, coworkers, bartenders, and... family."

Allyn's spine stiffened, and he instantly knew where Nolan was going and why he hadn't wanted to say anything. A voice inside him screamed, pleading with him to stop Nolan before he could continue.

"We spoke with your father, Allyn."

The words hung over Allyn like a dreaded diagnosis, his entire body tingling with contempt, and he would have done anything to go back thirty seconds and stop Nolan from continuing.

"I don't have a father," he heard himself say. "He died when I was young."

Nolan nodded, seemingly understanding that Allyn wanted the conversation to end there.

"Okay," Nolan said. "Can I just say one thing, though? He has a lot of regret in his life, Allyn. A lot of things he wishes he had done differently. I saw what it's done to him—what it can do to you. And I don't want that to happen. But what I really wanted to say, and the reason I brought it up in the first place, is even now, he understands you, Allyn."

Allyn started to speak, but Nolan held up a hand, stopping him. His father had long been an open wound, but Nolan was taking things to an entirely new level. Allyn could never let those feelings surface inside him, let alone discuss them with another person.

"I know what you're going to say, Allyn," Nolan continued. "He might not know who you are, but he *understands* you. You're more alike than I think you realize, and I don't mean that as a bad thing. But listening to him talk about you, the way he saw you, how he said you and your sister got along, the way you were inseparable, and the way you could be an insufferable little shit helped me realize that you could never be the monster Maddox thought you were. My point is, Allyn, those qualities are still in you. You're still the man who would do anything for his family, blood or otherwise. He saw it. I saw it. We all have. And we're still with you."

Allyn continued to trace the embroidered tablecloth, refusing to look up. He didn't want to meet Nolan's eye. He didn't know why exactly, but the confusing torrent of emotions inside made it hard to breathe. Hard to think. How could one person feel sad, embarrassed, angry, and disappointed at the same time? Shouldn't some of those contradict each other? But they were all there, powerful and suffocating.

Fearing they'd get the better of him, Allyn went through his old calming exercise, placing the palms of his hands on the cold tabletop, retreating into the sensation.

Nolan must have thought it was an angry pose, because he quickly apologized.

"It's fine," Allyn said between measured breaths. It wasn't fine, but Allyn knew Nolan's intentions were pure and that had to count for something. He did have one unanswered question, though. "Why now? We've lived together for several months, seen each other nearly every day. Why didn't you say anything before?"

"I don't know. At first, I wanted to wait for the right time. Then the longer I waited, the harder it was to bring up, and then I *really* didn't know what to do. I'm sorry, Allyn. I want you to know that. I should have said something a long time ago."

"It's okay," Allyn said, once again for Nolan's sake.

They sat in awkward silence for a time, avoiding eye contact. As the minutes ticked by, it became clear Nolan had more than Allyn's father on his mind. Nolan was similar to Kendyl in that way. Where Allyn needed time away, time to reflect, Nolan needed to talk. He needed to bounce thoughts and ideas off someone other than himself. "Do you think I should tell them?" Nolan finally asked.

"Tell who what?"

"The arch mage," Nolan said. "That I was the one who uploaded the videos."

"No."

"You heard him, Allyn. Those videos are the reason the Knights have returned. The reason there's been so much bloodshed."

"That's one man's opinion," Allyn said. "And I don't know

about you, but I'm beginning to appreciate that opinion less and less."

"Do you disagree?"

Allyn didn't respond.

"I didn't think so," Nolan said.

"Say that were true, Nolan. Say that the Knights saw those videos and used it as a catalyst for what's happened. What good would come from you telling the arch mage?"

"For all the time we've lived with each other, you still don't understand me, do you, Allyn? It's not about something good coming from it. It's about being a man and owning up to my mistakes. Taking responsibility."

"You want someone to punish you," Allyn said.

"No, I don't want to be punished. But there should be consequences."

It's my turn to talk him *off the ledge.* "You're a man of contradictions," Allyn said. "Didn't you just tell me leaving Liam behind wasn't my fault?"

"This is different."

"How?"

"We were all there, Allyn. I bear as much responsibility as you do. So does Nyla, Ren, and the rest. But this was *me*. All me. I found the videos, and I uploaded them for my own selfish reasons."

"To find me."

"To find out who I was," Nolan said. "To understand that I wasn't a freak. That I belonged somewhere."

"And you had no idea that any of this would happen as a result."

"Come on, Allyn," Nolan said. "You were a lawyer. When has ignorance ever been a legitimate defense?"

"'When the defining law isn't known, hasn't been published or made reasonably known to the defendant,'" Allyn quoted.

"I should have known better than to ask a lawyer," Nolan said sarcastically.

"No," Allyn said. "This is good; this is important. By withholding the knowledge of the Accord and its guidelines, the arch mage didn't allow for it to be published or reasonably known. You couldn't have known any better."

"Every magi knows to keep the secret, Allyn."

"Every magi, yes. But you said it yourself, you didn't know where you belonged. You weren't one of us, didn't even know we existed. More importantly, you weren't a part of this governing body, and are thereby exempt from its laws."

Nolan started to laugh.

"What?" Allyn asked.

"I've never heard you talk like a lawyer before."

"Ha!" Allyn said. "That wasn't talking like a lawyer."

"Sure sounded like it to me."

"That's because anytime anyone uses words instead of guns, cops scream, 'Lawyer!'"

"Or 'Liberal,'" Nolan said with a crooked smile. "And I wasn't a cop, dick."

"Fed, cop. Same difference."

"I should kick your ass for that."

"This coming from the man who's trying to date my sister."

"I guess we're even then."

"Like hell."

Nolan laughed, and Allyn found himself doing the same.

"I'll make you a deal," Nolan said. "I'll buy your lawyer bullshit, and I won't blame myself, but only if you do the same. I don't want to find you in here sulking again. We're in this shit together, Allyn, and that's the only way we're going to get out of it."

"All right," Allyn said. "I think that's a deal I can make."

"Good," Nolan said. "Me too. Now let's get some rest. The search begins tomorrow."

CHAPTER 15

THE PIECE OF CLOTH WAS a blight against the light gray of the rocky landscape. Torn, black, and stained with dried blood, it had called to Allyn like a beacon, and seeing the blemish, Allyn rushed for it. Kneeling above it, he took it in his hand. The fabric remained flexible even in the early morning frost, and it felt spongy as Allyn crumpled it in his fist.

"Compression armor," he said. "It's Liam's."

"Can you be sure?" Kendyl asked.

"I'm sure." Allyn stood, surveying the landscape again. There had to be more—another clue, anything that might indicate where the Knights had taken him.

Following his conversation with Nolan the night before, Allyn had felt a growing sense of resolve, which had firmed into a plan in the early hours of morning. The odds that the Knights of Rakkar had somehow missed Liam were impossibly low, but not so low that they couldn't afford to not explore the possibility. With Ren still recovering under the aid of a cleric chain, Allyn had assumed command and organized the expedition back to the Ferdii Village. He'd come prepared with two full squads of magi at his disposal, refusing to be taken unawares again.

In organized groups of four, magi searched the village proper, the citadel, and the hidden passage that led to the rocky outcropping a couple hundred yards away. With each passing minute and each incoming report, the small flicker of hope that kept Allyn going slowly diminished. When Nolan and his squad finally reappeared, missing a fifth member, the last flicker of hope solidified into a knot of disappointment that twisted in Allyn's gut.

"Anything?" Allyn asked as Nolan approached.

"There's blood and boot prints near the entrance to the tunnel. It looks like he was injured, and that's where they found him."

Allyn showed him the piece of compression armor he'd found, confirming Nolan's suspicions.

"There's not too much blood on here," Nolan said, looking at the cloth. "He couldn't have been too injured."

"Just enough to fall behind," Allyn agreed. "He's alive, though."

"He was, at least."

"He *is*," Allyn said, removing all doubt, both for himself and for those within earshot. "If they wanted him dead, they would have killed him and left him here for us to find like they did the others. We still have time."

"And a host of new problems," Nolan said. "Westarra said this was the only magi Family the Knights knew how to find. But with Liam being captured..."

The implication hung in the air, but it was worse than Nolan knew. Liam was the son of a grand mage, and he was well-versed in magi history. More importantly, he'd been in charge of the Family's library and the work to preserve their fragile history. In many ways, Liam was one of the most knowledgeable magi in the Order. Sedric, the Knight Commander of the Knights of Rakkar, wouldn't immediately know that, but once he got Liam talking...

"They could attack anywhere," Nolan said.

"It'll take time to organize," Allyn said, "but you're right. We need to tell Jaxon and the arch mage. We can't afford for another Family to be taken by surprise."

"He's alive," Allyn said, looking at the watchful magi on the computer monitor. Jaxon, Arch Mage Westarra, and Leira sat in Jaxon's study, framed by a pair of Elemental Guards in the background. "We found a piece of torn compression armor. It looks like he was wounded during our flight and fell behind, taking cover in a rocky outcropping out of view. The Knights must have found him following our retreat."

"Can you be sure it's his?" Jaxon asked. His voice had a metallic quality, a byproduct of the digital transmission.

"Yes," Allyn said. "We took inventory of the compression armor of every magi who joined us on the mission, and the torn fabric didn't match any tears of those who returned. It's Liam's."

"Good work," Jaxon said. "Anything else?"

"No," Allyn said with a sigh. "Like before, the Knights took their dead and injured with them. The only thing that shows they were ever there are their boot prints and spent bullet casings."

Jaxon cursed, and on the grainy image, Allyn could make out his hand rubbing Leira's back in a consoling manner.

"You said we know very little about the Knights, Arch Mage," Allyn continued. "But anything else you know might prove helpful. When they were founded, who they were founded by. That might help us narrow their location down."

"I had a chance to speak with the curator of my private library," Arch Mage Westarra said, "and I believe I can shed a little more light on this. As I said before though, much of this is speculation, so take it as such."

"Of course." Allyn leaned forward in his seat and felt Nolan, who was in the Klausner sitting room with him, Nyla, and Grand Mage Klausner, do the same beside him.

"By our best estimates," Westarra began, "we believe the Knights of Rakkar were founded in the late Middle Ages, around the fourteenth century. Tension between the Church and the magi order had been building for over a century. Prior to this time, the Church's official stance was that magi didn't exist, and that belief has been promoted since the fifth century, when Saint Augustine argued that God alone could suspend the laws of nature.

"But things began to change in the thirteenth century, with the formation of the Inquisition. Under the guise of trying heretics, the Church's Inquisitors rounded up thousands of those suspected of being witches and wizards and put them to trial, with those being found guilty put to the flame. The Protestant Church in Germany was the largest perpetrator of this, and toward the end of the fifteenth century, two Dominican inquisitors published what's known as the *Malleus Maleficarum,* or *The Hammer of Witches,* a handbook on how to detect and eliminate magi.

Following its publication, *The Hammer of Witches* spread throughout Europe, and the Inquisition's main purpose became the eradication of our people. Over the next two hundred years, anywhere from eighty to two hundred thousand suspected witches and wizards were burned at the stake. It's sometime during this time—likely around the fifteenth century, when the Inquisition was heating up—that the Knights of Rakkar were formed."

"And we don't know where?"

"Not exactly," Westarra said. "But there are clues. I mentioned before that the Knights of Rakkar let their presence be felt. They were thorough, methodical, and ruthless. It's well documented that near the end of the sixteenth century, near the city of Trier, Germany, the Inquisition murdered every woman in two separate villages, leaving a single survivor in each. And over the next few years, another twenty-two villages saw similar fates. In Germany alone, it's estimated twenty-six thousand suspected magi were executed, more than twice the next closest country."

"So you think the Knights were founded and operated out of Germany," Allyn said.

"I think it's a good place to begin our search," Westarra said.

Allyn chewed on his bottom lip, attempting to take it all in. The Accord. The Knights of Rakkar. The Inquisition. As impossible as it all sounded, it rang true. But even as *right* as it felt, he couldn't help thinking he was missing something. The motive felt off. Weak. There were a couple videos that looked like true magi, so the Knights murdered an entire village and renewed an ancient war? The videos couldn't have been the first of their kind. They couldn't even have been the first clue to the magi's existence. Either Allyn was missing something, or Sedric was an overzealous martyr primed for bloodshed.

Or both.

"Is there anything you can send us that might shed a little more light on this?" Nolan asked. "Something specific to Germany, maybe?"

"I'll have my curator send over the scans," Westarra said.

"Thank you."

"There's another piece of this that we haven't discussed,"

Allyn said. "You mentioned that the Knights knew of only one magi location—the Ferdii Village. But with Liam's capture, that's no longer true."

"Liam wouldn't do that," Leira said, cutting in.

"I'm sorry, Leira," Allyn said. "I really, truly am. I love Liam and will do everything in my power to get him back, but he doesn't have the capacity to hold up under... questioning. Not unless we get to him first."

Leira looked away, and for once, Allyn was thankful to be half a world away from the woman. He didn't know if he could have handled being in the same room with her. Didn't know if *she* would have been able to be in the same room without killing him.

"I've already spoken with the Forum," Westarra said. "The Families have been put on defensive alert."

"What did you tell them?" Allyn asked.

"Only what they needed to know."

Then you told them nothing, Allyn wanted to say, but kept the thought to himself.

"All right," Westarra said. "I'll send over the scans and have my team assist. We'll focus on known whereabouts and previous attacks to see if a pattern emerges."

"Thank you, Your Grace," Allyn said.

And with that, the transmission ended.

"You should get some sleep," Kendyl said.

Allyn tore his eyes away from the scans Arch Mage Westarra had sent over, to find Kendyl looking at him. They were alone in the kitchen, having migrated from the Klausner sitting room hours before. The room—all-white cabinets, marbled floors, and speckled ivory countertops—smelled of frustration and stale coffee, though he'd done his best to ignore the latter.

Working as a shop boy late in childhood, he'd often hitched rides from coworkers, and every morning, they'd smoke and drink cheap coffee on the way to work. The two unpleasant smells had become one terrible aroma, and years later, Allyn couldn't distinguish between the two or remember one without the other. Like the blue cloth interior of that late-eighties Buick Century, he'd soaked up the odor, and he knew he would never be free of it. So it said something about how exhausted he truly was when he had pulled a mug from one of the cabinets and poured himself a cup.

His eyes burned from the hours he'd spent poring over the digitized documents, and his back felt as though someone had driven a knife into it. Kendyl didn't look much better, with her bloodshot eyes and wild hair. Night had fallen outside, though to be honest, Allyn couldn't remember when exactly that had happened.

"Hey!" Kendyl snapped her fingers in front of Allyn's face. "Earth to Allyn. Did you hear me? I said you should get some sleep."

"No," Allyn said, blinking and sitting back to rub his eyes. "What I need is more caffeine." He took a sip of his coffee, grimacing. "How do people drink this crap? At least bad beer is served cold, which dilutes its flavor. This tastes like shit and is served hot enough to burn your tongue. It's not a winning combination."

Kendyl laughed. "Why are you drinking it then?"

"I didn't think they'd have a Coke."

"Probably not," Kendyl said. "But they probably have tea or something."

"I'll manage."

Kendyl took a sip from her own mug. "It's actually not that bad."

"If you say so."

Kendyl *would* know, he realized. One of the many short-term jobs she'd worked to support her art was as a barista at a small gourmet coffee shop, where even a small coffee, which they called a *short*, was nearly ten dollars.

"I bet Nolan likes coffee, doesn't he?" Allyn said with a mischievous grin.

In the dark room, it was difficult to tell for sure, but Allyn thought he saw Kendyl blush.

"We're not going to do this, are we?" Kendyl asked. "Am I going to have *the talk* with my brother?"

"Hey, I didn't want to talk about it, either," Allyn said. "But he keeps bringing it up. And it really says something about my current mental state that I'd rather talk about that than other things." He smiled, trying to show that he'd meant it as a joke, but there was so much truth behind the statement that it fell flat.

"What do you want to know?" Kendyl said. "He's a nice guy."

"I don't disagree. He's just not the normal tattoo-covered, bearded hipster type you usually date."

"Not everyone I date is like that," Kendyl said defensively.

Allyn gave her a skeptical look.

"What?"

"Name one man you've dated in the last two years who hasn't fit into the hipster stereotype."

"Compared to you, Allyn, everyone is a hipster. Just because they don't go to work in a suit doesn't make them a hipster."

"Nolan wore a suit to work too," Allyn teased. Then when

Kendyl just glared at him, he added, "You still haven't named one."

"I don't have to," she said. "You don't know the first thing about my love life."

"What's that supposed to mean?" Allyn asked, terrified of the answer.

"Nothing. I'm not going to get into this with you. You want to know why I'm attracted to Nolan? I'll tell you. He's kind, intelligent, passionate, can carry a conversation, and—to your point—different from other men I've dated. He might not have tattoos and a beard, but those things aren't important to me, and never have been. But he does have something else."

"And what's that?"

"Courage," Kendyl said. "He left everything he's ever known to be with us, Allyn, and I find that incredible. He gave up everything to fight for a cause that's important to him. That kind of quality is hard to find in *anyone*."

Allyn studied Kendyl for a moment. Her eyes had grown distant, and seemed to sparkle as she talked about Nolan. He wasn't just a possibility in a pool of limited options; she was truly interested in the guy.

"Okay," he said.

"Okay, what?"

"You have my consent."

"Your consent?" Kendyl asked. "What is this, eighteen-fifty? I'm a grown woman. I didn't ask for your consent."

"Either way, you have it."

Kendyl glared at him, and for a moment, Allyn thought she might hit him. Allyn's façade finally broke, and he began to laugh. Soft at first, it quickly gave way to true, infectious laughter, the kind that comes from deep inside one's chest. Before he knew it, Kendyl had joined in too.

"I thought you were going to slap me," Allyn said, wiping away tears.

"I wanted to," Kendyl said. "You really know how to get under my skin, don't you?"

"Please. You do it to me too."

"Well, you deserve it. I don't."

"I might flick you a little shit, Kendyl, but I really am happy for you. Nolan's a good guy."

She smiled at him, the sparkle in her eyes returning. "Thank you."

Their conversation devolved into a series of small discussions about nothing of consequence. In the end, each simply enjoyed the company of the other.

Happy not to be alone, Allyn watched as the stars faded and the sky turned from black to purple. The new day approaching, Allyn's mind slowly shifted to what came next. He began organizing squads, outlining tactics, and coming up with a list of questions to ask Nolan so they could maximize their efforts. The dark thoughts returned, bringing with them something else that Allyn hadn't wanted to confront.

"Nolan told me something interesting last night," he said. "Something I think you should know. When he was working our case with Agent Maddox—"

"Shhh!" Kendyl held up a hand, cutting him off.

He had been too preoccupied to notice it before, but Kendyl's attention was elsewhere. She was halfway off the chair, one foot on the floor, her body coiled as if ready to spring. Her attention was fixed firmly on the darkness beyond the window. Allyn followed her gaze, his own body tightening with worry. The wind blew outside, stirring thick branches of pine and strands of grass. The movement played with his eyes the same way shadows do in a dark room.

"It's just the wind," he said.

But Kendyl shushed him again, slowly rising completely out of the chair. She held her hand in front of her and closed her eyes, in what was a similar gesture to what Allyn had seen Nyla or Leira do when they used their abilities to feel for other life.

Kendyl was beginning to worry him, and he watched her intently.

"I feel something..."

"What?" Allyn whispered.

"Hatred." Kendyl opened her eyes and turned to him. "They're here."

Allyn stood sharply, grabbing Kendyl's arm and pulling her with him. "Away from the windows! Now!"

Keeping low, he dragged her from the eat-in dining room into the kitchen, ducking behind the large island in the center of the room.

"What are they doing here?" Kendyl asked.

"Finishing the job."

"I thought we had people on watch."

"So did I." Allyn risked a glance around the edge of the island, trying to see beyond the windows, but from the distance, the glass was reflective, and all he saw was a reflection of the kitchen.

"What do we do?" Kendyl asked.

"We have to warn everyone," Allyn said. "But we have to do it quietly so we don't let them know we know they're here."

"What good will that do?"

"It'll give us an advantage," Allyn said. "Come on."

"No." Kendyl grabbed Allyn's arm, stopping him before he could stand. "We should split up. You get Nolan. I'll get Klausner."

"I don't think—"

"We don't have time to argue." Kendyl squeezed his arm, easing his concern. "And we need everyone."

"Fine," Allyn said. "But be careful. And stay with the Grand Mage."

"Okay."

Allyn snuck another look around the edge of the island. Seeing nothing that would cause him to delay, he said, "Come on. Let's go."

Kendyl followed him into the hall, then the two of them quickly made for the nearest staircase. The bedrooms were located on the upper floors of the manor, with Klausner's taking up much of the northern wing of the third floor.

Allyn stopped on the landing of the second floor, where the McCollum magi were bunked. "Remember, no matter what happens, stay with the Grand Mage."

"I will." Kendyl offered him a small smile and disappeared up the stairwell.

Once she was gone, Allyn made his way down the hall. The bedroom doors to either side of him were closed, their rooms quiet, the magi inside having long since turned in for the night.

Allyn opened Nolan's door, entering his room.

"Nolan," Allyn said in a loud whisper. "Nolan, wake up." When his friend didn't move, Allyn stepped up beside his bed, grabbing Nolan by the shoulder and shaking him. "Nolan!"

The other man woke with a start, seizing Allyn's wrist with a firm hand and wielding with the other. A sharp white light filled the room, blinding Allyn.

"Put that out!" Allyn snapped.

"Allyn?" Nolan said groggily.

"I said put it out!"

The light dissipated, casting the room back into darkness,

though the afterimage of the light played games with Allyn's vision.

"What's going on?" Nolan asked, his tone more alert. "What's wrong?"

"The Knights are here. Rouse everyone."

"What? How do you know?"

"I don't have time to explain. Just wake up everyone on this side of the hall and meet us in the hall."

Without waiting for a response, Allyn rushed out of the room, trusting Nolan to do as ordered. He quickly roused Myanna and Braeburn, the latter now largely recovered from his wounds suffered the day before, and the three of them assembled with the growing mass of magi in the middle of the hall. As expected, Nolan had followed orders.

"The manor is under attack," Allyn said, loud enough for all to hear. "I don't have time to—"

"By who?" someone interrupted.

"The same people who attacked the Ferdii Family."

Murmurs and side conversations spread through the crowd.

"Right now," Allyn said over the din, "my sister is alerting Grand Mage Klausner, but I don't know how much time we have. The grand mage already put you on alert, correct?"

"Yes." A broad-shouldered, stringy-haired man separated himself from the rest of the group. "We have our orders."

"Good," Allyn said. "What's your name?"

"Bastien."

"Are you in charge here, Bastien?"

The older magi nodded.

"Assemble your magi and take this one with you." Allyn gestured to Myanna. "She's second in command in the Arch Mage's Elemental Guard."

"Okay."

Allyn turned to Nolan. "I think they're here for the grand mage. Find him and protect him." When it looked as though Nolan was set to argue, he added, "My sister will be with him too."

Nolan's expression resolved, and he nodded. "What about you?"

"Braeburn and I are going for Ren," Allyn said. "I won't risk leaving another person behind."

Bastien began shouting orders, organizing his magi into various squads, and almost immediately, the mass of people quickly became an organized force.

"Remember, they don't know we know they're coming. Use that to your advantage." Then, grabbing Bastien's attention, he added, "Our Family member, Ren, she was injured and is under the care of a cleric chain. Where can I find her?"

"The medical wing," Bastien said.

"Where is that?"

"Third floor, eastern wing opposite the grand mage's quarters."

"Thank you," Allyn said. "And good luck."

"You too."

CHAPTER 16

B Y THE TIME ALLYN AND Braeburn made it to the eastern
wing of the third floor, where Bastien had said Ren
would be, the manor was bursting with activity. The
mobilizing magi took defensive positions, massing near
windows and entrances, preparing for the assault. They did
so under great care, under the cover of night, and without
sound. So far, the Knights hadn't shown any indication that
they'd seen or heard the Klausner forces mobilizing.

They have no idea what they're about to walk into. Allyn
hoped it would be enough. The magi would be outgunned,
and likely outnumbered. Surprise and familiarity with the
grounds were the magi's greatest advantages.

The eastern wing was nearly an apartment in and of
itself, complete with sitting and dining rooms, kitchen, and
bedrooms. In the great room, Allyn found Ren. A single
cleric—a boy who couldn't have been any older than Liam—
with a narrow face made worse by a patchy beard, sat with
her. He looked up sharply as Allyn and Braeburn entered.

"Who are you?" the boy asked. "What are you doing in
here?"

"I'm with her," Allyn said, pointing at Ren's resting body.

They had her dressed in a thin gown and lying in a simple bed. Her eyes were closed, chest rising and falling slowly, wounds visibly healed. If Allyn hadn't known any better, he would have thought she was sleeping.

"You're not supposed to be here." The boy's eyes darted to the door, almost as if he expected someone to barge into the room after them.

The other clerics, Allyn realized. *He's expecting the other clerics to come and force us from the room. He doesn't know what's happening.*

"The manor is under attack," Allyn said. "We need to move her to a safer position."

"Attack? No it's—"

Gunfire interrupted the boy. Allyn raced to the hall, trying to pinpoint its source. It was distant and on one of the lower levels, but more specific than that, he couldn't be sure.

"Can she walk?" Allyn asked, re-entering the room.

The boy shook his head. "She hasn't woken yet."

"Then wake her."

"I can't."

"What do you mean you can't?"

"I mean I can't. She won't. Her body... you're not a magi, are you?"

Allyn wielded, and the boy's eyes went wide at the sight of the red coils. He looked from them to Allyn, then back to them in disbelief.

"Who are you?"

Allyn ignored the question, turning to Braeburn. "Can you carry her?"

"Yes." Braeburn stepped forward, took Ren in his arms, and gently rested her limp body over his shoulder.

Elsewhere in the manor, a new battle erupted, gunfire and explosions shaking the foundation.

"I think you should come with us," Allyn said to the boy.

For all his fear, the boy nodded then trailed them as they exited the clerics' wing. Allyn continued to wield, his coils lighting their way through the dark confines of the manor with a pulsating crimson light. It wasn't until he neared the stairwell that he realized he didn't know where to go.

"Where will the grand mage be?" Allyn asked.

The boy stammered, flinching at every burst of gunfire and explosion. A small part of Allyn empathized with the boy. He'd never been exposed to fighting like this, had never experienced battle, and at his age, he never should have. But he was now, and Allyn needed him to keep it together.

"Hey!" Allyn snapped his fingers in front of the boy's face. "Focus. Eyes on me, okay? Now tell me where to find the grand mage."

"He'll be in the main hall," the boy said.

"Good. Now listen to me. What's your name?"

"Petter."

"Okay, Petter. My name is Allyn, and this is Braeburn— he's a part of the arch mage's Elemental Guard. You'll be safe with us, okay? Just stay close and do exactly what we say. Can you do that?"

Petter nodded.

"Good," Allyn said. "Let's go then."

They stuck close to the wall as they descended the stairs, eyes locked on the landing below. The landing itself was dark, and Allyn let the coils dissipate—their light would have made him an easy target in the darkness.

Drawing close to Petter, Allyn whispered, "Where to now?"

"That way." Petter pointed down a wide hall. It shouldn't have come as a surprise—that direction was where the battle raged the loudest.

Allyn started down the hall, Braeburn and Petter in

tow. Once he was halfway down the hall, a group of dark silhouettes suddenly emerged in front of them, entering from the hall perpendicular to the one they were in. Their booted footsteps were heavy, and they moved together in a tight formation only months of training could perfect. They carried large assault rifles with mounted flashlights that lit the hallway.

Allyn ducked to the side of the hall, taking cover behind a long table that displayed decorative vases filled with yellow wildflowers. Braeburn and Petter quickly did the same, darting into a small alcove on the other side of the hall, but not before one of the flashlights illuminated their fleeing bodies. Gunfire followed immediately, peppering the wall inches from Braeburn's head.

Braeburn didn't so much as flinch, keeping himself as deep in the alcove as possible, readjusting Ren on his shoulder while attempting to shield Petter from the hail of bullets. Petter looked ready to bolt. The older magi must have sensed it too—he placed a hand on the boy's shoulder, both calming him and keeping him from fleeing.

Allyn risked a look around the table. The squad, five members in all, was already advancing. He cursed silently, wielded, and emerged from his hiding place, unleashing a wild volley of static charges. Without waiting to see if they landed, Allyn rushed backward, launching a second volley of attacks.

Light from one of the flashlights illuminated him and was instantly followed by gunfire. Allyn's ears rang as the bullets whistled past his head.

The Knights' attention diverted, Braeburn entered the fray. He had placed Ren on the floor and was wielding with both hands. He dropped the first Knight with a lance of ice to the throat and hit the second in the chest. Protected by Kevlar body armor, the second Knight only stumbled, recovered quickly, then swiveled back toward Braeburn. But the Elemental Guard was already wielding again. A second later, a massive fireball was covering the distance between him and the Knights. Those at the rear of the formation dove for cover, but the ones nearest Braeburn didn't have time.

The fireball exploded against the new lead Knight, throwing him and the next behind him off their feet, sending them sailing backward into the hall. Landing on their backs, they crashed into the wall, steam rising from their melted body armor and scorched clothing. They didn't rise again.

Before Allyn knew it, the two remaining Knights were on their knees, returning fire, and nearly cut Braeburn down before he could get back to the cover of the alcove. Allyn hit the first with a static charge and missed the second, but the last remaining Knight, seeing he was outnumbered and outflanked, retreated through the hall, firing bullets in a wide arc to keep Allyn and Braeburn at bay.

Once the last Knight had disappeared, Allyn rushed to Braeburn, standing guard as he repositioned Ren on his shoulder.

"They're inside the manor," Braeburn said.

"We have to get to the grand mage," Allyn said.

"Why him?" Braeburn asked. "Why not elsewhere? Get these two to safety?"

Allyn wanted to tell Braeburn the truth. That Kendyl and Nolan would be with Grand Mage Klausner. That he wouldn't leave without knowing they were safe. But he couldn't tell Braeburn that. It would mean admitting he was risking all of their lives for his own selfish desires and feelings. So instead, he lied.

"Because that's where we'll be needed," Allyn said.

He didn't wait to see Braeburn's reaction—it wouldn't

matter. Allyn wouldn't have listened to him anyway. He started back in the direction they'd been headed before running into the Knights, and coming to the intersection where the Knights had first appeared, Allyn stopped to consult Petter.

"That way," the boy said, pointing.

Allyn doubled their speed, pushing forward at nearly a run, using the rising sounds of battle as his guide. When they finally made it to the grand entrance, Allyn was immediately hit with an overwhelming sense of déjà vu.

The magi were losing the battle. The Knights, whom they had hoped to keep from entering the twelve-foot double doors, had pushed their way into the grand entrance, and despite being outnumbered, they were driving the magi back with their advanced firepower.

Entering an adjoining hallway, Allyn passed a number of retreating magi. Many were wounded, staunching blood from bullet wounds with their bare hands, their eyes wild with fear and pleading for help. The smell of smoke and blood was nearly overwhelming, burning the back of Allyn's throat.

Allyn saw Nolan before Kendyl. The balls of light he wielded easily separated him from the rest of the magi. Among the resistance force, he was easily the most effective, his attacks the most powerful. And unlike the other magi, Nolan's power was seemingly limitless—he didn't have to worry about burning himself out.

But greater power also meant he was a greater threat, and the Knights focused on him. Nolan took cover just as a barrage of gunfire laid waste to the wall he had ducked behind, and he was forced back even farther. The Klausner magi hadn't had time to construct barricades or choke points, or prepare other defensive measures. Being on alert had meant posting sentries and having a previously formed battle plan, but when it came to the battlefield, they were at the mercy of what the manor's architecture provided.

The rest of the Klausner forces were evenly spread among the grand entrance, forming a loose crescent around the doors. The room was in chaos. Fireballs and ice blasts streaked across the room with such intensity, the battle was hard to keep straight. Muzzle flashes answered, burning through the darkness with angry intention. Screams, shouts, and commands sounded overtop the din of battle.

Grand Mage Klausner was at the center of the mêlée, his fair skin and gray hair streaked red. He wore white, much like Graeme had the night he'd fallen, and in addition to being torn, tattered, and scorched, his clothes were painted with the blood of the dead and injured. Kendyl was with him, tending to those in the grand mage's squad. She tied tourniquets, applied pressure to wounds, drug the fallen out of harm's way, and if Allyn wasn't mistaken, kept the magi's confidence and courage up with a well-timed touch.

Surveying the battle from the distance, Allyn realized his initial impression had been incorrect. While the Knights had advanced into the main entryway, they weren't forcing their way deeper into the manor. They held their position, largely attacking from the doorway and through windows.

Something felt odd about that. They couldn't expect to take the manor fighting what was essentially a defensive battle.

Unless they're planning to flank us from behind. He thought of the squad they had encountered in the hall only moments before.

"I'm going to talk to the grand mage," Allyn said. "Help them keep the Knights at bay."

Braeburn nodded and found a sheltered place to lay Ren down. Petter remained with her as Braeburn quickly took up position with the squad nearest him, fire blossoming in his hands.

Allyn entered the grand hall from a separate hall and found Klausner immediately.

"What's wrong?" Klausner asked.

"They're inside the manor," Allyn said. "We need to get you to safety."

"Safety?" Klausner growled. "We don't have time for this."

Grand Mage Klausner stepped around Allyn, stopping only when Allyn grabbed his arm.

"They're after you, Grand Mage."

"Me?" Klausner asked. "What makes you think that?"

"You have answers to their questions."

"That doesn't change anything," Klausner said. "I'm not hiding. This is my home and my Family, and I won't see it fall like the McCollum or Ferdii. If you want to help, if you want to ensure my safety, take a small squad and search the manor. We can't afford to have them sneak up from behind."

One of Nolan's energy blasts detonated, rocking the floor, sending dust and debris into the air.

With a sigh, Allyn relented and let go of Klausner. The grand mage didn't miss a beat, slipping past Allyn and rushing to rally a squad taking heavy fire.

"My sister—" Allyn called after him.

"Will be safe with me!" Klausner shouted without turning back.

Allyn ground his teeth. He had risked life and limb to ensure his sister's safety, only to be dismissed moments after he'd arrived. It didn't seem fair. But if the grand mage was going to refuse to move to safety, he was right. If a second enemy force flanked their number, there would be no way the magi could hold them off, so the best way to ensure Kendyl's, Nolan's, and Ren's safety was to prevent that from happening.

Allyn rushed back to Braeburn. "Let's go. The grand mage wants us to patrol the manor."

"You!" Braeburn shouted at a square-faced, broad-shouldered man with a stony expression. "What's your name?"

"Roald," the magi said.

"You're with us."

The man looked back at his commander, who Allyn was surprised to see was Bastien, the same magi who had assembled the magi forces before. Bastien saw Allyn and Braeburn waiting and nodded his approval.

Allyn carefully picked up Ren and carried her to where a Klausner cleric was treating the wounded. After ensuring her safety, he set forth into the manor. "This way!"

For all its size, the manor consisted of only two main hallways that extended to both wings of the manor. Like the central living space, they were decorated with long runners and furnished with tables displaying various artwork. Roald proved helpful, not because the manor had an intricate set of hallways, but because it *did* have dozens of rooms, closets, and nooks. Being in a strange house in the early hours of morning meant they could easily miss a room or entrance, and that mistake could make the difference in the battle.

Moving toward the northeastern section of the manor, they quickly searched the formal dining room, den, mudroom, and washrooms before moving into the first-level suite, kitchen, and eat-in dining room where Allyn and Kendyl had first become aware of the Knights. They encountered many other magi, some pitched in battle, others wary it would find them next. Through it all, they continued moving. Their assignment was to patrol the manor and repel any Knights who had entered its walls, not assist those already fighting back—not unless it was clear they needed additional support.

The eat-in dining room connected with a secondary living space, which emptied into a game room complete with a wet bar and another master suite. Finding this devoid of enemy forces, they quickly turned back, retracing their steps through the manor and making for the western wing. Allyn surveyed the battle in the grand hall as they passed.

Grand Mage Klausner continued to hold strong, but Allyn could tell the magi number was even further depleted. Magi weren't made for extended battles. Unlike the Knights' guns, which could simply be reloaded, the magi required time to recover and replenish lost elements.

By not simply storming the manor, the Knights were stretching out the battle and effectively weakening the magi. When the magi were weak enough, the Knights would push in.

Moving into the western section of the manor, they quickly patrolled the formal office and living room, family room, foyer, private reading nook, two more bathrooms, and the western en-suite. Again, they found magi fighting back, but unlike the battle at the front entrance, these appeared to be little more than skirmishes—magi attacking as the Knights circled the manor grounds, searching for an entrance, or moving to reinforce another squad.

When they re-entered the hallway where Allyn and Braeburn had fought the first squad of Knights, they found the chamber empty—the fallen Knights nowhere to be seen.

"They're not here," Allyn said. "What the hell is going on?"

Braeburn crouched, tapped his finger in a droplet of blood, and rubbed it against his thumb.

"Why would they move the bodies?" Allyn asked. Were they afraid the magi would find something? Something that would help them identify the Knights? Something that could lead to their headquarters or expose who was truly in charge?

"I don't know," Braeburn said. "Maybe it was a rogue squad."

"But they were moving *toward* the battle."

"It could have been a coincidence," Braeburn said. "They could have been headed somewhere else."

"Where?"

Allyn thought back on the battle. The squad had been moving toward the battle, but what else had been in that direction?

"The stairs," Allyn said. "They were headed for the stairs. For the grand mage's quarters!"

Braeburn cursed.

The realization began to coalesce. The Knights weren't waiting them out. They were distracting the magi from their true purpose.

"They're not here to kill us," Allyn said. "They're here to rob us."

CHAPTER 17

Allyn bounded up the first set of stairs two at a time, keeping his eyes fixed on the stairwell above, ears straining to hear through the distant sounds of battle elsewhere in the manor. His arms were at his side, fingers splayed, ready to wield at the first sign of the Knights. He would have been more comfortable wielding, but the glow of the coils might also alert the Knights of his presence, that their ploy had been discovered, so he kept them at bay. If wielding was like firing a weapon, his finger was riding the trigger.

Roald and Braeburn followed half a step behind him, one behind each of his shoulders, and they were already wielding translucent shards of ice. The shards dripped water, and the steady tapping of water droplets hitting the hardwood of the stairs was the only indication they were headed up to cut off the Knights.

The third-floor landing was silent and deserted, and Allyn saw no sign that the Knights had been present. A tiny flame of doubt burned in the back of Allyn's mind. Had he been wrong? Were the Knights simply here to destroy another magi Family? Pushing aside the doubt, he continued to creep down the hall, careful not to make a sound.

Having been the private quarters of the Klausner Family's Grand Mage for generations, the wing was separated from the rest of the manor. The landing emptied into a single wide hallway cordoned off by a set of double doors. Allyn imagined that in years past, a magi guard had stood watch outside those doors, warrior's eyes fixed on the landing where he now stood, but tonight the post was unoccupied.

Their formation split wide, with Allyn taking the middle of the hall while Braeburn and Roald moved closer to the walls. At the double doors, Allyn stopped, placing an ear against the cold wood.

Nothing.

With a nod followed by a short countdown, Allyn pulled open the door, and the other two magi streamed inside. Allyn quickly followed, coils of electricity blazing in the darkness.

They entered into a small sitting room that adjoined the master suite. The room was empty, but the pair of leather-backed armchairs and side tables had been thrown aside. Pictures, paintings, and other wall decorations littered the ground, their frames and canvases shattered and ripped. The cushions to the chairs had been cut open, the stuffing thrown on the floor. Books and papers were strewn about, their pages ripped from their bindings.

Another set of double doors opened into the master suite, where a four-post bed with a canopy rested in the center of the room. Like the adjoining sitting room, the bedroom was empty, it too ransacked.

"No," Allyn said quietly, half to himself, half to anyone who was listening. He had been sure he would find them here. Sure he would catch them red-handed and find a clue to what they were after.

"We're too late," Roald said, voicing what everyone else was thinking.

Braeburn circled the room, using the light of a fireball to search the en-suite and master closet. Finding them in the same state, he made for the windows and tugged on the handles, trying to open them. "Locked," he said. "They didn't leave this way."

"They must have circled back the way they came," Roald said.

"Yeah," Allyn said. "But I don't think they found what they were looking for."

"Why do you think that?" Roald asked.

"If there was something so important that you were going to attack the manor to create a diversion, would you go back through the thick of battle, where you might be stopped?"

"No."

"Exactly," Allyn said. "If we hadn't seen them in the manor, nobody would have even known they'd made it inside. Who knows how long it would have taken us to realize they'd stolen something."

"I think we would have had a pretty good idea once we saw this room the way it is," Roald said.

"True," Allyn said. "But they wouldn't have torn the room apart if they'd found what they were looking for. Whatever they expected to find in here, they expected to find it easily. Almost as if they anticipated it being on display."

"If you're looking for something on display," Roald said, "you should look in the atrium."

"The atrium?" Allyn cursed—he'd been through that room twice. If the artifact had been displayed there, it had been right under his nose. He was halfway out the room before Braeburn called out, freezing him in his tracks.

"Allyn," he said. "Wait."

Allyn turned to the Elemental Guard. There was something in his voice—apprehension, bordering on regret.

The elder magi's brow was creased, thick lines of worry stretching the length of his forehead. "They're not after anything in the atrium," he said.

"You know what they're after?" Roald asked.

Braeburn nodded.

"Then tell us!" Allyn shouted.

"It's why I'm here, Allyn," Braeburn said. "Not to watch over you. Not to guide your hand."

The realization struck Allyn like a fall from a second-story window—a feeling he knew all too well. "You're here to keep us from knowing what this is really about."

Braeburn nodded again, his eyes darting away from Allyn's for the slightest of moments. He seemed... *ashamed.*

"What's going on, Braeburn?" Allyn asked.

"Later," he said. "Once this is over and the Blood Wand is safe."

"The Blood Wand?" Roald repeated. "What is the—"

"Come on," Braeburn said, moving toward the door. "We have to get it before they do."

Allyn fell into step beside the elder magi. He had a million questions, but Braeburn's locked jaw told Allyn he wouldn't be getting any answers before the magi had done what he intended to do.

Moments later, they re-entered the section of the manor where the McCollum magi had been housed. Braeburn went straight to his room, pulled a bundle from the trunk at the foot of his bed, and began to unwrap it. Black as a starless night, with red inlays set in a complex pattern, the relic was thin and about the length of Allyn's arm. At its end was a complex series of shapes not unlike the brand Jaxon had used during Allyn and Liam's magi initiation ceremony.

Allyn recognized it instantly as the artifact Braeburn had taken from the hidden chamber in the Ferdii citadel. "All of this for *that*?" he asked, incredulous. The relic was little more than a fire poker.

"It isn't what you think," Braeburn said. "And it's more dangerous than you can possibly imagine."

"That it is," said a voice behind them. A voice that was all too familiar.

Allyn's blood ran cold. He turned and found himself face-to-face with Sedric and an entire squad of Knights. They had Allyn's squad outnumbered by more than two to one—and that didn't include any additional Knights hidden in the hall. Sedric had removed his helmet, carrying it under his arm.

He was older than Allyn had first believed. The closer proximity revealed thick wrinkles in his face and a thinning head of gray hair that was in disarray from wearing the helmet. He wore a triumphant smile that didn't extend to his pale-blue eyes.

"Such an amazing piece of work, isn't it?" he asked as the Knights circled the room, guns raised. "And so... *plain*. Where's the flash? Where's the embellishment?"

Not knowing what the brand actually was, Allyn had no idea what Sedric was talking about. He couldn't say that, though. He couldn't let Sedric know he knew more about the magi than Allyn did.

"This isn't something we celebrate." Braeburn's hands gripped the brand, tightly enough that his knuckles went white. Despite being outnumbered as they were, the Elemental Guard showed no sign of relenting.

"I've never understood that," Sedric said. "You owe your life to it, do you not?"

"At great sacrifice."

"But not your sacrifice. We're here"—Sedric held his arms

out as if to include the squad of Knights around him—"walking in the light, our sins washed clean because of our Lord and Savior. We celebrate his love and compassion, and above all, the sacrifice he made so we can follow in his path. It's not all that different, I think."

"It is."

Sedric cocked an eyebrow. "You'll have to explain the difference to me sometime. But first, hand over the wand."

Braeburn fell into a defensive stance, holding the wand as if it were a sword.

"Come now," Sedric said. "This isn't a battle you can win."

But Braeburn wouldn't be talked out of it. Allyn could see the determination in his eyes. He was a member of the arch mage's Elemental Guard, and he would give his life defending that station, even if the odds were infinitely against him. Allyn went to call out, to order Braeburn to stand down, to reason with him. But he was too late.

Braeburn lunged at Sedric, the wand cutting through the air toward his face, but before the blow landed, the back of Braeburn's head exploded into a sea of red mist. The magi fell lifelessly to the ground, dropping the brand beside him with a dull thud.

"No!" Allyn screamed. He felt someone's hands on him, restraining him. He didn't know who. The world was spinning. He was drowning. Braeburn was down. Dead. And the answers he could provide had died with him.

Sedric stepped forward and grabbed the brand. He held it before him, tracing the red veins with a finger. "Heavier than I expected," he said to himself. "And still warm. A good sign, I'm sure." He then turned his attention to the fallen Braeburn, a look of pure hatred flashing across his face.

"'There shall not be found among you a sorcerer or a charmer or a medium or a necromancer or one who inquires of the dead, for whoever does these things is an abomination to the Lord.'" Sedric swung the brand in a vicious downward arc, hitting Braeburn squarely in the head. Blood exploded from Braeburn's skull, peppering Sedric's face and body armor with gore. He hit him again and again relentlessly, until Braeburn's skull cracked like a ripe melon.

Distantly, Allyn heard someone vomit.

"'And because of these abominations, the Lord, your God, is driving them out of you.'"

"Why?" Allyn heard himself ask, his voice little more than a whisper.

"'You shall not permit a sorceress to live,'" Sedric said simply, wiping Braeburn's blood from the wand.

Someone pulled the back of his shirt, and Allyn blinked, realizing he'd taken a step toward the Knight Commander. His arms tingled, and he knew without looking that he was wielding.

Sedric saw the coils, and his mask of anger vanished. He looked from the coils, to Allyn, and then back. His hand shot into the air, and it wasn't until then that Allyn realized the Knights had their guns drawn on him. He froze and instinctively held up his hands.

"What are you?" Sedric asked. There was awe in his eyes, fear too, and questions.

Allyn saw an opening, the smallest of chances. "I'll explain everything, but I need something in return."

"What?"

"Leave the manor. End this bloodshed."

"You'll come with me?"

"Willingly," Allyn said. "If this stops now."

"Yes." Sedric sounded conflicted. Confused. "Yes, of course." Then he blinked, the wonder in his eyes disappearing as quickly as it had appeared. "No. No, I should just kill you and the rest of your kind in this manor." He slipped into another biblical verse, repeating it more to himself than anyone else in the room. "'A man or a woman who is a medium or a necromancer shall surely be put to death. They shall be stoned with stones; their blood shall be upon them.'"

"I am not a medium or a necromancer," Allyn said. "And by killing me, you won't get the answers you're looking for."

"What makes you think I'm searching for answers?" Sedric asked.

"I can see the questions in your eyes." Allyn looked to the coils around his arms, watching as the bands of electricity writhed from his wrists to his shoulders, spitting sparks. "You don't know what I am. What these are. How it's possible. I'll tell you, but first, you need to leave this place and leave my people alone." Allyn let the coils wink out of existence. "Or you can live with the questions forever."

Sedric's eyes narrowed as he weighed Allyn.

Allyn steeled himself, meeting Sedric's gaze, refusing to look away, until finally, Sedric relented with a nod.

But before they could move, shouts echoed in the hallway. The *whoosh* of fireballs followed a split second later, and then the cacophony of gunfire. Sedric shouted a series of orders, and the Knights nearest the door raced into the hall. It left the two remaining magi only slightly outnumbered.

Allyn didn't hesitate. He wielded again, lashing out and blasting the two Knights nearest him with static charges, then dove across the room before the remaining Knights could fill him with holes. Bullets hit the ground behind him, slicing through the air where he'd just been.

Roald launched a strange fireball into the center of the room then quickly dove for cover. The fireball warped *inward* before it exploded, going supernova and throwing the remaining Knights against the wall. Two more Knights were down, the backs of their helmets cracked, faceplates bloodied, leaving three, including the Knight Commander.

Allyn was on his feet again, rushing toward Sedric, who had somehow avoided the blast. He took the Knight Commander in the chest with his shoulder, and the two of them fell to the ground in a tangled web of arms and legs, the wand falling out of reach. Gunfire filled the room, drowning out the battle in the hall.

Allyn grappled with Sedric, fighting for the advantage, but the Knight Commander was too strong, too well trained. Allyn found himself on his back, his arms pinned to his sides, Sedric on his chest. His vision went white, pain flaring in his face when Sedric punched him with a gauntleted hand. In an instant, Allyn's mouth was full of blood. He tried to breathe, inhaled blood, coughed violently.

Sedric hit him again. And again.

Allyn thrashed, kicking, flailing, fighting back with primal instinct—and found himself free. He rolled, rose to his knees, spat a mouthful of blood, and wielded, prepared to attack.

Glass shattered, and a rush of icy air swept through the room. A figure clad in black body armor leaped from the window, falling two stories to the soft ground below.

Allyn quickly scanned the room. Sedric—and the brand— were gone. Movement from the corner of the room caught his attention. He turned, hands ready to hit the enemy with a static charge, and found Nolan advancing toward him, assault rifle in hand.

"What happened?" Nolan asked.

"Where is he?" Allyn asked, ignoring the question. "Where's Sedric?"

"Jumped out the window."

Allyn cursed, rushing to the window, Nolan half a step behind. Broken glass crunched underfoot as they neared.

Outside, the world was dark and quiet. The eastern horizon had turned from purple to pink with the impending dawn.

Sedric was nowhere to be seen.

"Do we go after him?" Nolan asked.

"He got what he came for," Allyn said, exhaling deeply. "He's already gone."

CHAPTER 18

LIAM HAD THOUGHT HE UNDERSTOOD pain. He'd suffered countless cuts, scrapes, sprains, broken bones, and even a concussion after falling out of a tree as a young boy and hitting his head on an exposed root. He'd even suffered deep emotional and psychological pain after Lukas's betrayal, being ostracized by the Forum, the destruction of the McCollum Manor, and above all, his father's death. Allyn had once told him he had felt more pain than any fifteen-year-old had any right to experience. But nothing had prepared him for the pain Sedric subjected him to.

It started out cordially enough. Sedric's tone and demeanor was light and friendly, like that of a long-lost friend excited to share a cup of tea and catch up. Not that it eased any of Liam's nerves, of course. He could see through Sedric's false humility easily enough, but Liam also saw an opportunity to learn who was pulling the strings, and why. So he went along with it.

"Do you know who I am?" Sedric circled Liam to take a seat on the corner of the table at which Liam already sat. They were inside a small room with porous stone walls lit by a single fluorescent light. It reminded Liam of one of the rooms Nolan had described using to interrogate suspects, except that Sedric's room felt several hundred years older. In either case, it left little room for false interpretation of Sedric's intentions.

"Sedric," Liam said.

"Very good," Sedric said. "Though I suppose I should have asked if you knew who *we* are."

Liam shook his head.

"My name is Sedric Lang, and I am the Knight Commander of the Knights of Rakkar."

Sedric watched intently, as if he expected Liam to be surprised or show some sign of recognition, but Liam didn't know what a Knight Commander was any more than he knew who the Knights of Rakkar were. Sedric seemed a little surprised by Liam's lack of recognition. "So the Order hasn't entirely violated the Accord."

"I don't know what you're talking about."

The Knight Commander shrugged. "All you need to know is this, little devil. My Knights and your kind haven't been friends for a very long time."

"Then why did you bring me here?" Liam asked. "Why not kill me like you did the others?"

"Don't play dumb with me, boy," Sedric said. "You know why."

"For information."

"For information," Sedric repeated.

"I won't tell you anything."

"Now, son, I don't believe that any more than you do."

Liam flushed with anger and embarrassment. They weren't more than a few minutes into the interrogation, and Sedric could already see through him.

"Why don't we begin with something a little easier? What is your name, little devil?"

"Why do you keep calling me that?" Liam asked.

"Because even Satan can disguise himself as an angel of light."

Liam barked a false laugh and held up his hands, pointing at himself. "I'm not a demon. I'm barely a magi."

"You've been lied to your entire life, little devil."

"I won't argue with that."

"Tell me your name."

"Liam."

"Liam," Sedric repeated, rolling the name on his tongue as if he were tasting a fine wine. "Do you have a last name, Liam?"

"Hyland." The name, a practiced lie, slid out of Liam's mouth without hesitation.

Sedric's eyes narrowed with suspicion. "You're lying."

"No, I'm not."

"You're lying again." Sedric stood, his lighthearted demeanor vanishing. "Let me tell you how this is going to go, Liam. One of my Knights is going to ask you some questions, and you're going to answer him. If you lie to us again, we're going to hurt you and then ask the question a second time, a third time, as many times as necessary until you've answered fully and truthfully. You understand? Your well-being is completely in your hands."

Liam struggled to swallow the fear rising in his throat. "What happens when we're done?"

"Well, I suppose that depends on how helpful you are, doesn't it?"

Sedric's smile told him everything he needed to know. He'd known he was in serious trouble before, but the Knight Commander's eyes sparkled with unexpected mirth. It was one thing to carry out a mission; it was quite another to enjoy it. To relish in it. If Sedric's expression was any indication, he would have continued with his torture plans even without his weak justifications.

The Knight Commander left shortly after that, only to be replaced by two more members of his order, the second wheeling in a stainless steel cart with various knives, hooks, pliers, and other objects that could be used for torture. Liam's bladder emptied at the sight of the cart and the sheer casualness in which the two men handled the instruments. Part of him thought he should have been embarrassed, but the fear cut too deep. It rendered him silent, weak, and above all, submissive.

Liam had known he would break. He hadn't been trained to deal with this kind of torment, but he'd never expected to break so soon. It took only a few minutes, a single tool, and a couple basic questions. But the pain flared throughout his entire body, consuming him. Within minutes, he was giving the Knights anything they wanted—names, locations, numbers, and histories. He explained the McCollum Family's mission, how it had come from the arch mage, and why the Family had been so desperate to accept. He told them everything. Anything to stop the pain.

Not that it did. The two Knights continued to use the instruments in an attempt to draw more out of him or to ensure Liam wasn't holding anything back. They seemed particularly interested in the other Families—where they lived, how many were in each, and how they fit into society.

Liam didn't know how long they questioned him, but once they'd finished, Sedric returned, and they wheeled him to his cell.

The room was smaller than the interrogation room, with a low ceiling, no windows, and a stone slab with a thin blanket and pillow that did little to guard against the chill. A naked incandescent bulb flickered overhead, illuminating walls made of the same stone as the floor. Deep cracks and water stains marred every surface. The air itself was cold and damp, and had a foul smell he couldn't place. It gave him the distinct impression he was underground. Buried. Dying. A lone window cut into the heavy door that completed his imprisonment provided the only view of the world outside the room, but even the space beyond was dark.

He couldn't be sure, but he thought he slept, and when he did his sleep was plagued by nightmares of his torture that caused his body to ache even more—something made forever worse by the unforgiving bed. Worst of all was the guilt. He'd told the Knights everything they wanted to hear. He'd given up age-old secrets—information that could and would be used against them. A war was coming—no, the war had already started. And Liam had just outlined all of the major players. He'd condemned his Family and everyone he'd ever known to death. If anyone still stood when the bullets and magic stopped flying, they would remember his as the first betrayal.

Life continued like that for what felt like weeks, but the logical part of Liam's mind told him it couldn't have been more than a couple days, possibly even less than that if the number of meals they'd provided him were any indication.

Eventually, Sedric returned. The jangling of keys brought Liam out of a waking nightmare, but he remained on his bed when the ancient door squealed open. Sedric wore a black, loose-fitting long-sleeve shirt and his tactical bottoms. His face was scorched and bloodied, covered in fresh, uncleaned cuts and scrapes. Dry sweat glistened on his forehead, and despite his obvious injuries, he smiled and carried with him an aura of accomplishment.

"Bring him," Sedric said. "It's time for the test."

"Do you know what this is?" Knight Commander Sedric asked.

They were back in the interrogation room, joined by his two torturers and a handful of others. As before, Liam sat in the single chair bolted to the floor in the center of the room, his hands and feet bound to the chair with ropes tied so tightly, they bit into his skin through his clothing. Sweat dripped down his face and back, brought on by his apprehension and the overly hot room that was heated by a cast-iron furnace in the corner. Two of the Knights were working the furnace, bringing its temperature even hotter.

Sedric held a blackened rod inlaid with intricate red lines that reminded Liam of veins. It was much like the branding irons used by magi during initiations but somehow more decorative, more ceremonial.

"No," Liam lied. He remembered a passage from the lost book found in the Hyland Estate, and seeing the brand in Sedric's possession all but confirmed Liam's suspicions.

Unto each, they sacrificed their souls. Given freely, their heat, their water, and their blood. Their very lives. Seven in all, they sacrificed.

Liam had often wondered about its authenticity and had even gone so far as to attempt to verify it, but he'd never been able to do so. Until now.

Sedric's eyes didn't leave the brand. "Pity. It's beautiful, is it not?"

"It is," Liam admitted.

"It's amazing to me that something so powerful, something so important to your people, could go unrecognized. It could sit in a dusty corner of a rundown mansion, and you'd never recognize it. You'd never be the wiser."

One of the Knights behind Sedric approached. "It's ready, sir."

Sedric nodded and handed the brand to the man, who then placed the end of it in the furnace. Sedric sat on the only other chair in the room and leaned forward, his elbows on his knees.

"You've already been of enormous assistance, Liam. Without your information, tonight wouldn't have gone so well. And it's precisely because of your help that you're still breathing today. But your work isn't done."

Sedric's eyes flicked over Liam's shoulder, and he gave a silent command to one of the men behind him. Half a moment later, Liam's shirt was cut from his body, leaving him bare chested and vulnerable among his enemies. Though it provided him with temporary relief from the heat, he still broke out in a new, cold sweat.

A small look of surprise flashed in Sedric's eyes, and the Knight Commander was on his feet. He loomed over Liam, circling him, settling into a position behind him. Liam turned, struggling to see Sedric—he didn't like the man being out of his sight. Hated the feeling of dread and anticipation surging through his veins.

Sedric's cold hands took him by the shoulders, startling him. Liam wanted to shrug them off, swat them away as if they were a spider tickling his flesh, but his hands were bound. Sedric's hands slid down Liam's shoulders, becoming nothing more than a single finger tracing the outlines of the brands on his arms.

Liam stiffened.

"You've been *risen*," Sedric said.

The disbelief in his voice annoyed Liam. He sometimes questioned whether he'd earned his brands and place among his Family, but the Family had deemed him one of their own, and nothing the man could say or do would take that away. The seed of defiance gave Liam something to latch on to, and he fueled it with his anger and discontent. It wasn't enough to overtake his guilt, but it was a start, and for the first time since he'd been captured, Liam felt his will to fight returning.

"So you've been through this before," Sedric continued.

Realization ripped through Liam. They meant to brand him with the Blood Wand! Why? The Life Blood was centuries old. Surely the brand didn't still radiate with its power. And if it did, what would the Knights want with it? It only worked on those with magi blood... didn't it?

Suddenly, through all the questions, a new thought emerged.

By the First Families, what if it works? What will happen to me?

"It's ready, sir." The Knight who'd taken the brand from Sedric turned, holding it with a gloved hand. The brand glowed, radiating heat from its head, distorting the light of the room. Liam's questions were answered.

Even now, the cold iron glows with their lifeblood. White hot, it will burn for generations so that we may continue. Let it not be forgotten of the sacrifice of the seven.

"Good," Sedric said. He patted Liam on the shoulder. "This will be over soon, little devil."

"You haven't been honest with us."

Even to his own ears, Allyn's voice did little to hide the anger boiling inside him. He did his best to wait patiently, his right leg bouncing up and down nervously as his words were broadcast five thousand miles from the Klausner Manor to the Hyland Estate, where Arch Mage Westarra, Jaxon, and Leira waited.

Joining him in the Klausner study were Nolan, Nyla, Kendyl, Grand Mage Klausner, and Myanna, the last remaining Elemental Guard Arch Mage Westarra had sent. Nyla had ordered Ren to rest and hadn't permitted the magi to join them. Ren, of course, hadn't agreed with the order, but she'd found it difficult to argue with the cleric after Nyla forced her under.

When Allyn's words finally reached the arch mage, he stiffened slightly, reclining in his high-backed armchair, fingers steepled in front of his mouth. Jaxon opened his mouth to speak, likely in an attempt to stem the growing anger before it could get out of control, but Westarra beat him to it.

"What happened?" Westarra asked.

"The Knights happened," Allyn said. "They attacked a couple hours ago. We have fourteen dead, including Braeburn."

Westarra rose sharply to his feet and rubbed his eyes with the palms of his hands. "You defeated them?"

"No," Allyn said. "They fled once they got what they were after."

Westarra dropped his hands from his face. "They stole—"

"What is the Blood Wand, Your Grace?" He spat the last part, filling the words with every ounce of anger he felt.

Silence the size of the Atlantic stretched out before them. Jaxon, visibly uncomfortable, eyed Westarra, but the arch mage gave no indication he felt the gaze. He circled the armchair, came to a stop behind it, taking its back in his hands, and squeezed it hard enough that the leather creaked.

"Where did you hear that name?" Westarra asked.

"Your Elemental Guard," Allyn said. "Braeburn said we needed to keep it safe, that it was more dangerous than I knew, right before we were ambushed by the Knight Commander and a squad of his Knights. Braeburn gave his life protecting it, so I ask again, what is the Blood Wand? And why would the Knights of Rakkar want it so badly?"

Arch Mage Westarra shook his head, his fingers rubbing his temples in a circular pattern. Allyn had to give him credit; Westarra was taking the news better than he had anticipated. He'd expected anger, yelling, orders to return home—anything but this sullen, defeated, wilting man on the computer monitor. Allyn supposed that should have terrified him, but he couldn't think about that yet. He needed answers first. Needed to understand how scared he *should* be.

"What I'm about to tell you," Westarra said, "I tell you only so you can get it back. This information doesn't leave this room. Understood?"

Allyn bit back a retort pointing out that just by having the conversation, Westarra's words were leaving his room, but he kept it to himself. In fact, he remained silent, as did the others in the study—he wasn't about to make a promise he didn't know if he could keep, and if the arch mage took silence as an agreement, well, then that was on him.

Westarra took a deep breath and began. "The Blood Wand is older than the Accord or the Knights of Rakkar. It dates back to a time even before the Fracture. A time our history refers to as the Reaping."

Westarra paused, either for effect or because he expected questions.

"I've never heard of it," Allyn said, taking the bait.

"You wouldn't," Westarra admitted. "It's a term used only by grand mages and members of the Forum."

Allyn cast a sidelong look toward Klausner, but the grand mage avoided meeting his eye. *He knew. Maybe not everything, but he wasn't forthcoming, either.* Allyn would have to take that up with him later.

"Then what is it?" Allyn asked.

"Honestly?" Arch Mage Westarra said. "A time not unlike our own, though more dire, I suppose. The magi were dying. Our abilities, our *magic*, the very thing that sets us apart and makes us who we are, was fading. At our strongest points in history, nearly every child was born with some type of magi ability. Today, that number is roughly one in every two children. But during the Reaping, only one in ten magi children was born with magic, numbers that were obviously unsustainable.

"You have to know too that in these ancient times, the magi abilities were different. In addition to being more powerful, there were *other* abilities. Among them were the Granters, magi who had the ability not only to wield, but also to gift their various powers to another for a limited time. At the time of the Reaping, there were only seven Granters known to the Forum, and it was thought they could help find an answer to our declining abilities.

"After much investigation and deliberation, they came to an agreement, and at their consent, a brand was forged. The last remaining Granters sacrificed themselves, giving their power, their very lifeblood to that brand. It's said that after the final magi died, the brand glowed red, not with heat, but with power. From their essence. Aided with what would come to be known as the Blood Wand, the Forum selected from a handpicked group of Silent Magi to test the wand and see if the Granters' power could be transferred."

Westarra paused again, waiting for the inevitable round of questions.

"'You owe your life to it,'" Allyn repeated quietly, almost to himself.

"What did you say?" Westarra asked.

"Sedric said we owed our life to it."

"Then he was right," Westarra said. "The Blood Wand not only granted magi abilities to those Silent Magi, but it created some of the most powerful magi the Forum had seen in ages. And to their delight, those new magi spawned some of the strongest magi lines in the Order—many of which still exist today."

"Why isn't this celebrated then?" Allyn asked. "Why the secret?"

"You already know the answer to that question," Westarra said.

"Someone tried to steal it," Jaxon said.

Arch Mage Westarra turned to him, nodding. "Someone *did* steal it. It was surmised that the wand would not only grant magi abilities to those who didn't have them, but also enhance the abilities in someone who did, making them exponentially more powerful. Magi Families fought civil wars over it, and the wand exchanged possession dozens of times before the Forum finally recovered it. They lied to the Families, saying they destroyed it, but knowing the Blood Wand ensured a magi future, they hid it and tasked a single Family to protect it. To hold its secret."

"The Ferdii Family," Allyn said.

"Yes," Westarra said. "The Ferdii Family accepted a great sacrifice. To hold the secret, the Family limited their exposure to the rest of the Order, and to the rest of the world. You no doubt saw their primitive way of life. They lived that way not only because they chose to, but because they knew no other way."

"Seems a bit extreme, don't you think?" Nolan said. "I mean, I get hiding it and all, but after a hundred years, two hundred, everyone who knew about it would have died, and there wouldn't be a reason to hide it anymore."

"We couldn't take that risk," Westarra said. "Even today,

the wand is a rumor, a myth, something we have to deny. Can you imagine if Lukas had gotten his hands on it? Or Darian? The Blood Wand didn't come by its name because of the lifeblood that flows through it, but because of the blood shed in the magi wars fought for its possession. A war that continues today, it seems."

"What I don't understand," Allyn said, "is if this has been a magi secret for thousands of years, and no one knows it exists except for you and the arch mages who have come before you, how the hell do the Knights of Rakkar know about it?"

"That's the larger question, isn't it?" Westarra said.

"You have a mole somewhere," Allyn said.

"It's not so simple," Westarra said. "Yes, this secret has been held for thousands of years, but the information could have leaked out anytime in the last two or three millennia. Knowing about the Blood Wand's existence alone isn't enough to incriminate anyone; we need to determine how long the secret has been out."

"They also knew its location," Nolan noted.

"Which narrows it down to the last thousand years," Westarra said. "In either case, our priority isn't determining how the Knights knew about it, but getting it back."

"Wait," Allyn said. "Why is it so important we get it back? It obviously works on magi. Are you suggesting it might work on normal people too?"

Westarra held his hands up to the side as if suggesting he didn't know. "It was never used on your kind. Could it grant abilities to someone who isn't of magi blood? Perhaps. Trace magi and human lineage back far enough, and you'll find we came from the same bloodlines. You're approaching a larger philosophical question about what it means to be magi and where the first magi came from that I don't want to get into now. But I think it's safe to say the chances of it working on Silent Men are pretty high. And if it does, the magical community is about to get a lot larger and a lot more dangerous."

Liam nearly passed out from the pain. The brand burned into his skin, hissing and smoking, and the combination of the pain and the smell of his own burning flesh made his eyes water. He fought the bonds that held his hands and feet in place, trying to rock himself free, but it was to no avail. The Knights, it seemed, were well versed in holding people against their will.

Unlike the branding at the Kaplans' cabin, when Jaxon had been there to talk him through it, this was a solitary experience. A handful of Knights still occupied the room, but it was Sedric whom Liam wanted to spit venom at.

The Knight Commander sat in front of Liam, leaning forward, with his elbows resting on his knees, focused on the branding. Liam had trouble placing the emotion in his eyes. Something between expectation and anticipation. Sedric knew what he expected to happen, what he wanted to happen, but wasn't yet convinced those wants and expectations *would* happen.

Halfway through the branding, the pain disappeared. *They held it on for too long*, Liam thought. *Burned me too deep. Damaged the nerves.*

But that wasn't it. Immediately after the pain stopped, something strange happened. The brand seemed to come alive. To glow. Not just the end, but the entire rod. First, the red inlays turned from a dull maroon to a rich crimson, then the brand itself turned from black to white, like the light from a cleric's touch.

Energy poured into him, making the pain little more than a distant memory, and Liam's exhaustion disappeared, replaced by a reservoir of power he'd never felt before.

Sedric leaned forward in his chair, eyes wide. Liam closed his eyes, pushing away the distractions of the room, and focused solely on the new power. It felt somehow familiar.

It's the same feeling I have when I'm coding. But that wasn't specific enough. It was the same feeling he had when he went *beyond* simple coding and interfaced directly with the computer. When he used his machinist abilities.

Liam probed the new reservoir, poking it with an invisible hand. It pushed back. Both confused and curious, Liam changed tactics, pulling on the power, willing it outward and—

Shouts filled the room. Liam opened his eyes to find a roomful of armed Knights with their guns aimed toward him. He pulled back, instinctively covering his head with his arms, finding they were suddenly *free.*

Liam blinked, baffled. When had the Knights cut him loose?

And then he saw it. His hands and arms were encased in fire. He screamed, waved his arms, then patted them, trying to snuff out the flames. That's when he realized the fire, which had burned through the ropes and singed his clothing, didn't burn him. There was only one kind of fire that could do that.

Magi fire.

Liam paused, holding his hands before him in amazement.

"Stand down!" Sedric shouted. "Stow your weapons!"

Liam looked up to see the Knight Commander on his feet, hands raised as if to repel any discharged bullets. His Knights obeyed, albeit a little slower than usual.

"It worked," Sedric said, his voice filled with disbelief. "It actually worked."

Liam looked at him, his dormant anger rising, fueling the fire. Before, he'd been weak, unable to fight back. That same weakness had prevented him from being able to protect himself, from being able to protect his Family—and his father. Not anymore. *Never again!*

Liam struck, and uncontrolled fire filled the room. Men screamed as smoke billowed and flesh burned. Liam smiled and stood, ready to advance, then tripped and found himself on the ground.

Stupid! Your feet are still bound!

One hand still aimed at the remaining Knights in the room, Liam used the other to burn away the ropes binding his feet. He stood again and turned to survey the room, arms still outstretched, fire pouring from his palms.

Distantly, he knew he needed to be careful. If he wielded too much fire, pulled too much heat from his body, it would kill him. But in that moment, he didn't care. The power was intoxicating. Addictive. And it was his.

The small room was in chaos. Bodies and guns littered the stone floor, and more fell as the remaining Knights dove to avoid the inferno. Those closest to the door struggled to open it, then once they did, they tumbled into the hall.

Liam moved to follow—that door was the first step to freedom—when something smashed into the back of his head. Liam's vision flared white. The room spun, and for the second time in as many moments, he found himself on the floor.

He saw the butt of the rifle just as it slammed into his face. Stars filled his vision, and he tried to roll away. To his horror, the fire had dissipated. Not knowing how to call it back, he reached for something, anything to protect himself with.

He found something cold and rectangular and closed his fingers around it just as the butt of the rifle came down a third time. Darkness came next, leaving an afterimage of the object in his hand.

A cell phone. One of the Knights must have dropped it.

With his last ounce of strength and final moments of consciousness, Liam rolled onto his stomach and slid the phone into his pants.

CHAPTER 19

LLYN'S HEAD WAS SPINNING BY the time he left the study. He didn't know where he was going exactly, only that he needed to get away. Away from his fellow magi. Away from the lies and half-truths and deceit. As far away from the situation as possible. The problem was no matter where he went, he would be drawn back into its horrors. From the blood-soaked rugs and carpets to the charred and bullet-riddled walls. From the smell of wood smoke, piss, and blood to the continuous murmurs and cries of pain, suffering, and loss.

His favorite stories of heroism and adventure celebrated the cause to fight and glorified the violence, but they always seemed to avoid the aftermath—the point when the heroes were too exhausted to walk, their minds too muddled to think. The consequences of battle weren't pretty, they weren't glorious, and they sure as hell didn't feel heroic. So the last thing Allyn wanted to do was return to the manor proper. Instead, he found himself heading out the back door of the study, into the brisk air of the Alps.

"Allyn," someone called out after him. It could have been either Kendyl or Nyla—both were so exhausted, he couldn't tell their voices apart anymore. Or maybe it was a symptom of his own fatigue. It didn't matter. He didn't want to talk to either of them. "Where are you going?"

"Somewhere to think," he said, closing the door behind him.

Guilt for leaving gnawed at his insides, and he did his best to fight it with logic. He wasn't a cleric, and he didn't have any medical training, so he would be worse than useless at helping with the wounded and injured. He wasn't a counselor, psychiatrist, or priest, and he didn't have any emotional-crisis training, so he wouldn't feel comfortable consoling victims or their loved ones. Moreover, he didn't know how the members of the Klausner Family would take his presence. Would they blame him for bringing the Knights to their doorstep, or would they view the McCollum magi as champions who'd helped fight them off? He was too scared to find out.

The grounds outside the Klausner Manor were less cultivated than the McCollum grounds had been. The grass, thick and tall, was moist with early morning dew, and colorful flowers that could have been either winter flowers or the first signs of spring sprouted from the few remaining patches of snow. They were beautiful and resilient at the same time, unlike the delicate things he was accustomed to back home.

He followed a natural pathway down the hillside, descending into a small thicket of trees before coming to a stone outcropping that overlooked Schwyz. The low-hanging morning sun bathed the town in a golden light, glistening off white homes and buildings. It was picturesque, stunning, and fake all at the same time.

Members of the town would be waking up and starting their day, oblivious to the horrors Allyn and the rest of the Klausner Family had experienced just a couple hours ago.

Allyn couldn't place it, but something didn't feel right about that. Whether they realized it or not, the townsfolk were in danger. The Knights of Rakkar, the same men who had just murdered fourteen of the Klausner Family, drove the same roads as the men and women below. They breathed the same air and drank the same water. Did that make the townsfolk unwilling participants in this, or did their ignorance keep them safe?

It didn't for Emelina or her Family.

But then again, the Ferdii Family hadn't been truly ignorant. They understood the risk they took. But did it even matter? Evil was evil, death was death, and it afflicted the ignorant and the educated without prejudice. The only way to stop it was to stamp it out. Prevent it from ever taking root.

Allyn sighed, his breath billowing out before him in a puff of white smoke. His orders had been to uncover who was behind the attacks. He'd done that. That had evolved into discovering what they were after. He'd solved that riddle too. Now they were tasked with recovering the Blood Wand before the Knights could use it.

There was a glaring problem with that. He had no clue where the Knights operated. No one did. Not Grand Mage Klausner. Not the Forum. Not the arch mage. It was an impossible task. Beyond impossible.

"Come on," he said to no one in particular.

He wasn't a religious person, never had been. Believing in a higher power that could provide miracles hadn't set well when he'd lost his mother. Neither had the argument that it was all a part of God's plan or that he was somehow better off. He couldn't imagine how two young children without a father or other family could be better off without their mother. Children needed their parents. And no good had come out of him and Kendyl losing theirs.

So it wasn't God he spoke to. It was the world. To anyone who was listening.

He was talking to Sedric, pleading with the man to make a mistake.

He was talking to the fallen Knights back at the manor, wishing one of them had something on them that would lead Allyn to their base.

He was talking to the arch mage and the Forum, hoping they would discover a long-lost piece of information buried in their archives.

He was talking to Liam, trusting the young magi was still alive.

"Give me something," he pleaded.

And when his phone vibrated, he realized someone had answered. Stunned by the coincidence, Allyn slid the phone out from his pocket and, with a trembling hand, read the message. His eyes welled with tears of relief, happiness, and fresh determination.

Liam had heard him.

"This," Allyn said, angling the computer monitor so the rest in the room could see it, "is where Liam is. And presumably where we'll find the Knights of Rakkar and the Blood Wand."

"A church?" Nolan asked, his disbelief clear in the tone of his voice.

"It makes sense, doesn't it?" Allyn said. "The Knights began as a secret subset of the Church's inquisitors. It stands to reason they remain affiliated in some way."

"I just..." Nolan stammered. "It's just not what I was expecting."

The church in question had more in common with a castle than it did most churches Allyn had seen before. Made up of light-gray bricks, arched windows and doorways, and a pair of spires that reached toward the heavens, the structure easily dwarfed the buildings around it.

"Walk me through it again," Ren said, sitting up in her bed with a wince. Grand Mage Klausner had given her a private room to recuperate in, and while she had regained some of her color and strength, she still hadn't fully recovered.

"A short time after our call with Arch Mage Westarra, I received a strange message from an unknown number that said, 'I stole a phone. They have the wand. Get us out.' And before I could respond, the map on my phone opened up, giving me the GPS location of what I suspect is Liam's whereabouts. That's when I got the other message. 'Don't write back. Too dangerous. Just get us out.'"

"And you believe it's authentic," Ren said.

"I think we have to treat it as such," Allyn said. "But yeah, I do."

"I don't disagree," Ren said. "We're weak and in disarray. They gain nothing by setting a trap. How long before we can have eyes on the church?"

"If we left now," Allyn said, "an hour."

"Good," Ren said. "Myanna and Nolan, I want you two to go now and scout the area. Watch only. Do not enter and do not engage."

"What if they leave?" Nolan asked.

"Then follow," Ren said. "But do not engage. We're only going to get one shot at this, and we can't mess it up by acting prematurely."

"We'll have to let the grand mage know," Allyn said. "We don't have a car."

"I know. But keep the circle small for now, at least until we know what we're dealing with. Once the location is verified, we can inform the rest and prepare our assault."

Allyn nodded.

"Anything else?" Ren asked.

Allyn surveyed the room, but nobody spoke up.

"Okay then," Ren said. "Let's get our Family back."

The others filtered out of the room, Allyn bringing up the rear.

"Allyn," she said. "Hold up."

He stopped, turning to face her.

"Close the door."

He did as instructed and returned to the foot of her bed. "What is it?"

Ren's mask of strength faded slightly, and she bit back a curse as she tried to sit up again. Allyn almost told her to take it easy but stopped himself before he made that mistake. It would have only ended in an angry look or firm rebuke, neither of which he was in the mood for.

"You're going to have to lead them through this, Allyn."

"Don't say that," Allyn said. "I'll speak with the grand mage and get a cleric back in here. By the time we're ready for the assault, you'll be ready."

"Are you blind or naïve?"

"Uh... neither?"

"Then what's your excuse?" Ren asked. "Look at me, Allyn. A bullet tore through my stomach and intestine. It took a full *chain* to heal me, and even that incapacitated seven clerics. I won't even be at half strength for another few days, and I hope this is all finished by then. No, you'll have to lead them."

"Why not Nolan? He has a better handle on this stuff."

"Nolan is even more of a stranger to our ways than you are."

"Myanna then."

"Do you trust Myanna?" Ren asked.

240

"I don't distrust her," Allyn said.

"Words with no meaning, Allyn. Answer the question."

"I... I don't know."

"Which is an answer in itself," she said. "And a feeling felt by the rest of us, I assure you. Make no mistake, Allyn, we have two targets to recover here—the wand *and* Liam. Myanna will give her life to accomplish the first; do you think she'd do the same for the other?"

"Probably not," Allyn admitted.

"Would you?"

Allyn looked away. Ren had a valid argument, and one he didn't disagree with, but he couldn't shake the feeling it was the wrong move.

"You've experienced battle," Ren continued. "You've led magi through it, and you've won. What makes this any different?"

"I froze," Allyn said quietly, ashamed. "At the Ferdii Village. I froze."

Ren studied him, biting her bottom lip in contemplation. "Have I ever told you how I got my scar?" She traced the white line that ran nearly the length of her face. Her voice was soft, intimate if also a little uneasy, as though it belonged to a girl about to make love for the first time.

"No," Allyn said.

"Well, contrary to what you've experienced, the magi people are traditionally non-violent. This isn't normal. Lukas, Darian, the Knights, it's all as new and frightening to us as it is to you. Maybe even more so because it isn't who we are. It isn't who we want to be."

"Then—"

"Let me finish. Violence may be unusual, but it's not unexpected. We live a solitary life, Allyn. Always hiding. Always threatened. We never know what to expect, so we have to be ready for everything. So we train. We practice. We fight mock battles, and we keep our skills sharp so we can stay prepared. And for some who have never experienced the horror of battle, and don't understand the difference between simulation and reality, it can make us overconfident."

Ren's words hit on something he'd long been confused by. He'd wondered how people who lived in secret with limited numbers and seemed so at war with themselves hadn't been exposed earlier and how they kept their numbers at a sustainable level. If what Ren was saying were true, and war was new to them, then the magi he was about to go to war with—had been to war with—were as green as he was. Some even more so. And yet they were expected to take on a well-trained force on their own turf.

Despite Ren's intentions, her moment of honesty did little to instill him with confidence.

"There was a lot of buildup to Lukas's splinter," Ren continued. "For as quick as it seemed, there were a lot of signs along the way. Arguments. Fights. Some of which got out of hand. This"—Ren ran another finger down her scar—"happened one night when I interrupted a private disagreement between Lukas and Graeme. They were in Graeme's forest study, away from the manor. I don't know if Graeme had moved there intentionally or if that's where Lukas found him. In either case, that's where they were, and they were alone. Which was odd, because by then, tensions were growing, and Jaxon had ordered Graeme watched at all times, even positioning someone inside Graeme's room every night while he slept.

"I heard shouting, recognized Graeme's voice, and came running. Graeme and Lukas were *this* close to each other." Ren held her thumb and index finger only a couple inches apart. "I don't think I'd ever seen either so angry. So I did what any hotheaded, overconfident fighter would do—I got in the middle of it and protected my leader."

"Which only made the situation worse," Allyn said, seeing where the story was headed.

"Exactly," Ren said. "Though, looking back, I'm still not convinced I made a mistake letting my presence be known. Graeme was in danger, even if he didn't want to admit it. Where I erred was not that I stepped in, but how I did so—without thought. Without first assessing the situation. Instead, as you said, I only made the situation worse. What was originally a shouting match became physical. And what was originally a shoving match quickly escalated into something far more dangerous.

"I wielded first, blasting a lance of ice toward Lukas. It missed, but I was already preparing another one. Graeme was shouting at me, ordering me to stop, but I didn't hear him, didn't listen. Before the new blast of ice left my hand, Graeme had hit it with one of his own, shattering it in my hand. Ice shards peppered my hand, but a larger piece of shrapnel did this."

"It was Graeme?" Allyn asked, genuinely surprised.

"It was Graeme," Ren repeated. "I was angry. I felt betrayed. But above all, I was disappointed. I'd made a grave mistake, had endangered myself and my grand mage. All because I'd acted without thought and without assessing the situation."

"Maybe you didn't though," Allyn said. "What if—"

"What if I'd killed Lukas?" Ren asked. "All of this would have been avoided, right?"

"Yeah."

"Perhaps," Ren said. "Trust me, I've thought about it. But I doubt it. I think something far worse would have happened. If I'd killed Lukas, he would have become a martyr, and that would have been the tinder to a larger inferno."

"I guess we'll never know."

"No," she said. "We won't. But this is what I *do* know, Allyn. I made a mistake, but I learned from that mistake and haven't made it since. There's no better teacher than our own failings. You understand that. And that's why you'll succeed in this. You won't make the same mistake twice."

Ren was the last person Allyn had ever expected to give him a pep talk. Until this trip, she hadn't spoken more than fifteen words to him, and those fifteen words hadn't exactly been the encouraging or supportive type. Surprisingly, though, her words resonated with him, somehow telling him exactly what he needed to hear. And wasn't that what great leaders did? Not only understand their own strengths and limitations, but also the strengths and limitations of those under them?

If so, then much of leadership could be boiled down to reading people and understanding them. That was something Allyn could do. That was something he *had* done. Suddenly, the burden didn't feel so heavy, the task as impossible.

Allyn met Ren's eye, and an understanding passed between them. He didn't need to speak the words—they both already felt them—but he did anyway.

"I'll see it done."

CHAPTER 20

ONFIDENCE, ALLYN HAD LONG SINCE learned, was a fickle beast. As far as he had experienced, one either had it or they didn't—there was no in between. Fortunately for him, there had been a time earlier in life when he'd overflowed with it, strutting around campus as if he could walk not just on water, but on the very air itself.

The world came easy because he expected it to. His fellow classmates listened to him because he believed what he said and spoke in a way that scared away potential challengers. He'd scored his first job at one of the most prestigious firms in the Pacific Northwest based on the strength of his interview and his reputation among the faculty.

The problem was that confidence hadn't been earned, and unearned confidence was little more than simple arrogance. Thinking back, he realized that one of the most important lessons in his life and professional career had been losing his first case. Inexperience and arrogance were a volatile combination, and the result had left him humbled and shaken, if not more than a little angry. It had taken weeks of reflection before he'd begun to see his error. Confidence shaken, he'd swung the other way. Indecision plagued him, and with the loss of his self-confidence, his colleagues and clients began to question him too. It wasn't until someone told him, "Sometimes you have to fake it until you make it," that he'd regained what he'd lost. The false bravado re-earned the trust he'd lost, which in turn provided him with more confidence. It was a self-fulfilling prophecy built on a lie, but by God, it worked.

So standing in front of the remaining McCollum magi, Grand Mage Klausner, and the select group of Klausner magi the grand mage had assembled, Allyn channeled that false confidence. He kept his face hard, eyes stern, back straight, chin raised, and voice level and assured. And like his time back in law school, his partners didn't question him.

"Nolan and Myanna arrived at the site a little over two hours ago," Allyn said. He was in the middle of his briefing. "So far it's been quiet, nobody going in or out."

"How can you be sure he's in there?" Grand Mage Klausner asked, his tone skeptical. He'd changed clothing since the battle and now wore the same compression armor as the rest of the magi.

"The signal hasn't moved," Allyn said.

"Which only means the phone hasn't moved," Klausner pressed. "Not that Liam himself hasn't moved."

"He'll have the phone on him," Allyn said. "Hidden somewhere. If the Knights knew about it, they would have destroyed it. And like I said, nobody has gone in or out. As far as I'm concerned, as long as that signal is transmitting, there's still hope."

"I suppose," Klausner said, then gestured for Allyn to continue.

Allyn turned back to the crude drawing on the wall behind him, depicting the structure. "There are two main entrances—here and here—and then a third at the rear of the structure. It's here where we believe many of the offices are and where Liam will be. We won't enter from the rear. Instead, we'll station two magi outside the rear entrance to ensure nobody slips out while the operation is underway."

"We're walking in through the front door?" Nyla asked.

"Yes."

"It's the only way to be sure we thoroughly search the building," Ren said. They'd found her an old wheelchair and rolled her into the study. She seemed to be growing stronger by the minute, but Allyn suspected her strength was much like his confidence—a façade.

"Like we did with the rear exit, we'll station two magi at the front and side entrances while the rest search for Liam and the wand," Allyn said.

"Two at each of the entrances, for six total," Grand Mage Klausner said, "leaving fourteen to battle the Knights and recover your magi and the wand."

"That's correct," Allyn said.

"Doesn't give us a lot of room for error."

The grand mage hadn't come out and said it, but Allyn understood the implications. There was no way they would all be walking away from this assault, and with their numbers already limited, every loss would be exponentially more damaging.

"Outside of the main structure," Allyn said, "the church will be narrow. Larger numbers won't necessarily be to our advantage. That said, if you have other magi to spare, we'd be happy to accommodate them."

Klausner winced and shook his head. "I wish we did, but we're leaving the manor exposed as it is. We can't spare any more."

"Then twenty will have to be enough," Allyn said.

"Do we know what to expect inside?" Nyla asked.

"Yes and no," Allyn said. "The church is a traditional design, so we know what to expect there, but beyond the altar, and hidden from view, are the various offices and administrative rooms. Once in there, we're flying blind."

"Then what's your plan there?" Grand Mage Klausner asked.

"Once we're beyond the church proper, we'll rely on your training and expertise."

Klausner pinched the bridge of his nose and exhaled a long, deep breath. "I'm not going to lie, Allyn. The plan is weak."

"It's the best we could come up with in the time we were given," Ren said, coming to Allyn's defense before he could speak. She was taking ownership of the plan, which wasn't altogether fair. They'd come up with it together, even if she had taken the lead.

She knows how fragile I am.

"Then why not wait another day?" Klausner said. "Like you said, the signal hasn't moved."

"Two reasons," Allyn said. He had been the one to push for the compressed time frame. "First, Liam's phone will die if it's not charged, and it's already been transmitting for a few hours, so we have no idea how much longer his battery has. The moment it dies, the transmission dies along with it. We'll be blind again, and we'll have no idea if he or the wand is transported.

"Secondly, we could wait a day, or two, or three—it doesn't matter. Except for the main chamber, we're blind to the rest of the church. We've searched for pictures, plans, schematics, anything that would give us an idea what to expect inside, but all we've found are pictures of the church proper, nothing from the administrative areas."

"I wasn't advocating for more time for more scouting,"

Klausner said. "I think we all understand and accept the challenges there. I was thinking the extra time would allow us to enlist the aid of another Family. The Bachmann Family is near Zurich. They could augment our numbers."

"As much as I'd like that," Allyn said, "you and I both know the arch mage has made it explicitly clear that nobody beyond this room is to know about the Knights of Rakkar or the Blood Wand."

Klausner nodded. "It's decided then. Twenty magi, two at each entrance, leaving fourteen to explore the church, and the offices beyond. Seems simple enough. What else do you need from me?"

"Beyond the magi in this room?" Allyn asked. "Cars."

"Done. When do we leave?"

"Now."

CHAPTER 21

NIGHT HAD FALLEN BY THE time Allyn and his squad arrived in Zurich. According to Kendyl, the city was the largest in Switzerland, though only half the population of Portland, and had a mixture of modern and old-world architecture that Allyn had never seen before. Churches and monuments, thousands of years old, sat alongside coffee shops, restaurants, and boutiques. It was the opposite of home, where everything was new, newer, or in the process of being remodeled.

He'd never thought about it before, but in the States, nothing was more than a couple hundred years old. Nothing could be—the country itself wasn't much older—and the Pacific Northwest, where he'd lived and grown up, was even worse. There was no history. Nothing that said, "this is our country" or "this is who we are."

The church itself looked much like it had on the computer monitor, an ageless, imposing light-gray structure with twin spires that stretched toward the heavens. What the monitor hadn't given justice to, however, was the sheer size of it. The church was massive, stretching larger than a full city block in both its width and depth. In many ways the church was Goliath to the surrounding area's David.

They parked the two 4x4 vehicles they'd borrowed from the Klausner Family on a cobblestoned street a few blocks from the church and approached on foot. It was late enough that most of the foot traffic had died down, and the little that remained was mostly relegated to a riverside promenade a couple of blocks away. Nolan was parked adjacent to the church, the front of his vehicle facing its double doors.

Always the cop, Allyn thought, imagining Nolan and Myanna with cups of cold coffee and a half-eaten box of donuts. Something about that made him want to laugh, and if it had been any other night, he might have, but his sense of humor had escaped him, replaced by an intense, unshakable focus.

Nolan and Myanna met Allyn's squad in an alleyway near his car.

"Updates?" Allyn asked quietly.

"Nothing's changed," Nolan said.

"Nobody in or out?"

"Couple of tourists," Nolan said. "No one of note. Anyone who's gone in has already come out. Should be empty except for the Knights."

"Good." Allyn turned his attention back to the church. "We proceed as planned then."

At his command, the magi quickly arranged themselves into a pair of previously agreed-upon squads of seven. Thinking it was the best way to ensure they secured *both* targets, Allyn had split the McCollum and Klausner magi as evenly as possible between the two groups.

As the squads organized and readied themselves, the remaining six magi stepped from the alley and moved into position, keeping to the shadows as they made their way forward.

"Let's go," Allyn said once they'd disappeared.

On his command, the remaining magi followed Allyn from the alley, jogging across the deserted street.

The main entrance to the church was made up of an arched doorway that housed a pair of bronze double doors, easily twelve feet tall. Pausing outside the doors, Allyn turned to Nyla and Kendyl.

"Anything?"

The two women mimicked each other, holding a hand up and closing their eyes. While the physical expression looked similar and would achieve the same result, Allyn knew they were sensing different things. Nyla felt for people inside while Kendyl felt for their emotions—neither seemed to sense anything though, opening their eyes and shaking their heads.

Content he wasn't about to step into a hail of bullets, Allyn pulled open the door and slipped inside, the rest of his squad close on his heels, alert and ready to strike. The church's interior was made up of a similar light stone and marble. Grand arches lined either side of the nave, opening into a pair of hallways that paralleled the pews and central aisle.

As Allyn stepped forward, he descended a small stairwell from the antechamber into the nave, and made for the aisle to his left. Nolan and his squad mirrored his movements, disappearing into the aisle to the right. The church was empty and quiet, save for the faint rustle of footsteps from their two squads.

They advanced toward the apse and came to a pair of painted doors near the rear of the structure. Biblical paintings conveying the light of God obscured the doors, matching similar paintings that lined the aisles. Without hesitation,

Allyn pulled open the door, allowing Nyla and Myanna to rush through the opening into the adjoining hallway. The rest of the squad followed, with Allyn bringing up the rear.

They entered a narrow L-shaped hall with whitewashed walls and simple decorations, a stark contrast to the public areas of the church. Two doors lined the hall. The first opened into an empty parish room, and they quickly moved on to the second, which Allyn expected to be the priest's private quarters.

As they moved into position, the door suddenly opened, exposing a short priest who wore simple black robes. Allyn started, taking an unconscious step backward. The priest mirrored Allyn's movements, his eyes wide with shock. Those same eyes flashed with fear an instant later when he saw the rest of the magi squad waiting in the hall.

Nyla swooped past Allyn and into the room, subduing the priest and covering his mouth with her hand. The priest yelled, his protests muffled by Nyla's hand, and tried to shake himself free, but the cleric was too strong.

The magi squad streamed into the room, ready for a fight. As Allyn had expected, the room belonged to the priest, but it was smaller than he anticipated, and save for a few meager furnishings, surprisingly empty.

"Where is he?" Allyn asked the priest, his voice oozing with unspoken threats.

"Who?"

"You know who." Allyn took a menacing step forward, wielding for effect.

Terror blazed in the priest's eyes, and he fought to get free, reaching, grasping, twisting, kicking, but it was useless. Nyla had him in a vise.

"Don't make me ask you again," Allyn said.

The priest didn't answer, but again his eyes, which flicked downward, told Allyn everything he needed to know.

He was across the room in an instant, sliding the small cot away from the wall, exposing a hatch cut into the floor.

"They're under the church," Allyn said. "Myanna, find Nolan and bring his squad to me. We're going underground."

If stepping into the church had been like stepping into the past, then entering its bowels was like stepping into another world. While the upper levels had been immaculately preserved, the lower levels showed their age. Stone bricks, two feet thick and four feet long, made up the foundation of the church. Their edges were worn, the stone porous and crumbling. The uneven floor sloped in various directions, and the ceiling, only inches from the tops of their heads, seemed to weigh down on them with the full weight of the structure.

The only signs of modern technology were the naked bulbs spread evenly through the space. They burned with a yellow light, casting long shadows through the room. There was only one direction to go, and Allyn led the two squads through an arch into the space beyond.

They entered into a long corridor without embellishment or decoration. At its end was a modern blockade meant to keep anyone from continuing beyond. Allyn ignored it, noting the disturbed ground, hoping it was a sign of the Knights' boot traffic.

Beyond the long corridor was another chamber similar to the one they'd originally dropped into, though wider and without electric lights. Allyn wielded, letting the pulsating red light of his coils illuminate the room. His breath immediately caught in his throat. Human remains—full skeletons with skin, muscle, and sinew long since decayed—rested ominously in holes cut directly in the walls. There was no telling how many there were. Fifty. One hundred. Allyn couldn't stomach the idea of counting.

"What the fuck is this place?" Nolan said.

"Catacombs," Kendyl said. "It's a burial ground."

"How deep do these go?" Allyn asked, stepping deeper into the hall. The chamber seemed to open into another that held even more of the dead.

"No idea," Kendyl said. "I didn't know Switzerland had anything like this, but in Paris, there's hundreds of miles of these things, and even more in Rome. I doubt Zurich has anything that complex, but this could go on for a while."

"That changes things," Allyn said, turning back to the two squads. "We need to stay together. We can't split up and risk getting lost, and seven of us won't be enough to take on a full contingent of Knights. We'll need our full strength."

"That's going to add time," Nolan said.

"I know," Allyn agreed. "But Liam's signal was coming from this position. He won't be far, regardless of how deep these catacombs might go. Come on."

The ground sloped gently downward, and as they continued, Allyn let Myanna, whose hands were encased in fire, take the lead. They passed through tunnel after tunnel, chamber after chamber, each the final resting place of hundreds of bodies, until they finally came to a long corridor lined with unlit torches. The hollow beyond glowed with the steady light only modern technology could provide.

Allyn had the magi replace fire with ice, and then holding a finger to his lips, he pointed at Nolan then at the opposite wall. Nolan understood immediately and broke his squad away from Allyn's to take position where Allyn had directed him. Together, just as they'd done in the church, the two squads pushed forward at equal speeds, careful to remain as silent as possible—though that was growing increasingly difficult as the stone floor had deteriorated enough that it almost resembled walking on a gravel-strewn road, loose rock crunching underfoot. Halfway through the corridor, Allyn began to make out the soft echoes of voices.

They're here.

He more than half expected to spring a trap, to stumble across a hidden guard or somehow alert the Knights in the adjoining chamber to their presence. None of it happened, though. The Knights hadn't set up a perimeter or placed anyone on guard—and why would they? The Knights were a specter of the past, little more than myth. Who would come looking? *How* would anyone come looking? Where does one find a living legend?

Coming to the end of the corridor, Allyn took a short moment to make eye contact with each member of his squad, verifying that each was ready for what came next. He received nods from everyone and, satisfied, turned to Myanna and gave a small hand signal ordering her to get eyes on the adjoining chamber.

Myanna stepped beyond Allyn, her slender frame as nimble and silent as a mountain lion. She inched toward the opening, and once in position, she peered beyond the corner of the wall. Allyn watched as she surveyed the room and then slowly retreated.

Four, she signaled then mouthed, "Armed. Distracted."

"Sedric?" Allyn mouthed.

She shook her head.

Allyn cursed silently, but nodded. He pointed at Myanna and Andrick, a Klausner magi with a pinched face, who was only a few years older than he was, and signaled for them to advance. They'd prepared for this, and each knew their role.

Stealth and silence. Don't give the Knights the ability to fight back or to alert the others.

Myanna and Andrick stepped into position, wielding slowly. The usual sound of pooling water and the crack of forming ice was largely absent with their lack of haste. The slowness of it made the hair on the back of Allyn's neck stand on end. It left so much to chance. Any of the four Knights could look into the opening and see Myanna or Andrick. Someone could walk into the room and do the same. Hell, someone could enter the corridor from behind and see their entire magi force ready to strike.

But the possibility of being seen didn't outweigh their need to take the Knights by surprise. Botch this and the Knights' entire cadre would descend on the magi like a swarm of angry hornets. Outnumbered and outgunned, the magi *needed* that surprise. They didn't stand a chance without it.

Myanna and Andrick recoiled as the first ice blasts shot into the chamber, then immediately recovering, they stepped into the doorway, their hands already filling with ice again. Unable to see, Allyn could only imagine what was happening inside the room.

Two Knights would be taken completely by surprise as lances of ice took them in the head or neck, causing wounds that would prevent them from calling out. The other two would watch in confusion, unable to see the nearly translucent spears of ice dug into the back of their companions' bodies until they went limp and their heads drooped, exposing the magi weapons. By then, their attention would turn to the doorway, where Myanna and Andrick were already advancing.

Allyn heard a muffled cry that was cut short as the second blast of ice struck the Knight, the sound of alarm dying as he did.

Myanna stepped back into the corridor, her body relaxed, and waved Allyn forward.

The room was the size of a large living room, and a set of chairs surrounded a collapsible table. The four Knights, all dead now, had been in the middle of a card game.

With the aid of two other magi, Myanna and Andrick drug the fallen Knights into a dark corner of the corridor. There was nothing they could do about the blood that had pooled on the floor, but in the dim light of the room, that would be less noticeable than four fallen bodies.

A network of corridors extended from the chamber, two from the far wall, and one each to Allyn's left and right. The two squads of magi had already filtered through the room, each taking up position outside the corridors, ready to strike if any other Knights came looking.

Nyla raised a hand, catching Allyn's attention, and pointed down the second corridor against the far wall. As Allyn stepped over a fresh bloodstain, he heard additional voices.

This is it.

Allyn waved his squad forward, and they fell into step behind him. The corridor was so narrow that Allyn could touch both walls at either side at the same time. *A choke point.*

Full magi squads wouldn't be an advantage there, and worse, if they were cornered, the tight confines of the hall would turn the battle into a magi massacre. At the far end of the corridor he could see what looked like another hall that ran perpendicular to the one they were about to enter. That one would probably meet up with the other corridor several feet to Allyn's left.

Stepping close to Nolan, Allyn whispered, "Split your squad into two subsquads. Leave half here and take the other half down that second corridor. I'll do the same, only with this hall. I think they mirror each other and empty into the same hall on the other side."

"Okay," Nolan said. "Be careful."

"You too."

Allyn returned to his squad as Nolan's formed up behind him.

"Subsquads," Allyn ordered. Myanna, Andrick, and Kendyl fell in behind him, while Nyla commanded the remainder that were rounded out by two Klausner magi. "Hold this chamber until I say otherwise."

Nyla nodded and ordered her magi to take up position just outside the corridor, ready to defend or aid Allyn's squad as needed. Mirroring them outside the other corridor was Nolan's subsquad.

Only a few steps into the corridor, Allyn realized his first mistake. The corridor was actually a hall with several rooms lining either side, each marked by an ancient wooden door, reinforced with steel bands that were as thick as they were imposing. Age and rot had taken its toll, however, and many of the doors hung awkwardly, had fallen, or were missing altogether.

Allyn stepped up to the room nearest him and looked through an eye-level, steel-barred window. Inside was a tight room without furnishings or embellishment—just a plain square room with a hard floor and a stone slab for a bed. *A cell.*

A chill ran down his spine. The catacombs were more than just an ancient burial ground. They were a prison. How many of the dead they'd passed had been prisoners or heretics?

No time for that now. Find Liam. Ask questions later.

Allyn continued, slowing at every cell to poke his head in and make sure the Knights weren't using them for their personal quarters. Each was empty, but he found himself drawn to one farther down the hall. The door was in better shape than the rest. Refurbished. Sturdy.

He stopped outside the cell in question. The door was cracked open, and he slowly nudged it open even more. The wood creaked, but gentle and slow as he was, the hinges didn't squeal. Once it was open far enough that he could enter, he slipped inside.

The cell was tighter than he'd first thought—he wouldn't have been able to lie down without touching one of the walls. He had a sudden image of a prisoner spending his final days in this cell, curled in a ball to protect himself from the chill, and unable to stretch out. It would have been agonizing on the joints and spine, and sleep would come only in fits and spurts. The pain and lack of proper rest would slowly drive a man into madness.

He knelt, placing the palm of his hand on the stone floor... and touched something wet. Turning his palm over, he rubbed the wetness with his other hand. It was cold and tacky, little more than a black smudge in the darkness.

"Myanna," he whispered, and a second later, she appeared. "I need a little light."

She wielded a wisp of fire, a single flame about the length of his finger, and held it above Allyn's hand as if it were a lighter. The black smudge became something more ominous.

"Blood." Allyn looked past his hand, to the floor, where more of it dotted the pale stone. Not big puddles, but drops. Several spaced throughout the room. "Liam."

And as if saying his name aloud in the cell triggered something in the universe, Liam answered. It wasn't a yell. He wasn't calling for Allyn, Nyla, or anyone else in their number. It was a scream of pure misery. Of absolute torment. Agony beyond comprehension.

And that's when the first burst of gunfire rocked the catacombs.

CHAPTER 22

SHOUTS AND GUNFIRE ECHOED THROUGH the catacombs as Allyn rushed out of the cell. At first, he'd thought Nolan had encountered resistance in the other corridor, but stepping into the corridor, he realized the gunfire was coming from back in the original chamber, where they'd left the subsquads. Bursts of muzzle flashes lit the dim chamber, and the more steady light of fireballs flew in return fire.

Half of him wanted to rush to their aid; the other half needed to push forward to find Liam. In the end, reason won out. He'd left the subsquads behind for a reason—to keep the remainder of his and Nolan's squads from getting ambushed. He'd also known that in the event their cover was blown, they would need to hold the exit so they would have a chance to escape once they'd found Liam and recovered the Blood Wand. He had to trust that the other magi would do their job and give the rest of them a chance to succeed.

"Come on!" Allyn shouted, rushing in the direction of Liam's scream.

Before they reached the end of the corridor, they encountered their first squad of Knights. Four in total, they lacked the tactical armor Allyn had seen them wear before. Their black pants and shirts made them less intimidating, some-how more human and less menacing. They were still armed, though. Assault rifles raised, fingers on the triggers, they rushed toward the sounds of battle.

Myanna and Andrick wielded before the Knights could squeeze off a shot, and in an instant, they had a pair of fireballs soaring down the narrow corridor. The surprised Knights had nowhere to go. The fireballs struck, exploding and hurling the Knights back through the corridor. Three remained down, but a fourth staggered to his feet, only to be met with a shard of ice, piercing him through the chest.

No sooner was the last Knight down than more gunfire echoed through the corridor where Nolan's squad was advancing. Allyn did his best to tune it out, waving his own squad forward. Like the subsquads behind, Nolan was prepared for the possibilities.

At the end of the corridor, Allyn paused, taking a moment to look in both directions. The passageway was wider than the one they'd just passed through, with a room to Allyn's right and another series of cells to his left. He left those for Nolan to search, deciding to head toward the room to his right. He waved his squad forward, and Myanna and Andrick pushed ahead, hands burning with flame. Kendyl trailed closely behind, bringing up the rear.

Allyn had originally wanted to leave her in the subsquad he'd left behind, but they didn't know what kind of psychological condition Liam would be in. If he was too scared or had suffered deep psychological abuse, nobody would be able to help him in the way Kendyl could.

Allyn followed the squad toward the room, running backward, keeping his eyes on their six, where a pair of Knights were suddenly hurled out of Nolan's corridor. The former FBI agent emerged a moment later, white orbs of power glowing in his hands. He saw Allyn and paused, awaiting instruction. Allyn pointed down the hall. Nolan nodded and ordered his magi in the opposite direction.

Allyn flinched as more gunfire ripped through the corridor. He spun, dropping to a crouch and throwing his back against the wall.

"Get behind me!" Allyn shouted, pulling Kendyl back so that his body was shielding hers. In front of them, Myanna and Andrick huddled as close to the wall as possible, the flames in their hands forming into fireballs roughly the size of a man's head.

A pair of Knights popped out from around the corner of the room, firing a barrage of bullets in their direction. Bullets ricocheted off the walls, but amazingly, no one was hit. They couldn't count on that kind of luck a second time. They had to strike before the Knights let loose another hail of gunfire.

If Nolan had been with them, he would have been able to use one of his energy blasts and level anyone waiting in the room, but Allyn had ordered him in the opposite direction. He briefly thought about calling out to him, ordering him back, but quickly thought better of it.

"Myanna!" Allyn shouted.

"Already on it!" she shouted back. "Andrick! Now!"

"Where?" Andrick cried.

"The center of the room!"

"But—"

"Just do it!"

Andrick flung his fireball forward, straight down the center of the hall. Half a beat later, Myanna let hers fly too, and just as the first crested the threshold of the room, Myanna's fireball struck. The two exploded in a flash of orange and white, and tendrils of flame lashed out, kissing the stone face of the room.

Two Knights staggered into view. One was covering his burnt face with his hands; the other dropped to the ground, rolling in an attempt to smother the fire blanketing his black clothing. Myanna advanced, shards of ice crystalizing in either hand, and in a moment it was over, the two Knights each pierced by the Elemental Guard's latest creation.

The room they'd been guarding was completely vacant, save for a pair of collapsible chairs sitting outside another door. It was metal and of a more modern design, and didn't fit properly in the frame. The only reason the door remained closed was because of a thick steel latch that slid into a metal bracket fastened to the wall. A single shadow paced inside the room, visible through the crack beneath the door.

"Sanders?" the person behind the door said. "Sanders, report!"

The squad looked to Allyn, who shook his head. He knew that voice.

"Sanders?"

Myanna and Andrick waited outside the door, ready to strike as Allyn stepped closer.

"Three, two, one," he mouthed silently, then slid the metal latch out of the bracket and yanked open the door. There was no gunfire, only shouted commands from Myanna and Andrick.

"Freeze!"

"Don't move!"

Allyn rounded the doorway, wielding. Inside the door, standing slightly wide-eyed but still very much as though he were in control, was Sedric. He saw Allyn and *smiled*.

"Hello, Allyn," he said. "I must say this is a surprise."

But Allyn barely heard him, his eyes finding what lay behind the Knight Commander. Stretched out and shirtless, strapped to a metal table, was Liam. His pale skin was covered in yellow and purple bruises and littered with fresh and half-healed cuts and scrapes. His body twisted, almost as if he were attempting to turn and look, but the straps held him in place.

Liam groaned, moaning something that only faintly resembled, "Allyn?"

Allyn snarled. He had enough adrenaline pulsing through his veins that he probably could have ripped Sedric's head from his body with his bare hands. "What have you done to him?"

"Oh, we've become very acquainted, haven't we, Liam?" Sedric's voice lacked even a hint of fear.

Allyn closed the distance between them, stopping when his face was only inches from Sedric's.

"I'm going to kill you," Allyn whispered. But even as he said it, he knew it wasn't true. Oh, he wanted to. He wanted to burn Sedric's flesh from his bones as he'd done to Lukas, but he needed the Knight Commander for questioning. He needed to understand how big the Knights of Rakkar were, outline the command structure, identify bases, determine their affiliation with the Church, and more. They couldn't trust a simple soldier would have all the information they needed.

"One of us will surely die today," Sedric said. "But I don't plan on that being me."

Allyn circled Sedric and gave him a push in the back, shoving him toward Myanna and Andrick. "Watch him," he said. "If he moves, kill him."

Allyn moved toward Liam and began undoing his bindings.

Liam grunted, trying to speak, his voice oddly muffled. Allyn cursed and leaned down to find Liam gagged.

"Allyn?" Liam said once Allyn had removed the gag. "Is that really you?"

"It's me, buddy."

"I knew you'd come."

"We couldn't have done it without your help," Allyn said, returning to the bindings.

"I didn't know if it would work," Liam said. "It feels like we're underground. I didn't know if the signal would get out."

"It did."

"How many are with you?"

Allyn shot a glance at Sedric, who was now in Myanna's grip, his hands safely behind his back.

"Twenty," Allyn said, quiet enough that only Liam could hear him. "How many Knights are there?"

"I don't know," Liam admitted. "The most I've seen were at the village. Thirty maybe. Forty."

"Well they don't have that many anymore."

Once Liam was nearly unstrapped, Kendyl entered the room and placed a bare hand on Liam's back. A soft glow of light appeared at the point of contact.

"What are you doing?" Allyn mouthed.

"Confidence," Kendyl mouthed back.

"They did something to me," Liam said.

"Not now," Allyn said. "We'll talk about it later. Let's get you out of here first." He removed the final band at Liam's ankles. "All done. Can you sit up?"

Liam pushed himself up into a sitting position.

"Easy," Allyn said. "Take it slow."

"We don't have time," Liam said. "The brand, Allyn. It's not a normal brand. It's called the—"

"Liam—"

"No, Allyn, this is important. The wand can grant abilities. Magi abilities."

"Liam, I know."

"It's... wait. You know? How?"

Allyn went to answer, but shouts from the adjoining room

interrupted him. He turned just in time to see an explosion—and Myanna and Andrick being thrown away from Sedric.

Allyn struggled to make sense of it. How would the two magi be thrown *away* from Sedric?

The Knight Commander turned, smiling, holding the impossible. Two fireballs danced in his hands. Sedric Lang, the Knight Commander of the Knights of Rakkar, could wield.

Time slowed, and Allyn moved just as Sedric brought his hands up. "Down!" he shouted, diving for the door before Sedric had time to unleash his newest creations. He slammed the door closed... only it didn't close.

Since the door didn't fit properly, it swung outward and slammed into Sedric with enough force to send the Knight Commander sprawling. He landed on the ground with a groan, several feet deeper in the room.

The door rebounded weakly, swinging back toward Allyn. He caught it, holding it so it shielded them from Sedric while he checked on Liam and Kendyl.

"You all right?"

The two had ducked behind the metal table.

"Yes," Liam shouted, then pointed. "He's getting away!"

Allyn swung open the door just in time to see Sedric rushing across the room. He broke into a run after the Knight Commander, then had to duck as Sedric shot a wild fireball in his direction. By the time he rose again, Sedric was halfway down the corridor. Allyn wanted to go after the Knight Commander with nearly every ounce of his being, but it was the little logic that remained that held him in place. He couldn't leave Liam and Kendyl behind again. Couldn't leave without checking Myanna's and Andrick's injuries. Couldn't abandon his squad. So he remained in the room, watching as Sedric disappeared into another corridor.

"What are you doing?" Liam shouted, stepping out of the torture room. "You let him get away!"

"He hasn't gotten away yet," Allyn said simply, kneeling down beside Myanna. The Elemental Guard was regaining consciousness, her eyes unfocused and blinking. "Don't move."

Sedric's fireball had taken her directly in the chest, leaving a hole in her compression armor and irritated pink flesh beneath. The skin on her neck and lower face was worse off, inflamed and red, but not yet blistering.

She should be dead. Luck, it seemed, was finally on their side.

Across the room, Andrick stirred, sitting up. He was in similar shape, though his burns extended to his hands, as well. "What happened?"

"Sedric used the Blood Wand," Liam said. "He has magic."

Andrick grunted. "Then thank the First Families he's untrained. Otherwise, we'd be dead."

"What do you mean?" Allyn asked.

"His fire was weak," Andrick said. "He doesn't have control yet. If he did, we wouldn't be talking about it." The Klausner magi saw Liam and asked, "What now?"

"We need to get you and Myanna back to safety," Allyn said. "Then I'll take the other squad and find the Blood Wand."

"I'm going with you," Andrick said.

"No you're—"

"I've burnt myself worse on the stove," Andrick said. "I'm going."

"Fine," Allyn said. "Help me with her."

Andrick began to lift the dazed magi, but Myanna shook him off. "I'm fine," she said. "I can walk." She rose to her feet, growing steadier and steadier by the second.

"Let's go," Allyn said.

They headed back to where the rest of their subsquads remained. Even with Myanna's injuries, they made good time and arrived back in the original room without incident. A handful of fallen Knights lay dead in the corridor, but it seemed the most intense fighting had been relegated to the deeper passages of the catacombs, where Nolan's squad was pressing forward.

The six members of the two remaining subsquads had obviously seen battle, but despite the scorched walls peppered with bullet holes, their number was whole. No one down. No one injured.

"Liam!" Nyla shouted, crashing into the young magi with a fierce hug. "You found him." Then, perhaps thinking better of the embrace, she pulled back, surveying his injuries. "What happened?"

"He's been tortured," Allyn said. "But he seems good."

"I'm fine," Liam said.

But Nyla wasn't listening. Light already emitted from her touch as she probed his injuries.

"I said I'm fine," Liam said, trying to pull away.

But Nyla had him now, and Liam wasn't getting away until she was done with him. A few moments went by before, finally satisfied, Nyla broke the connection and let Liam go.

"Nothing too serious," she said, her voice still thick with concern. The implications were clear—Liam's real injuries wouldn't be physical.

"Like I said—"

"We have other problems," Allyn said, then told Nyla about Sedric. "We don't know if he's the only one or if he's branded others, so don't let your guard down, even if they appear unarmed."

"Where are you going?" Nyla asked.

"Going to find Nolan," he said. "He's alone in there. How many can you spare?"

"How many do you need?"

"Assuming Myanna and Andrick are still good, two should be enough." Leaving Kendyl behind, that would give him a squad of five. Coupled with Nolan's squad of four, that would still leave five to guard their exit.

"Yann! Theo!" Nyla barked at two nearby magi. "You're going with Allyn."

The two magi nodded, their attention shifting immediately to Allyn, awaiting orders.

Liam appeared at Allyn's side. "I'm going too."

"No," Allyn started. "I can't risk—"

"Incoming!" someone shouted.

Gunfire billowed almost instantly.

Allyn darted past Liam and rushed to the corner of the wall, wielding and readying a pair of static charges. The gunfire was relentless. Bullets buried themselves in the wall near Allyn's head.

Just as Allyn was about to enter the fray, a fireball easily three feet in diameter sailed past him, into the corridor. There was a shout, followed by an explosion, then silence. Allyn rounded the corner, prepared to throw the two static charges, but all he saw was a smoke-filled corridor and two motionless figures lying on the ground.

Allyn turned his attention back to the room. "Who..." Allyn faltered when his eyes found Liam.

The young magi wore an expression of deep satisfaction, and he held another fireball in his hands, the orange light illuminating a bloody wound on his upper arm.

No, not a wound, Allyn realized. *A brand. They branded him too!*

"I told you I was going," Liam said.

270

"You... you can wield?"

"I was his guinea pig," Liam said. "Had its advantages. Now are we going to do this or not?"

Speechless, Allyn turned to Nyla and Kendyl for support. The two women wore matching smiles. His sister even raised an eyebrow at him. He shook his head. After everything it had taken to rescue the damn kid, he couldn't believe he was even considering taking him back into the belly of danger. But Liam could wield. He'd seen battle and kept his head. And most of all, they needed the additional support.

"Fine," Allyn said. "Let's go."

CHAPTER 23

NOLAN CURSED, DUCKING AS A bullet zipped uncomfortably close to his ear. He and his squad were pinned down in an adjoining corridor between the Knights' makeshift armory and barracks—not an ideal location to dig in. He was here now, mostly because he and Allyn had deviated from the original plan of sticking together, Allyn deciding to split off in a different direction while ordering him deeper into the shit.

It was hard to tell how many corridors they'd passed through or how many rooms they'd entered, and if push came to shove, he *thought* he could make his way back to the rest of the magi. But every damn room looked the same. The same deteriorating walls. Same uneven floor. Same low ceilings. Same narrow corridors. Each hall led to larger rooms that had been retrofitted into new purposes by the Knights.

Nolan and his squad had fought a series of small skirmishes as they moved into the heart of the Knights' compound, until they'd passed through the armory. There, they'd run into the larger Knight force regrouping within the barracks. After Nolan's magi engaged the Knights, a second force had appeared behind them, pitting Nolan's squad of four against a good dozen. Not good odds by anyone's standards.

Fortunately, the corridor they were pinned down in was one that had alcoves and small rooms cut into its walls, offering some degree of cover and hope.

Between bursts of gunfire and the occasional hiss, roar, or thunderclap of magi return fire, Nolan heard the sound of men advancing, their heavy military-style boots thumping and scraping against the stone floor. He chanced a look beyond his alcove, spying a foursome of Knights hugging the walls and closing in on their position. He pulled back just as a pair of them fired, and got peppered with rocky debris in his face for his efforts.

Nolan breathed a series of short, sharp breaths, steeling himself, then popped out of the alcove to send an energy blast at the advancing Knights. He ducked back into the alcove before it detonated, narrowly avoiding a second barrage of bullets, this time coming from *behind* him.

They're advancing too, Nolan realized, letting out a series of curses. *That's how you fight, Allyn. Coordination. Tactics. Not every man for himself.*

"Get dow—" one of the Knights shouted before the energy blast ignited, cutting him off. It was powerful enough that dust and loose rock fell from the ceiling, but noticeably less powerful than the ones before it had been. Nolan's power was weakening. And quickly. Very shortly, he wouldn't be of any help to the other members of his squad. Depleted—out of ammo, so to speak—he would be dead weight.

Why didn't I bring my gun? Magic was great, but he had other skills that could have been just as effective. *You're an idiot, Nolan. A goddamn idiot.*

Without further thought, Nolan shot a glance down the corridor where he'd sent his energy blast. Dust hung in the air, giving off the faint impression of smoke. The Knights were down. Two were moving, albeit slowly. On the ground, and well out of reach, were their assault rifles.

"Asa! Elov!" Nolan shouted, the Klausner magi names coming off his tongue unnaturally. They met his gaze from their alcoves across the corridor, and Nolan pointed back to where the new squad remained, then signaled with an exploding fist—the sign for a fireball.

The two magi nodded, and Nolan counted down from three with his fingers. On zero, Asa and Elov shot a pair of fireballs toward the Knights, and Nolan darted into the corridor, racing toward the fallen Knights and their weapons. The nearest gun was only six feet away. He dropped, sliding the last few feet as a series of bullets hissed through the air above his head. His hands found the gun, and it was as if he were in bed with an old lover again. Hands and fingers moving deftly, he pulled the gun into position and fired off a triple burst.

He smiled as the enemy shouted curses.

With the short reprieve, he snagged the other rifle, wrapping its strap over his shoulder, and then buried bullets in each of the nearest Knights' chests.

At least four down now, he thought, ducking into the nearest alcove and reassessing the situation. *Two to one.* The odds were swinging in their favor. *Finally!*

And then because fate could be a cruel bitch, a new salvo of gunfire ended in a magi cry. Nolan spun, turning back to look where Asa and Elov were hiding. Elov was down, unmoving, the lower half of his body exposed in the corridor.

There went your improving odds, asshole.

"Asa!" Nolan shouted. But the magi didn't hear him. Bullets sprayed his alcove, blasting away the little bit of cover he had. Asa pushed himself to the very back of the recess, as if willing the wall to give way and provide him with a couple additional inches of cover. "Asa!"

But the other magi didn't respond.

"Hagan!" Nolan shouted at the fourth member of their squad. He occupied the same wall as Nolan, and as such, was entirely out of sight. He also had the most direct route to Asa.

"Occupied!" Hagan shouted back.

Grinding his teeth, Nolan pushed himself into the back of the alcove, placing a foot against its wall for leverage. Before he could think better of it, he shoved off the wall, hurling himself across the corridor, angling toward Asa's alcove. Gunfire immediately erupted, and a bullet tore through his upper arm.

Nolan crashed into the recess occupied by Asa's fallen body. Doing his best to ignore the rush of pain, he dropped his gun, letting it dangle from the strap around his shoulder, and took Elov by the arm, dragging him fully into the temporary safety of the alcove. The magi groaned, obviously dazed. He was in bad shape. His compression armor was sticky with blood where two bullets had ripped through his chest and leg.

Nolan let out a frustrated breath, taking stock of his own wound. Blood poured down his compression armor where the bullet had grazed his upper arm. Though it hurt like a bitch, the wound was barely worse than a bad cut.

Hagan whistled from across the corridor. Catching Nolan's attention, the stocky magi shook his head and pointed outside his alcove. Venturing a peek, Nolan saw what had Hagan discouraged. The Knights from the armory were advancing again, moving from alcove to alcove in a coordinated, methodical effort. Nolan glanced in the opposite direction—the other squad of Knights were doing the same.

We're in a vise, Nolan thought. *They're squeezing us.*

Nolan brought up his gun again, checked his ammo—*running out*—and fired off a burst. He missed as the advancing Knight jumped into the nearest alcove for cover. *Is this it? Is this how it ends? Here, in an ancient tomb, of all places?*

Nolan wanted to laugh, but dying wasn't funny business. He sighed instead. They didn't have the numbers. He didn't have the ammo. And they sure as hell didn't have the terrain. But he still couldn't bring himself to give up. If he could pick off a couple, slow them down, then... then what? Hope someone saved them?

Goddamn right.

Using the corner of the alcove for cover, Nolan brought his gun up again and was immediately met with a barrage of gunfire. He cursed, retreating, his breath ragged. He made a fist, flexing and unflexing, trying to release the tension and stop his hands from trembling. Three more sharp breaths, and he swung his gun back into position just as an explosion rocked the corridor.

The Knights advancing from the armory flew forward, crashing against the walls at unnatural angles, and before Nolan could register what had happened, a series of fireballs ripped through the corridor at incredible speeds. There were explosions. Cries. Gunfire. The corridor erupted into full battle.

"Nolan?" someone shouted.

Allyn? It's Allyn! "Here!"

Allyn appeared a second later, saw Nolan, his gun, and Elov crumpled against the wall behind him. He cursed, kneeling, and placed his fingers on Elov's neck, checking his pulse.

"What happened?"

"Got pinned down. He got hit."

"How bad?"

"Not good. Bullets took him in the chest and leg. He hasn't been fully conscious since."

Allyn shook his head, visibly torn about something. "Have you seen Sedric?"

"Sedric?" Nolan asked. "No. Not yet. Why?"

"I almost had the bastard," Allyn said. "He's one of us now. He used the wand on himself and can wield."

"One of us... what does that mean?"

"We'll figure it out later," Allyn said. "There's no time right now. We *have* to stop him and get that wand back. I don't think this was only about stealing it from us anymore. He's using it."

"How many do you have with you?"

"Including me? Six."

"It won't be enough."

"It has to be."

The sounds of battle, which had been dissipating for several moments, finally ended, and Allyn's other magi, including Liam—*Allyn saved the kid, thank God*—advanced down the corridor to make sure the Knights were down for good.

"What's beyond this hall?" Allyn asked.

"Barracks," Nolan said.

"He won't be there," Allyn said. "The wand will be in his personal quarters, and he'll be with the wand. Get ready to move out."

"What about him?" Nolan nodded toward Elov.

"We'll have to get him on the way back."

"He won't last that long, Allyn."

Allyn took a deep breath. "Andrick!" The Klausner magi appeared a moment later. "Get Elov to Nyla and meet us back here. You have two minutes."

Andrick drew his lips into a line, irritated, but did as instructed.

"We're almost there, Nolan. Take a minute, regroup, and reload."

As Nolan reloaded and stuck additional magazines into his waistband, Allyn searched the barracks. Like the rest of the catacombs, it was sparsely furnished with light, transportable furniture—in this case, a series of foldup cots, with tactical armor neatly arranged at the foot of each bed.

He picked up one of the helmets, the seed of an idea blossoming in his head.

"Look what I found," Nolan said, stepping into the room. He held a thick, flat black, four-foot-long steel shield—the kind that Allyn had seen SWAT teams carry as they stormed houses or managed riots.

"Very nice," Allyn said. "Can I see it?"

Nolan handed him the shield, and Allyn's arm drooped under its unexpected weight.

"It's heavy," Allyn said. "Bulletproof?"

"You bet your ass it is."

"Good," Allyn said. "Because I have a plan."

CHAPTER 24

THE TACTICAL ARMOR WAS RESTRICTIVE. The helmet, even with its glass faceplate, cut off Allyn's peripheral vision and made the sound of his breathing heavy, nearly drowning out all other sounds. Combined, the sensations gave him the impression that he was somehow experiencing the world secondhand. The Kevlar in the chest and back plates weighed down on his shoulders like the weight of responsibility; but worse were the arm and leg pieces that covered his elbow and knee joints, limiting his movements and pinching the soft flesh on the back of his arms and legs.

Everyone had donned the tactical armor, doing their best to find the closest approximation of size, then rounded out the ensemble with an assault rifle. Allyn's was slung over his shoulder as he carried the heavy shield; Andrick was at his side doing the same. Nolan and Hagan were behind them, towing Liam, who hung limply, pretending to be wounded. The rest brought up the rear. Nine in all, they comprised the largest squad Allyn had led during the assault, moving toward a force that would again outnumber them by more than three to one.

They moved as fast as they dared, feigning the need to get

Liam medical attention. The problem was they were blind. Allyn didn't know where to go—or where the Knights were regrouping. They marched down corridors, finding other burial chambers and barracks, each as empty and quiet as the last. Finally, after what seemed like an hour's worth of wandering, they came to a long corridor guarded by a pair of armed Knights.

Allyn didn't hesitate, didn't slow, and continued to march down the corridor. He shouted for help as Liam wailed in false agony, dragging his legs behind him as he'd been instructed.

The pair of Knights lowered their weapons and raced down the hall to meet them.

"What happened?" one of the Knights asked, his voice thickly accented.

"Ambushed." Allyn kept his voice low and thick as if he too were injured, hoping it would mask his own accent—or lack thereof.

"Fucking witches," the Knight said. "Come on. Let's get him to the infirmary."

The Knight turned and led them down the hall, his counterpart allowing their squad to slip past him as he guarded their rear. Allyn breathed a sigh of relief. The ploy had worked—so far.

"The Knight Commander is at the back of the chamber," the Knight said. "I expect he'll want to debrief you."

"Of course," Allyn said, surveying the hall. He didn't see any other Knights, and feeling confident they were the only two, he gave the signal.

With each of the Knights' backs turned to them, they were simple enough to dispatch. Yann and Theo buried a pair of ice shards into their backs, and caught the two men before they could crash to the ground. With no other guards in the hall, they quickly carried the Knights into an adjoining chamber and hid them among the dead. Once they returned, Allyn led the squad to the end of the hall, where Yann and Theo assumed the defensive position the two Knights had held before.

The hall emptied into the largest chamber Allyn had been in yet. Easily forty feet in length and width, the chamber had a series of pillars spaced every five or six feet, holding up the low-hanging ceiling. Knights filled the room, some already in tactical armor, and others putting it on, preparing for battle. Lining the wall to Allyn's right, the injured—nearly all of whom suffered from burns and puncture wounds—were clustered into two groups: those being actively treated and those who weren't. The latter rested and had likely been given some sort of sedative.

Allyn turned to his squad, who watched him attentively, their eyes hard behind their visors. Not counting the injured and sedated, there had to be thirty people in the room. It was impossible to say how many Knights there were in total, but one thing was becoming increasingly clear: unless their entire number was in that room, the magi had grossly underestimated the Knights' strength.

"Over there." Allyn pointed to an empty corner in the room, and Nolan and Hagan drug Liam to it, letting him slump to the ground.

Another Knight was on them in an instant. He wore no tactical armor, and his pale face and blond hair were slick with blood and sweat. "What's wrong?" he asked in a hurried voice.

"Fell," Nolan said. "Twisted a knee."

"No other injuries?"

"No."

"Then keep it straight and try and find something to build

a splint. I'll check on him after..." He moved away, rubbing his forehead, smearing more blood across his pale skin.

"Take up places throughout the room and try and keep a wall to your back," Allyn said once the medic was out of earshot. "Wait for my signal."

"There's a lot more in here than we expected," Nolan said.

"Just means our job is more important," Allyn said. "Let's go."

Their group dispersed, spreading throughout the room as instructed. Allyn stayed close to the wall, circling the chamber, taking the long way to where Sedric and his apparent council were in active session. He stood with four other Knights, huddled around a small table, looking and pointing at something on its top. As Allyn got closer, he recognized it as a map of the catacombs, but his attention was quickly drawn to something in Sedric's hand.

The Blood Wand.

Allyn cursed silently. He'd hoped the wand would be locked away in a private room or set aside somewhere where he could steal it, but it seemed Sedric wasn't going to make things so simple.

Slowing so as to not come upon Sedric too quickly, Allyn turned, surveying the room. He found his magi easily enough—they'd each smeared blood across their helmets, distinguishing them from the rest, and save for those nearest the door, they were also the only ones still wearing their helmets. How long would it take before someone thought that was odd?

After getting each of their attention, Allyn gave the signal, and from across the room, near the entrance to the chamber, a shout rose.

"Here they come!"

He recognized it as Nolan's voice, but he was close enough

to the entrance that nobody noticed it hadn't come from the Knights guarding the entrance. If anyone *had* noticed, that suspicion was quickly quashed as Yann and Theo opened fire down the corridor.

Nobody was there, of course, but the unknowing Knights still jumped into action. They assembled into squads with military precision, spreading throughout the room into defensive positions. The members of Sedric's council left the Knight Commander, barking orders as they assumed command of their various squads.

Allyn stepped from his position near the wall and made his way toward the man holding the Blood Wand. Unconcerned about the apparent battle, Sedric barely looked up from the map. Still holding the shield, Allyn raised the gun, took aim at Sedric, and fired.

The bullet struck the wall behind him, and Sedric looked up sharply, his hand going for the pistol at his hip, realizing for the first time someone was approaching. Seeing Allyn in full Knight armor, he froze, confused. The helmet covered Allyn's head, but the faceplate was large enough to reveal his features, and recognition slowly dawned in Sedric's eyes. He shouted, but gunfire from the entrance drowned it out, and then seemingly realizing he was on his own, Sedric brought his gun up to fire.

Allyn broke into a run, protecting as much of his body behind the shield as possible, watching through the small window as Sedric fired. Bullets slammed into the shield with more force than Allyn had anticipated, ricocheting at odd angles, throwing off sparks.

Allyn squeezed off three more rounds, but the weight of the shield and his awkward grip on the gun threw off his aim. After missing Sedric again, Allyn changed tactics and charged, crashing into Sedric with the full force of his run.

The Knight Commander fell back, the gun and wand falling to the ground in opposite directions.

Falling atop Sedric, Allyn held onto the shield then rolled to the side. His helmet was slightly too large, and twisted, obscuring his vision. With his free hand, he yanked it off, quickly getting his bearings.

Sedric was already moving, diving for the gun a few paces away. Seeing his opportunity, Allyn moved in the opposite direction, grabbing the Blood Wand from the ground. He turned, putting the shield between him and Sedric just as the Knight Commander squeezed off a few more rounds. The shield deflected them easily, and Sedric growled, throwing the gun aside.

Allyn lowered the shield, watching, and before he could blink, the Knight Commander wielded a fireball.

Oh shit! Forgot about that!

Allyn pulled the shield up just as the fireball struck. The force threw him off his feet and hurled him backward. He hit the ground hard, the force knocking the wind out of him. By the time he could think about something other than the pain, Sedric stood above him, the Blood Wand in hand.

Without hesitating, Sedric swung the wand through the air at incredible speed. Allyn vaguely remembered Braeburn's head bursting like a melon, and brought his hand up instinctively, *catching* it. Pain exploded as the bones in Allyn's hand shattered, but somehow, miraculously, he held on. It wasn't a conscious decision, but he wielded, and coils of electricity sprang to life around Allyn's arm, extending up the wand.

Sedric screamed, recoiling from the shock, and let go of the wand. His hand broken, the wand slipped from Allyn's mangled fingers, falling to the ground again. He reached for it with his good hand, but Sedric crashed into him before he could grab it, and they rolled across the ground.

"Knight Commander!" a voice shouted. Someone had spotted them.

Allyn turned to see four Knights running in their direction, guns raised. Before they could fire, something bright exploded against their backs, throwing them aside and exposing an armor-clad Liam behind them.

He was a single source of light and hope within a sea of black. Allyn hadn't realized it, but the orderly chamber had erupted into chaos. The Knights near the corridor continued to fire, believing they were holding off an advancing magi force, when in fact the true enemy was already in the chamber with them.

Allyn watched as Liam slipped back in among the swirling mass of Knights, and even though Allyn focused on him, Liam was hard to keep track of. The only way Allyn could spot him was through the wake of death he left in his path. He wielded ice among the mass, keeping it low and hidden, striking only when he was in close proximity to another, burying a shaft of ice through a kidney here and a stomach there. He was the blade of an assassin, silent and deadly.

Elsewhere, the rest of the magi worked in similar fashion, though Allyn could only make out three more. Where were the rest? Were they down? Injured? Dead?

Focus on your own mission, a voice somewhere inside chided him. *Get the wand.*

Allyn blinked, snapping his attention back to the fight he was engaged in. He was on his stomach, his broken hand throbbing beneath him. He pushed himself up, turning to face Sedric... only he wasn't there.

And neither was the wand.

Allyn spun, searching the chamber frantically. He didn't see him. Couldn't make anything out. There were too many people. The room too frantic.

He wouldn't have run into the chaos. Not with the wand. He would have run away *from it.*

Allyn whirled, spotting an adjoining corridor at the back of the chamber, and thought he briefly saw a shadow of movement. He jumped to his feet and rushed toward the corridor, snatching the map off the table as he passed.

He barreled into the corridor without thought, and it wasn't until he had fully crossed the invisible barrier into the hall that he realized how truly stupid he had been. Sedric could have been waiting for him. He could have taken his head off with one swing as Allyn recklessly crossed the threshold into the chamber. He needed to be more careful, somehow find the balance between speed and caution.

Slowing to a guarded jog, Allyn slipped through corridor after corridor, eventually coming to his first intersection. The corridors split in two different directions, neither of which more noteworthy than the other. He surveyed the map, tracing the maze of lines with a finger, until he found something that looked like it could be an exit. He traced it back to the intersection he was at. *Left.*

Folding up the map and sliding it into a safe spot within his armor, Allyn took off. Did Sedric know his way through the corridors? Could he find the exit without the aid of the map? If not, he could be lost within the catacombs, and Allyn might never find him.

Allyn passed through more burial chambers and corridors, only slowing to double-check his position on the map when he came to intersections. Once he was close enough to the exit that he could memorize the rest of the way, he put the map away for good. Throwing caution to the side, he broke into a full sprint. Without having to fear damaging the map, he wielded, providing himself with more light.

Something echoed ahead. *Sedric. Almost there!*

Allyn pushed harder, keeping his ravaged hand close to his chest to minimize movement and pain. It slowed his speed, but that was something he could make up since he didn't have to stop at every intersection to consult the map, and as Allyn flew out of another chamber, he saw Sedric round a corner ahead of him.

He dug in, grinding his teeth as he pulled his bad arm down from his chest to push himself even harder. He gained ground, and by the time he rounded another corner, he had full sight of Sedric. Coils of electricity already cording his arms, Allyn flung a static charge after the Knight Commander. It struck the wall near Sedric's head with a hiss.

Sedric started, rolled, spun, and shot a fireball back through the corridor in Allyn's direction.

Cursing, Allyn dodged, narrowly avoiding it as it sped toward him faster than he had expected. *Aided by air*, he realized. A trick used by experienced magi. And Sedric had already picked up on it. *How?*

Sedric rose to his feet, watching Allyn intently, fire burning in the hand that didn't hold the Blood Wand.

"You left all of your men behind," Allyn said.

"I have more."

"Will you throw their lives away as easily?"

"Allyn, some day you'll understand that this wand is more important than any man I command. More important than even me. They're all prepared to die for it, and so am I."

"Why?"

"Why?" Sedric asked, feigning confusion. "To win the war."

"What war?" Allyn asked. "We just want to live our lives. We *were* living our lives before you showed up. You're not fighting a war, Sedric. You're fighting a crusade. Committing genocide."

"You think the war is over, Allyn?" Sedric asked. "You're wrong. Wars are moments of battle broken up by longer periods of waiting, and this war has been going on for centuries. It never ended. You've just been living in a period of waiting."

"I refuse to believe that," Allyn said.

"Believe what you like," Sedric said. "It doesn't change the truth."

"Why do you hate us so much?"

"You're a perversion of God's plan, Allyn. Nobody but God should have supernatural abilities."

"If you truly believed that, why did you turn yourself into one of us? Why soil yourself?"

Sedric shrugged, looking down at the fire burning around his arm. "To defeat a monster, sometimes you have to become a monster."

"What do you really want, Sedric? What's your real plan?"

"I don't owe you anything, Allyn. And I wouldn't tell you even if I did." Sedric's eyes flickered past Allyn, into the corridor behind him. "How long until the rest of your squad catches up?"

"Won't be long," Allyn lied. For all he knew, his squad was still fighting for their lives inside the chamber with the rest of the Knights.

"Well then," Sedric said. "I won't be tricked into waiting until they arrive. Until next time, Allyn."

Sedric's hand shot up, and Allyn flinched, ready to dodge. But the fireball didn't fly toward him.

"No!" Allyn screamed, rushing forward. Too slow.

The fireball exploded against the ceiling, collapsing the tunnel and bringing down centuries of rock and soil between Allyn and Sedric. Allyn stumbled and backed away, coughing up the gray dust that filled the air. When it finally dissipated, he saw that the entire corridor was completely blocked.

"No!" Allyn yelled again. "No! No! No! No! *No!*"

Allyn yanked out the map and quickly looked for a way around the collapsed tunnel. If he backtracked and took the opposite fork at the previous intersection, he could loop around the barricade and connect with the adjoining tunnel just before the exit. And Sedric, thinking he'd slipped Allyn, wouldn't be moving at the same pace he had before. If Allyn hurried, he still had a chance.

Not bothering to return the map, he took off through the corridor. When he came to the intersection near the exit, Sedric was nowhere to be seen. Allyn proceeded with caution, slipping the map back into the secure place within his armor. The passageway ended abruptly, but fastened to the wall was an old wooden ladder. Forty or fifty feet above was a ray of artificial light—whatever normally covered the entrance to the catacombs had been removed and not returned.

The aged wood, slick and moist, groaned under his weight as he started up the ladder. He climbed quickly, only pausing when he neared the top of the tunnel, straining his ears to listen. And when he didn't hear anything, he continued.

The room was of a modest size and furnished with equally humble furniture, simple chairs and tables, all handcrafted of natural timber. Flickering candlelight gave life to the empty room.

Shuffling across the room, Allyn stopped outside the door to listen. When he didn't hear anything, he pulled it open with a soft creak. The main living space was empty, and the front door to the small home was open to the night air.

Allyn abandoned all caution and rushed forward, exiting the house and finding himself on a quiet cobblestoned street. Colorful buildings three and four stories tall loomed over him, their windows dark. The distant, soft sounds of traffic hummed through the city, but nothing moved on the street. No cars. No bicycles. No pedestrians.

Allyn finally succumbed to the realization that Sedric was gone... and with him, the Blood Wand.

CHAPTER 25

SEDRIC'S ASSERTION THAT HIS KNIGHTS would die happily to protect the Blood Wand had been an exaggeration. By the time Allyn returned to the chamber, he found the remaining Knights bound and lined against the wall, their weapons safely stowed. The dead were piled on the opposite end of the room. Andrick and Nolan, both bloodied and clearly exhausted, added another fallen Knight to the pile.

Liam was speaking with another Klausner magi, directing a final sweep of the catacombs, while Nyla and the Klausner clerics verified the dead and administered aid to those in need—magi and Knight alike.

Allyn made for Liam as the Klausner magi moved away to undoubtedly carry out Liam's orders. Liam saw him, smiled, and took a hopeful breath.

"What happened?" Allyn asked.

"We won," Liam said simply. "Not without a stroke of luck and some insubordination, but we won."

"Explain."

"It was Kendyl," Liam said. "She convinced Nyla to come, and if it hadn't been for her, we would have been overrun, and it would have been us taken prisoner or in that pile over there."

Kendyl. His sister, ever the troublemaker, had ensured their victory. He wanted to smile, to laugh, but he couldn't bring himself to do it. Not with his own failures weighing so heavily on him.

"How many dead?" he asked, not wanting to know the answer.

"Them or us?"

"Both."

Liam winced, his cheerful disposition disappearing. "Five for us. We're still counting the Knights."

"Who?" Allyn asked.

"Do we have to do this now?"

"Who?" Allyn asked more forcefully.

"No one from our Family," Liam said.

As if that made a difference—though, if Allyn were being honest with himself, it did. He hated himself for it, but the feeling of dread was unknotting in his chest.

"Thank you," Allyn said. "Continue." He moved to leave Liam to his work, but Liam grabbed his arm.

"What about the wand?" Liam asked softly.

Allyn shook his head.

"Sedric?"

"No."

Liam sighed, a thin veil of determination sweeping over his face. "We'll find them."

"Yeah," Allyn said, and was relieved when Liam let him go. But halfway between Liam and Kendyl, he stopped, turning back to his friend.

"Liam?" When the younger magi looked at him, he added, "Good work."

Liam nodded, his eyes twinkling with pride, and Allyn

was suddenly struck by how much Liam reminded him of Graeme. A weight had been lifted off Liam's shoulders, only to be replaced by a new heavier burden, and Liam had risen to bear it. Graeme would have been proud. *Allyn* was proud. For an instant the gloom faded, and a tiny smile tickled the corners of Allyn's mouth. He continued toward his sister, feeling slightly better than he had only a few moments before.

Kendyl saw him approaching and closed the distance between them.

"Hey," Allyn said.

"Hey." She gave him a tight hug. "You look like hell."

"I feel like hell," he said as the embrace ended.

"What happened to your hand?"

"Broken, I think."

"You should get it looked at."

"Later," Allyn said. "Worry about everyone else first." He surveyed the scene again. "Liam said all of this was because of you. I guess I owe you one."

"No," Kendyl said. "You already saved me, remember? This makes us even. Though you *should* be happy I'm not holed up back in the Hyland Estate, being useless."

Allyn grunted a laugh. Kendyl never missed an opportunity to let him know when she was right. "Good point," he conceded. "What happened?"

"There were too many Knights," she said. "So I sent a runner to bring the magi down from the exits to protect our injured and sent some of them and our remaining magi to reinforce you."

"You convinced Nyla to disobey her orders," he said. "That couldn't have been easy."

Kendyl's cheeks flushed at the veiled accusation. "It might have taken a little *convincing*."

"Does she know?"

"I don't know," Kendyl said. "I don't think so."

Allyn whistled, impressed. Kendyl had successfully used her abilities on Nyla, one of the most perceptive clerics in the McCollum Family, not only to carry out her wishes, but to disregard orders to do so.

"Good job."

And then it hit him—the hug and the way her hand continued to rest on his shoulder where his compression armor was torn. He stepped away, breaking Kendyl's contact.

"You're doing it right now, aren't you?"

Kendyl looked at him as if he'd just accused her of cheating at a board game. "What are you talking about?"

"You are! Wow. I'm not even mad, Kendyl. I'm impressed. Very subtle."

Her shocked expression gave way to self-satisfaction. "Like I said, you looked like hell."

Without Kendyl controlling his emotions, the feeling of despair returned twofold. "Yeah, well, I failed, Kendyl. Sedric got away, and he still has the Blood Wand. I don't know what we're going to do."

"It wasn't a complete failure." Kendyl nodded toward Liam. Another magi handed him something roughly the size of a hardback book, though thinner and dark in color. Liam ran a finger along its glass face as he listened to the magi's report. "He's changed," she added.

"He's been through a lot," Allyn said, but he knew she was right. Something about Liam *was* different. He'd seen it only a few moments before when the young magi had reminded him so much of Graeme. Allyn nodded toward the prisoners against the wall. "What about them? Think they'll talk?"

"Oh, I'm sure we can pry something out of them."

"Good," Allyn said. "Because this isn't over. Not even close. And we need information."

They spoke for a few moments more before exchanging goodbyes. Kendyl returned to helping Nyla while Allyn circled the room, getting updates from the remaining magi. When the Knights' underground base had been thoroughly searched and catalogued and the injured were ready for transport, they began to move out.

"What about them?" Nolan asked, gesturing toward the pile of dead Knights.

"Leave them," Allyn said. "They're already with the dead."

———————•••———————

The drive back to the Klausner Manor was silent and subdued, broken only by the moans and cries of the injured. Bullet wounds were difficult for magi to heal, and attempting to often inflicted more pain than the initial wound itself, so for the time being, the wounded magi were made as comfortable as possible, but left untreated.

Grand Mage Klausner met them outside as they arrived. The early morning sun bathed the landscape in a golden hue that openly contradicted their feeling of despair. The squad of clerics waiting at the grand mage's side immediately jumped into action, helping their exhausted comrades out of the vehicles and attending to the injured. Klausner himself was focused on something else.

"You brought them *here*?" he hissed as Andrick and the other magi pulled the prisoners from the vehicles.

"We didn't have a choice," Allyn said. "Sedric got away before we could retrieve the Blood Wand. We need them for information."

Klausner rubbed his forehead irritably. "I don't like this. How long do you plan on holding them?"

"They're prisoners of war," Allyn said. "I'll hold on to them for as long as I need to."

"This is my home, my Family."

"Then you can ensure that our security is up to your standards," Allyn said. "But until we have the information we need, they stay. If you don't like it, take it up with the arch mage."

Klausner glared at Allyn but didn't push the issue further. Allyn couldn't blame him—the Knights *were* a danger to him and his Family, and they didn't have a great place to keep them locked up. Unfortunately, necessity and convenience rarely aligned.

Once the injured were situated in the cleric's wing and the prisoners were under guard and stowed away in an unoccupied quarter of the house, Allyn called Jaxon to give him his report. It went as he expected. Though Arch Mage Westarra's priority had been recovering the Blood Wand, Jaxon's primary concern had been Liam's safety, so one man was in better spirits than the other.

In the end, they came up with a course of action: Arch Mage Westarra and Jaxon would meet them in Switzerland, and in the meantime, Kendyl and Nolan would pull what information they could out of the prisoners and begin to map out the Knights' organization—bases of operation, financial backing, and most importantly, Knight Commander Sedric Lang himself.

———————————

Allyn woke to a series of loud, insistent knocks on his door. He was lying facedown on his bed, still fully clothed in his compression armor. The warm afternoon light had dimmed considerably. How long had he been out? He remembered lying down, but not falling asleep.

The knocks continued.

"Yeah, yeah," Allyn said, his voice thick with fatigue. "I'm coming."

He pushed himself off the bed and walked across the room. His knees and joints ached and seemed to crack and pop with every other step. His head pounded, and his legs, dead and shaky, crying under his weight, felt as though he'd just run a marathon.

Allyn pulled open the door to find Liam in the hall. He didn't have time to speak before Liam stormed into the room.

"I found it," Liam said excitedly. "This is it."

Allyn closed the door and rubbed the sleepiness from his eyes, his groggy mind struggling to catch up. "Found what?"

"This." Liam held up the black device Allyn had seen one of the Klausner magi hand him back in the catacombs.

Seeing it up close, Allyn realized it was a tablet.

"It's the Knight Commander's logbook. It has everything. Lists of Knights on assignment, supply caches, financial information. Their entire organization."

Allyn blinked. This wasn't happening, was it? He still had to be sleeping, his mind coping with their failed mission by manifesting happy dreams. He ran his hands through his short hair.

"Aren't you going to say anything?" Liam asked. "Allyn, this is exactly what we needed."

"Just give me a second." Allyn spotted a glass of water atop his bedside table and downed its contents in four large gulps. "Where did you find it?"

"In the catacombs," Liam said. "In what looked like the Knight Commander's private quarters. What's wrong?"

"It's too convenient," Allyn said. "It almost feels like we were supposed to find it."

"No. You're just exhausted. They had no idea we were coming. He left this behind because he was too focused on the Blood Wand. It was a *mistake*, Allyn, and one we're going to take advantage of."

Hope swelled in Allyn's chest. It tasted sweet, refreshing, like the first iced tea of summer. He couldn't remember how long it had been since he'd felt something so wonderful. But a little voice in the back of his head told him not to relish in it. That it was false. A trick. Some sort of trap concocted by Sedric.

No, Allyn thought, burying the rising feeling of cynicism. *Enjoy this.*

"What about bases?" Allyn asked. "Does it say where the Knights of Rakkar are headquartered?"

"Nothing so explicit," Liam said. "At least not that I've found. But I'm sure if we look at supply movements and deployments, some sort of pattern will emerge."

"And you can send the information to other devices?"

"Of course."

"Excellent," Allyn said. "Then assemble the rest of our squad. I want to know everything on that tablet by the time Jaxon and the arch mage arrive."

"Okay."

"Good work, Liam. We're going to war, and we just had our first victory."

The story continues in...

EXPOSURE

The Machinists, Book Four
Coming Soon

To receive *Heritage*, a free prequel novella
set in the world of The Machinists, sign up
for the Craig Andrews mailing list at:

http://eepurl.com/IEjIr

For additional bonus content, and to be the first to hear
about giveaways and
promotions, follow Craig Andrews on Facebook at:

https://www.facebook.com/craigandrewsauthor

ACKNOWLEDGMENTS

I HAVE AN UNHEALTHY TENDENCY TO make things more difficult than they need to be. My wife and I got married the same summer I decided to direct a feature-length, independent film. We bought our first house a month before our first son was born, signed papers the day after he entered this world, and started moving the day before we brought him home. And in typical fashion, I made writing this book more difficult than it needed to be too.

Truth be told, I sometimes struggle to balance my day job with my author career. When one is particularly consuming, the other falters. During the writing of *Martyr*, I accepted a promotion, then accepted a second, pseudo-promotion, and took on a lot of additional responsibility. As a result, 2015 was great for my professional career, but my author career languished, and despite my intentions, *Martyr* wasn't released in December 2015 as I'd hoped. Instead, you're getting it now, in October 2016, nearly a full year after I anticipated.

The silver lining, I suppose, is that I'm very happy with how the book turned out. In many ways I wrote the first two books in The Machinists so that I could write *this* book.

This is where the story shifts. This is where the small bits of foreshadowing pay dividends. This is where characters, Families, and the world of the magi are set down a path that will leave them forever changed. I hope it's exciting. I hope you enjoy it. Because I had a blast writing it and can't wait to share where we go next.

As with before, *Martyr* wouldn't have happened without the love and support of so many. And as always, my thanks must begin with my wife. Tiffany is my best friend, my partner-in-crime, and my biggest fan—even if she hasn't read everything I've written. ☺. She's there when I need to wake up at 5:00 am to write. She's there at 10:30 pm when I can't sleep because my mind is racing about a sticky plot or character point. And she's always supportive when I tell her I need to take away from family time to write for the weekend.

Next up are my boys, Ender and Callan, to whom this book is dedicated. They are two of the best boys a father could ask for. When I need to take one of the aforementioned weekends to write, they're always willing to let daddy work, and then happy to drag me away from the computer when I've taken too long and been too selfish. I strive everyday to be a better person, better father, and set a better example so that one day, they'll be better men than I ever was.

An enormous thank you must go to my Mom and Dad, and Gary and Gala, for their continued support and excitement— and being understanding when I'm cranky and short after being asked how the book is coming along. I wish I had a better excuse, but I'm afraid I'm just a cantankerous ass sometimes. I'm working on that, remember?

Then there's my extended family, for whom there's too many to name, who I must thank for their continued enthusiasm, liking and sharing my Facebook posts, loaning, giving out, and donating paperback copies to friends, coworkers, and local libraries. I need to get better at thanking them in person, but in the meantime, I hope this will do.

To my former colleague, Kate, who listened to my frustrations about what to name this book, and took my half-baked ramblings and came up with the perfect title. I hope you find the book as good as the title is fitting.

To Lynn and Stefanie from Red Adept Editing, we're three books in now (and a novelette) and I can't imagine working with anyone else. Here's to many more!

And finally, thank you, dear reader. I go to great lengths, to write the best books I can write, and have them professionally edited, proofread (multiple times), formatted, and designed to make your experience as enjoyable as possible. Without you these stories wouldn't exist, these characters wouldn't live, and my ultimate dream of becoming a full-time author would never become a reality. I'm forever grateful for your support. If you like these books, please consider leaving them an Amazon review and help other readers find them. Every review, every shelf-add and rating on Goodreads, and every time you mention them on Facebook or in an online forum, helps others discover this series and supports this crazy dream of mine. If we ever meet in person, please let me know you're a fan so I can shake your hand or give you a hug (your choice).

If there's anyone I missed—and I'm sure there is— please know I greatly appreciate you too. I can't possibly name everyone here (or even remember everyone—my memory isn't that great!), and already I've turned what's supposed to be a small acknowledgments page and stretched it out to 850 words...

I look forward to our next adventure!

—Craig Andrews

CRAIG **A**NDREWS GRADUATED FROM PORTLAND State University with a Bachelors of Arts in English. Growing up on a healthy diet of fantasy and science fiction, some of his favorite childhood memories include being traumatized by the TV shows *Unsolved Mysteries* and *The X-Files*. He currently lives in a small, rural town outside of Portland, Oregon with his wife and two boys.

Say "hi" at any of the following:
craigandrewsauthor@yahoo.com
http://www.craigandrewsauthor.com
https://www.facebook.com/craigandrewsauthor
http://eepurl.com/IEjIr (mailing list)

www.ingramcontent.com/pod-product-compliance
Lightning Source LLC
Chambersburg PA
CBHW021321250626
47155CB00002B/572